Ready

Shoot

ACCLAIM FOR THE KIKI LOWENSTEIN SCRAP-N-CRAFT MYSTERY SERIES

Paper, Scissors, Death

* An Agatha Award Finalist *

"A well-turned cozy with loads of scrapbooking tips."

—*Kirkus Reviews*

"Scrapbookers will love the whole idea of forensic scrapbooking and will relish the tips on the craft sprinkled throughout the story."

—*Booklist*

"With plotting as tight as the seal of a decompression chamber and a flow to the narrative that is as smooth as silk, this is a wonderful read."

—*Crimespree Magazine*

"A proper pacy mystery with plenty of tension (and red herrings) that kept me guessing to the end."

—*ScrapBook inspirations Magazine* (U.K.)

"An engaging mystery."—Donna Andrews, Agatha and Anthony Award-winning author of the Meg Langslow and Turing Hopper series

"Charming, funny, and very enjoyable!"

—J. A. Konrath, author of *Whiskey Sour*

"A page turner who-done-it, filled with colorful characters and scrapbooking tips. The story is filled with insightful glimpses into the heart of a true scrapbooker and a touch of romance."

—Rebecca Ludens, Scrapbooking Guide for About.com

"If you like mysteries, quirky characters, and scrapbooking, you will love this book."

—Angie Pedersen, The Scrappy Marketer, ScrapbookMarketing.com

"Pick this one up if you love scrapbooking or cozies."

—Fresh Fiction

"Fun to read, with laugh-out-loud humor along with tensions and true friendships."

—Mysterious Women

Cut, Crop & Die

"A nicely crafted cozy full of amusing moments, real-life insecurities, and scrapbooking tips."

—*Kirkus Reviews*

"Slan fulfills all the promise of her first novel . . . and the book is filled with characters who we care about."

—*Booklist*

"Another enthralling, interesting, fast-paced mystery."

—ReviewingTheEvidence.com

Photo, Snap, Shot

"A cut above the usual craft-themed cozy."—*Publishers Weekly*

"Slan writes with a wonderful knack for characters and the plot is laid out in a great classic style . . . Treat yourself to a wonderful traditional feeling mystery with characters you will love."

—*Crimespree Magazine*

"Intricate and fascinating. Readers will find realistic characters and plenty of tension to keep pages turning right until the end. Award-nominated author Joanna Campbell Slan's series continues to be strong." —Bookreporter.com

Make, Take, Murder

"The characters are so well developed that each installment leaves the reader yearning for the next."

—*Kirkus Reviews*

"Topically relevant and chock-full of side stories."

—*Library Journal*

"There are chuckle-out-loud moments as well as wonderful scrapbooking tips and recipes scattered throughout the book."

—RTBookReviews.com

Joanna Campbell Slan

Ready

scrap

Shoot

A Kiki Lowenstein
Scrap-N-Craft
Mystery

MIDNIGHT INK
WOODBURY, MINNESOTA

FIRST EDITION
First Printing, 2012

Book design and format by Donna Burch
Cover art : Utility Knife © iStockphoto.com/Blanka Boskov
        Pencil © iStockphoto.com/rambo182
        Calla Lily © iStockphoto.com/Diane Labombarbe
Cover design by Kevin R. Brown
Editing by Connie Hill

Midnight Ink, an imprint of Llewellyn Publications

Library of Congress Cataloging-in-Publication Data

Campbell-Slan, Joanna.
  Ready, scrap, shoot : A Kiki Lowenstein scrap-n-craft mystery / Joanna Campbell Slan. — 1st ed.
      p.   cm. — (A Kiki Lowenstein scrap-n-craft mystery ; 5)
   ISBN 978-0-7387-2747-9
  1. Lowenstein, Kiki (Fictitious character)—Fiction. 2. Murder—Investigation—Fiction. 3. Scrapbooking—Fiction. I. Title.
   PS3603.A4845R43   2012
   813'.6—dc23   2011044061

Midnight Ink
Llewellyn Publications
2143 Wooddale Drive
Woodbury, MN 55125-2989
www.midnightinkbooks.com

Printed in the United States of America

To the wonderful ladies of The Mystery Book Club that meets at the Barnes & Noble in Fenton, Missouri—Mary M. Cotton, Jeanne Dagne, Judy Dawes, Barbara Green, Ruth G. McMahon, Angie Reeder, Doris C. Sipe, and Jeanne Yochim—with my deep appreciation for suggesting that I add a "scrubby Dutch" character to this series.

ONE

Saturday, May 1

A BLOOD-RED SPLOTCH FLOWERED slowly on Edwina Fitzgerald's chest, marring the cornflower blue of her St. John Knits suit.

I notice things like that—colors, textures, and patterns. My name is Kiki Lowenstein, and I'm a scrapbooker.

I admired the growing red blossom as I peered through the viewfinder of the video camera. But I didn't realize what I was seeing. Not at first. I was mesmerized by the colorful spectacle before me, the annual Charles and Anne Lindbergh Academy's May Day Celebration. Actually, I was deep in concentration. This was the first time my mother-in-law, Sheila, had trusted me with her new camera, and I hoped to do a good job of capturing the amazing pageantry.

Only later I would realize that the strains of Mozart's "Turkish March" had masked the sound of that first shot.

Pop! Pop! Pop! came the percussive series that followed. The blasts were rhythmical as taps on a snare drum.

A scream pierced the dulcet music. "She's been hit!" yelled someone.

Another loud *Pop!*

I instinctively turned toward the sound, but all I saw was a nearby stand of trees.

"It's Edwina!" another voice cried. "Get help!"

I panned the camera back to Edwina and watched her slump over in her chair. Blood gushed from her chest onto her lap.

With a jolt, I figured out what was happening.

"Sniper!" I yelled to my mother-in-law, Sheila. "Hit the ground! Grab my mom! I'll get Anya!" I tossed the video camera to the grass and started running. I could smell my own sweat, a combination of exertion and fear, as I pumped my arms.

The music continued, but screams pierced the melody.

I raced toward my daughter, Anya. She and forty of her class-mates stood holding colorful ribbons that twisted partway up the Maypole. Sprinting past the other girls, I grabbed my kid's hand, and shouted, "Run!"

Ping!

A shot hit a folding chair not ten feet away. The peppery scent of gunpowder filled the air.

Anya hiked her lacy white skirt above her knees and jogged along beside me. I pulled her back toward where I'd been sitting. I briefly considered running away with my daughter, to make sure she was safe. But I couldn't leave Sheila with responsibility for my mother. I had a hunch Mom was not going to see the urgency in our situation.

Anya and I dodged spectators and stunned families frozen in place as they tried to make sense of what had happened. The crowd

2

was collectively shocked and unable to act. Several turned to stare at me and my kid as we zigged and zagged.

"She's hit! She's hurt!" Deanna Fitzgerald stood over her mother-in-law's body. "Help! Somebody help!"

"Call nine-one-one!" yelled Edwina's son, Peter, to no one in particular as he bent over his fallen mother. He'd no more than gotten out those words when a bullet pierced his left thigh. With a yowl, he jumped and grabbed his upper leg. Crimson blood flowed through his fingers and covered his slacks.

"I've been shot!" Peter Fitzgerald roared. "Turn off the music! Someone call nine-one-one!"

A *Zing!* and a *Ping!* indicated another metal chair had been hit.

A sniper was in the trees, shooting at people.

This couldn't be happening.

But it was.

TWO

From the trees on our left came two more explosions. *Pop! Pop!* The fresh spring-green leaves ruffled in the wind.

My mother and my mother-in-law sat shivering under their overturned gray metal chairs.

I called out, "Get up! Those were gunshots! We have to move!"

Sheila hopped to her feet. My mother didn't move.

"Come on!" I handed Anya over to Sheila. I reached toward Mom and her familiar scent of Chantilly. She fought me, pushing me away and crying, "My purse! I can't find my purse!"

"Forget it!"

The music had stopped. The May Day dancers froze in their positions, looking frantically for direction. A couple of the girls burst into tears, and a few more cried out for their mothers.

Panic started in earnest. Parents snatched up children. Women screamed and grabbed their purses. Men shouted orders and tugged at their wives. Students headed toward the shelter of the main building.

We were ahead of the pack, but not by much. Behind us, metal chairs clanged and banged as people knocked them over in their haste. A security guard pointed at the stand of trees and yelled into his walkie-talkie, "We've got a situation here!" A few Good Samaritans stayed to help Edwina and her son. Someone yelled, "Get an ambulance!" The older girls broke formation on the sidelines, huddled together, and hugged each other, crying.

Once confusion gave way to fight or flight, we'd be trampled.

"Move it!" I screamed, grabbing Mom's elbow.

I started dragging her. She fought me every inch of the way, tossing her head and throwing up her arms.

She'd always been a pain in the butt. I had half a mind to leave her there. But she was my mother, and I loved her.

Anya forced Sheila to turn around and come back for us.

"Grandmére, we have to run! Please!" My daughter bent to my mother, reaching out for her hand. Fear pitched Anya's voice higher than normal.

"Which way?" panted Sheila, as she doubled over with her hands on her knees, trying to catch her breath. We both scanned the area, trying to make sense of this impossible situation.

"Parking lot!" I yelled. The crowd surged toward us like a wounded beast, roaring with pain and anger.

Running for the cars wasn't much of a plan, but it was the best I could muster.

THREE

ANYA KEPT PACE WITH Sheila. They were half a football field ahead of the crowd, but I was losing ground. I had my arm around my mother, and she was literally dragging her heels. "My purse! I need my purse!" she whined, turning and pointing behind us.

I did the best I could, but it was hard to hurry someone who was protesting every step of the way.

Sheila made a fast assessment of the situation. "We need to carry her."

Without discussion, we formed a chair with our arms and scooped Mom up from behind. Sheila and I staggered under Mom's weight. Miraculously, we caught our balance and stumbled forward.

Sheila held up her end, and I mine, as we struggled over stones and uneven ground. Despite our burden, we made headway. We'd almost cleared the top of the hill. The lot wasn't far away.

"Stop it! Put me down!" Mom batted at us with both hands. "My shoes! I've lost my shoes!"

She swatted at us as though we were pesky mosquitoes.

"Stop it!" Sheila hissed at her.

That only made Mom angrier. "Kiki, no!" she yelled. She hauled off and slapped the side of my face with her open palm. The pain staggered me. I lost my grip on Mom and dropped her. For a second, all I could do was massage my stinging skin in wonder and spit blood on the ground. I felt the imprint of her hand glowing red on my cheek.

"My word," said Sheila. "How dare she?"

She dared.

Mom had always cared too much about the little things and too little about what mattered. Here we were, trying to run for our lives, and her only concern was her purse and her shoes. My child—her granddaughter—could be killed, but my mother wasn't about to lose any parts of her wardrobe.

My eyes watered in response to the pain. (And, yes, in part to her cruelty.) But it wasn't the first time she'd struck me or the last. So I pulled up my big girl panties and wrestled with my emotions. This was no time to break down or fall apart. I needed to act decisively. We stood on the crest of the hill. The parking lot sprawled before us. The crowd nipped at our heels. Our only option was to move forward. The slope was in our favor. Worst-case scenario, I could roll Mom down the hill. Gravity was my friend.

Mom had other plans. She started crawling back the way we came.

Fortunately, I'm faster than she is. That and weighing ten pounds over the number on my driver's license served me well. Those additional pounds gave me leverage. Without thinking, I grabbed the back of Mom's jacket and her belt. With a mighty heave, I lifted her.

Her feet scrabbled the ground, but she came along with me. I carried her much the way a mother cat does her kitten.

If you asked me to do that again, I probably couldn't. But I managed during the crisis, and that's all that mattered.

"You're going too fast," Mom whined. "Slow down!"

Instead, I picked up the pace.

An hysterical mob trailed behind us. Their fear announced them, in a swelling cacophony of snapping twigs, mewling cries, and tramping feet. I turned my head to see a blur of faces, drawing nearer with each step.

I hustled Mom along, barely keeping up with my mother-in-law and daughter. Every muscle in my body screamed in protest at the dead weight I carried. My right fingers froze in a grip on Mom's collar. My left locked onto her belt. Somewhere in the scuffle, I'd lost both my shoes. My feet throbbed and blood covered my right big toe. But all that pain paled in contrast to my will to live.

If we stopped now, if I caught my breath, we'd surely be trampled. I wanted desperately to live. I had a child to raise. I had a man who loved me.

I muttered to myself, "Detweiler, Anya, Detweiler, Anya," and their names kept me going.

Despite the pain in my clenched fingers and tortured feet, I kept moving, half-carrying Mom along with me.

Behind us, men yelled, women shrieked, students sobbed, and children cried.

Somewhere in the distance a siren wailed.

The cavalry was coming, and not a moment too soon.

FOUR

WHAT A DIFFERENCE TWENTY-FIVE minutes can make. Back then, my priorities were entirely different. Less than a half an hour ago, the only "safety" that concerned me was the safety pin holding up the skirt of my borrowed navy suit. Its head dug into my skin, pinching me.

My control-top panty hose cut off my air supply. The only pumps I could find at Goodwill were too small. Not only did my heels sink into the soft ground, but my big toes screamed in pain with every step.

Other than that, I was having a jolly good time.

Um, not so much.

"Kiki, quit digging at your waistband," my mother hissed. We rode side-by-side sharing the back seat of Sheila's car, traveling to the May Day Celebration. "Try for once to act like a lady. Well-bred people do not adjust their wardrobes in public."

"Sorry," I mumbled.

"For goodness sake, Kiki," Mom continued her rant. "Anyone would think you were brought up in a barn!"

Yada, yada, yada. Mom kept up a steady harangue about my lack of couth. My ill-mannered behavior. My general worthlessness.

Usually this was Sheila's job. But in light of my mother's superior snarky qualities, Sheila held her tongue. Finally, even she had enough.

"Mrs. Montgomery, please. Kiki's a Lowenstein now. We don't treat each other that way."

Since when? I wanted to ask.

Browbeating me was Sheila's primary form of recreation. Maybe watching my mom give me "what for" made Sheila feel left out. Or maybe she realized how she herself acted when Mom wasn't around.

Whatever.

I sighed and enjoyed a few moments of blessed silence. Mom harrumphed and stared angrily out the window of the Mercedes. Unconsciously, she clutched her purse to her chest. Looking over at her, I noticed again how frail she seemed. Once upon a time, my mother towered over me. These days, I stared down on her head of thinning hair. When I helped her into Sheila's car, I was shocked by how pronounced her bones were, how clearly I could feel her skeleton through her mottled skin, and how light she was. In more ways than I could count, my mother was a shadow of her former, formidable self. Old age was taking her away from me, slowly but surely.

However, Mom was still determined to be independent. And she still had her pride. As we drove up to the fancy school Anya attended, a tiny gasp escaped her. "What is all this? A city park?" she asked.

"No, these are the school grounds. CALA owns more than 100 acres," said Sheila proudly. She began detailing the various captains of industry who were alums, explaining about the $94 million endowment, and extolling the virtues instilled by CALA.

When Sheila slowed to a stop, Mom turned to me and said, "I knew you had money."

FIVE

WHAT MOM DIDN'T SAY, but she left hanging in the air were the words, "You are so selfish not to take care of me." Mom and my sister Amanda campaigned vigorously for me to send my mother a monthly allowance. The amount they "suggested" was exactly what I took home each week from my job at the local scrapbook store.

"Mom, I'm broke. We are fortunate that Sheila pays for Anya's tuition," I said. "She also takes care of all my daughter's books and most of her clothes. Plus her cell phone and any extra fees like her lunches and the yearly donation that's expected of families."

That shut Mom up. But I knew she wouldn't be quiet for long. She was determined to prove that I should be giving her financial assistance, and that I was a bad daughter by not helping her out more. She and Amanda had decided I was living the high life. Nothing I said would change their minds.

In fact, I was pretty sure that the entire purpose of Mom's visit was to expose me as a tightwad and a fraud. As best I could tell, my mother had decided that an unannounced visit would be the best way to verify that I was holding out on her. Once she could prove I had money, I'd be shamed into honoring her requests for a generous monthly allowance.

If, indeed, that was the plan, so far their scheme had failed miserably.

Mom quickly saw the painful truth: I was barely getting by. If she thought my life was a picnic, well, she'd underestimated the number of ants swarming my basket. I worked overtime to make ends meet. I cut corners whenever possible. I wore clothes from resale and thrift shops. I ate leftovers. I drove a creaky BMW with a leaky convertible roof. In short, I was a nickel and a dime away from going under. Shoot, I wasn't just underwater, I was twenty thousand leagues beneath the sea.

My mother also learned that my mother-in-law was nearly as critical and demanding as she was. Mom actually had the nerve to ask me why I put up with Sheila.

"After all," Mom sniffed, the day after they met, "your husband is dead. The two of you aren't really related. And the woman is obnoxious."

I have to admit, Mom was right. Sheila could be a real pill.

Albeit, a well-dressed pill at that. More than one admiring glance came her way as Sheila slid her long legs out of the Mercedes sedan. Her lovely periwinkle bouclé suit brought out the silver highlights in her hair and the blue of her eyes. She looked every inch a lady. Which she was, until she was provoked. Then she could be a real harridan. She had demanded I wear a suit, blouse, and pumps to the May Day Ceremony. "I don't care if it is out-of-doors, it's a venerable and important moment in the school year.

You need to make more of an effort to be part of the school community. I won't have you embarrassing Anya ... or me."

Yep, no doubt about it, Sheila could be a real stinker. Sometimes I wondered why I put up with her.

I pondered this as Anya kissed both of her grandmothers goodbye.

Sheila stood on tiptoes and waved after my child, "Have a good time, darling. Enjoy yourself! You look lovely! You'll be the prettiest girl here!"

Okay, *that* was why I put up with my mother-in-law.

After her son died, I decided that no matter how she treated me, Sheila was good for my child. She positively doted on Anya. The education my daughter received at CALA was the finest money could buy. Correction: the finest Sheila's money could buy.

My mother-in-law's affection and her willingness to foot the bill for my daughter's pricey tuition forced me to suffer the thousand slings and arrows that Sheila lobbed in my direction. Sheila's generosity helps my daughter fit in. She makes sure Anya has whatever extras she needs, all the little extras that her peers take for granted. This was very, very important at a school where most of the families owned vacation homes in Aspen or Jackson Hole or Palm Beach, or wherever the rich and trendy go to oppress the poorer classes these days.

(Me bitter? Heaven forfend!)

Thanks to Sheila's support, no one would ever guess that the fashionable Anya Lowenstein went home at night to a teensy one-bathroom house. Or that Anya's mother made little more than minimum wage while working at Time in a Bottle, a scrapbook store.

So, yes, I put up with Sheila. We've had our moments, but over-all we supported each other because in our heart of hearts, we agreed on what was important: Anya.

SIX

Because we arrived late, all the spaces near the ceremonial grounds were filled. We circled around and drove over to the auxiliary school lot. School security waved us into a makeshift spot along the pickup lane, then ushered a Hummer in behind us. The huge vehicle blocked our egress. I hated the idea we couldn't leave when we wanted—and I anticipated Mom would whine and want to go home way before we were ready—but there was no help for it. The annual May Day celebration was the biggest event of the CALA (that's local speak for Charles and Anne Lindbergh Academy) school year. If you wanted a primo parking space, you needed to arrive at least an hour in advance of the ceremony.

Despite my warning it was time for us to leave, and in spite of Sheila's urging her to "hurry up," my mother had taken her own sweet time primping and running to the bathroom. As a result, Anya arrived a good forty-five minutes after the time specified by her advisor. I would have to call the school and beg them not to send her to detention.

Sheila was furious.

Mom didn't care that she'd inconvenienced us all.

When she realized she'd have to climb a small hill to get to the natural amphitheater where the festivities took place, Mom turned to me and said, "I'm not going. You can't make me."

I tried cajoling her. "I know it looks like a hike, but really, the pageantry is worth it. Come on, Mom. Watching this will take you back to your days in show business. Wait till you see the dancing."

"No." Her mouth formed a flat unyielding line. "Take me home."

"I can't. First of all, this is Sheila's car, not mine. Second, look around at the parking lot. See the Hummer blocking us in? We can't get out. And third, I would miss the ceremony. I want to see my daughter dance around the Maypole. Anya's so excited about her costume," I said.

My daughter wore a full white skirt with a lace overlay, a blue blouse with poet sleeves, and a multi-colored sash tied in a big bow at the waist. In her hair were silk daisies. She looked like a fairy princess.

"I don't care. I want to go home. Right now. Call a cab for me. Or a limo service."

Even if I wanted to, I couldn't afford either. It shocked me that my mother *still* didn't have a clue about how I lived. She had visited me once shortly after George and I married. I thought she wanted to get to know my new husband and his family, but she wasn't interested in meeting my in-laws. After several invitations, she consented reluctantly to have dinner with Sheila and Harry Lowenstein. During the meal, she and Sheila sniped at each other incessantly. Tempers flared and they both raised their voices so loudly that nearby diners turned to stare.

Mom also used her visit to criticize every part of my life: the house, the furniture, the books I was reading, and my clothes. Each day the list grew.

Worst of all, she took potshots at George. Okay, he wasn't perfect. None of us are. But he was her new son-in-law. You'd think she'd want to make nice. Instead, she laughed at him when he spilled his morning coffee. She sneered when his beloved Cardinals were creamed by the Cubs. She predicted he would lose all his hair by the time he was forty. (Sadly, George didn't live to see forty.)

The visit had gone about as well as a rout by marauding Vikings. At long last, I was able to drive Mom to the airport. I nearly clicked my heels together with joy. I spent the whole ride praying that her plane hadn't been delayed. If it had, I would have gladly booked her on the next flight, even if it took her to Timbuktu. I would have sent her anywhere, anywhere in the world to get her out of my life—with George's blessings.

Even the stalwart Lowensteins were happy to see my mother leave.

And she accomplished all that animosity in a mere five days.

Think what she could do in a couple of weeks!

I wasn't sure how long she was staying, but this time, she arrived with six overstuffed suitcases. Anya sat under two of them in the back seat. One was in my trunk, and the other three would be delivered to my home at a princely sum. (Clearly I was in the wrong business. I mean, how can it cost so much to deliver a suitcase? They don't bark, pee, or chew your furniture, but the porter charged more for the trip than I did to dogsit for a day.)

"Um, are you planning to be with us awhile?" I asked.

"It depends. This might be a long visit," she said.

I wanted to say, "How long is long to you?" so I could count down the days and hours. But Anya jumped in and started narrating the drive for her grandmother. I had to admit, my daughter made a good tour guide, pointing out where Bob Cassilly, our most famous local artist and eclectic sculptor, revised a section of historic fencing by turning it into a chorus line of ghostly figures. (The neighbors were not pleased. I guess some folks don't have a sense of humor.)

Mom listened politely to Anya's commentary, not saying much. When Anya asked if she'd be here long enough to visit the local sights, such as the City Museum, the St. Louis Art Museum, and our fabulous zoo, Mom hesitated. "Maybe. Maybe not."

"You certainly brought a lot of suitcases," I pointed out helpfully.

"I like to make a good impression," said Mom. "The right clothes are important. One never knows what functions one might be invited to attend."

Hmmm. Definitely sounding like a long visit.

Ben Franklin once observed that "fish and visitors both stink after three days." But I had a sinking feeling that the carp in the passenger seat was here for the duration. Swimming around and fouling up my personal fishbowl.

I wondered if my sister Amanda had gotten fed up with our mother and given Mom the old heave-ho. Mom had always doted on Amanda, but given my mother's mercurial temperament of late, that could have changed.

When we pulled onto my street, Mom focused on the big house on the corner. "Look at that! It's a mansion!" She jutted out her chin and said, "I knew it. You moved from one big house to the other, didn't you? All this poor mouthing was just an act!"

I said nothing. Anya reached up from the back seat and squeezed my shoulder gently three times, our secret code for "I love you." I might be a rotten daughter, but I was raising an empathetic, kind young woman. Anya's compassion touched me. I couldn't speak for the lump in my throat.

Mom kept on about how palatial my "home" was as we pulled around the block and onto the driveway of my real domicile, a converted garage.

"These are your servants' quarters?" Mom asked, as I turned off the engine.

"Nope," said Anya. "No servants. Just us. This is where we live." She jerked a thumb over her shoulder at the big place. "That's Mr. Leighton Haversham's house. He's really nice. Famous, too. He's an author. Authors make tons of money, you know. One of his books was made into a movie."

"But you own part of that store!" Mom had persisted, staring at me.

True, I was proud to call myself part owner of Time in a Bottle, St. Louis's premier scrapbooking store. But I've quickly come to learn that being a minority stockholder means I have bragging rights and not much more. I'm holding out for the promise that if the store does well, I might bring home a bonus. Holding out? Actually, I count mightily on that possibility.

Because if I don't, I won't be able to buy new tires for my car, pay off my credit card, get my dog her rabies shots, or even eat for the next couple of months.

Yeah, it's really that bad.

SEVEN

ANYA AND I HAD brainstormed a list of activities we might do with Mom.

Running from sniper fire had not been on that list. Clearly, an oversight on our part.

Because we'd certainly done exactly that. We had raced our way over rough terrain away from the shooting and toward the parking lot. I had the bloody feet and aching muscles to show for our efforts. Sheila's perfect coiffure showed signs of dishevelment. Anya's cheeks glowed pink and a sheen of perspiration dotted her upper lip.

My mother looked fresh as a newly opened tulip except her stockings sported runs and her shoes were missing.

"To the car?" Sheila managed between huffs and puffs, while catching her breath.

"I think that's our best bet." I nodded toward Mom. Sheila obliged me by doing another basket carry and off we went. The crowd still nipped at our heels, but fortunately, we'd gotten a good head start.

Bless Sheila's heart. She'd had the good sense to slip her keys in her pocket before we took off running. With the remote unlock, she clicked the doors open before we arrived. My mother-in-law bundled Anya inside, protecting my kid with her body. I fought my mother, finally shoving her head down and upending her into the back seat.

"How dare you! What will people think?" she screamed at me. "How could you?"

I imagined that other people thought we were lucky. Around us, folks pounded on their car doors in vain. They hadn't thought to grab their keys. Women set to wailing. Men cursed, and children cried. But we sat there safely in the nearly soundproof Mercedes.

Of course, we couldn't go anywhere. The mass of the crowd swept past us and moved toward the school building. I quivered and shook. My legs turned to a wobbly bowl of Jell-O. As the adrenaline stopped flooding my body, my teeth started to chatter. "Keep your heads down," I shouted to Sheila, Anya, and Mom as I locked the doors. "We don't know that we're in the clear yet."

There we remained, safe and yet not safe, exposed and yet sheltered. Sheila handed her cell phone over to Anya and instructed my daughter to text message Robbie Holmes, the St. Louis Chief of Police, on Sheila's behalf: *We're at CALA. Gunshots. Safe in car in lot.*

Like any kid her age, Anya could text with two thumbs faster than I could type. I knew Robbie would respond as soon as possible. He and Sheila were not only longtime friends, they'd gotten engaged over the holidays. Their wedding was set for next month.

If we lived that long. I snaked my arm between the front seats and gave my daughter's hand three quick squeezes. She returned my signal. I had to withdraw my arm because the twisted position was too painful. Anya and Sheila huddled in the foot well of the passenger's side. My mother and I were in the back seat where I was stretched out over her like a human tent.

Robbie texted back immediately: *Stay put. Units at scene. Cordoning off area.*

A few minutes later, he added: *Shooting has stopped. Believe shooter has fled. Stay put until escort comes.*

I didn't feel relieved. I worried that Robbie was wrong. Maybe the shooter had merely changed position. If so, could bullets penetrate the quarter panels of the Mercedes? I didn't want to find out.

How had such a beautiful scene turned to such a nightmare so quickly?

What more could I do to protect my child and my family?

From inside the usually soundproof German car, we could hear shouts and screams. Horns honked. Glass crashed. Metal crunched. Bumpers crashed into other bumpers and light poles. People struggled to flee, heedless of the damage inflicted on their own cars and the vehicles of others. From my position on top of my squirming mother, I watched the side panel of the neighboring Hummer pass us by. The driver clipped Sheila's bumper, aimed his car directly over the curb, and drove up onto the grass.

The impact of the Hummer rocked our car, and Anya whimpered.

"Sh, sh," whispered Sheila. "We're fine. He's just an awful driver, that's all."

Mom whined and shoved me, "Get off. I need to tinkle! Who cares what that man says!"

"That man is the police chief," I said. "I trust his judgment over yours any day."

Robbie sent another message to Sheila: *Is Kiki with you? Anya?*

My daughter texted back on our behalf: *Yes & Kiki's mom.*

His response was: *Sit tight.*

The crashing and honking and yelling continued outside our windows. I heard Sheila humming a song to my daughter. I'd never heard her sing before, but oh how I appreciated the attempt! I couldn't believe I was stuck here with my complaining mother instead of holding my child. A million, zillion fears zinged through my mind. I thought about how close the gunshots had come. How I might have missed grabbing Anya. How we could have been trampled.

A shudder seized me as I realized I'd been watching Edwina Fitzgerald bleed to death. That poor woman had departed this earth before my very eyes. I'd also seen her son, Peter, take a direct hit to his thigh. I wondered, could he be all right? What if the shot hit a major artery? Again, my teeth chattered uncontrollably. But no one could hear my dental clacking over the racket outside.

Really, it was like something out of one of those catastrophe movies.

That's what it was: a catastrophe.

EIGHT

WE HEARD A NEW symphony of sirens. Sheila reached up and switched on the radio. The reporter announced there'd been a shooting incident at CALA. Police were on the scene. As a result, roads were blocked off and drivers were encouraged to seek alternate routes, but no other details were available.

I took some comfort in the increased presence of the police. I wondered if Detweiler was out there. If so, I prayed he'd be safe. Realizing how selfish I was being, I prayed for everyone else on the scene, too.

Soft sounds of my child crying filtered through from the front of the car. I couldn't reach her. The feeling of desperation nearly swallowed me whole. If we were dying, I wanted to spend my last moments comforting her, holding her hand.

At least she had Sheila. I, however, did not have anyone except my own mother who was muttering curses at me.

If we were going to die, I took comfort from knowing that I'd finally told Detweiler how much I loved him. But oh, what I'd give to kiss him one more time! To unburden my heart to him.

Although that might make this infinitely worse.

A bullhorn scattered my thoughts: "Stay where you are! Do not, we repeat, do not attempt to leave the area."

An authoritative voice shouted this message over and over.

The radio announcer explained that the area was being secured by police. "If you are on or near CALA property, stay put. Authorities will let you know when it's safe to leave."

We were stuck. I tried to quell my restlessness. I wanted to look around. To survey the situation. But if I got up, Mom would too. That also meant I couldn't use my cell phone because it was clipped to my sagging waistband. I couldn't even text Detweiler to say, "I love you" one more time.

So I stayed there in the well between the front and back seats. My legs cramped fiercely as I tried to keep my weight off of Mom. She, on the other hand, wiggled and complained.

What else was new?

"Get off me," she howled. "Your elbow is in my back."

"Better that than a bullet," mumbled Sheila. "Although I'd swear it was a mercy killing."

Anya snickered a little. I smiled and thought, *Okay, she's going to be fine. Really, we all are.*

The radio reporter explained that police had blocked off both ends of the street, and diverted local traffic. Another voice, calling in from the scene, said that the shooting had stopped. One person was confirmed dead and another victim had been taken to a local hospital with gunshot wounds.

I raised my head and peeked out the back window. Uniformed police escorted people inside the school. Officials in SWAT jackets approached cars, copied down license plate numbers, took notes about the occupants, and ushered hysterical families out of the vehicles and into the CALA gymnasium. Would they do that if the shooter was still at large? I thought a minute. The reporters and Robbie might be wrong, but then again, the shooter could have gotten away. Otherwise, the SWAT team would concentrate on taking the gunman out. Instead, the police conducted a car-by-car search. This felt more to me like the aftermath of a tragedy, an attempt to catalog who was on the premises, whether they belonged here, and who might be missing.

"I want to see!" Mom said.

"Stay down," I warned her. "What if there were two shooters?"

It was, after all, a distinct possibility. The incident at Columbine had confused the rescuers in part because they couldn't tell how many gunmen were involved. The two boys removed their trench coats. The hallway cameras recorded shooters wearing different apparel. This discrepancy led outside observers to believe they were dealing with four separate perpetrators. The miscalculation slowed down the rescue process considerably.

Mom kept up a litany of complaints about her shoes, her ruined suit, and how uncomfortable she was.

All the while, Sheila talked quietly to Anya, reassuring her, protecting my daughter with her own body. I thanked God for my mother-in-law. Her quiet, matter-of-fact manner went a long way toward keeping Anya calm.

A tap on the driver's side window startled us. Sheila reached up from her spot on the floor, flicked off the radio, pulled herself onto the driver's seat slowly, and lowered the glass. Keeping one hand on Mom to hold her down, I rose in concert with Sheila. A policeman wearing SWAT gear spoke to us through the clear shield over his face. "Sheila Lowenstein? Anya Lowenstein? Kiki Lowenstein? Police Chief Holmes told me to escort you out of the area."

Sheila frowned. "Are we safe? Is he getting everyone out?"

I could tell she didn't want to take unfair advantage of their relationship. Sometimes Sheila could be very selfish, but she was learning to think strategically. Since their engagement, she'd taken more of an interest in Robbie Holmes's career and the fine line he trod between personal interest and the good of the city.

"Not exactly, ma'am. He's worried the gunman was aiming at Kiki Lowenstein."

NINE

My stomach clenched.

So this was my fault? How? Why?

The SWAT team member added, "He wants all of you to follow us. Now. Those are his instructions."

Walking backwards and using his hand to wave us through, the cop from the Special Weapons And Tactics team helped us maneuver around cars and onto the main street. From there we followed a motorcycle escort to a crossroad. The cycle led us through back streets of Ladue, St. Louis's toniest suburb, and finally to the police station.

Mom squawked and complained the entire time.

I wasn't worried about her, but I was concerned about my daughter. A natural blonde, Anya was always pale. The policeman's announcement, however, turned her pallor even whiter. Sheila, to my relief, acted with aplomb. She drove with one hand on the wheel and the other grasping Anya's. "Not to worry," she said to my child. "Robbie will take care of us. Remember, this is just a precaution."

Anya nodded, her face wan but composed.

I felt positively, utterly sick. All this was because of me? Mom muttered dark warnings under her breath. Anya didn't say a word. Sheila's hands clutched the steering wheel so tightly, I thought it might break.

A vibration along my waistband notified me of a text message. It was from my boss: *"Dodie: How's it going? Did they luv the album?"*

I clapped my phone closed. The album? I'd run off without the May Day album!

Crud.

I dropped my head into my hands and groaned. I had left my beautiful album, my purse, and Sheila's camera behind in our mad dash.

That album had taken me two weeks to finish.

The first page was devoted to the history of May Day:

May Day began in 1843, when Mrs. Theodosia Stephens founded the St. Louis Arts Academy for Young Women. Mrs. Stephens believed that a genteel outdoor "Ceremony to Welcome Spring" provided fresh air, sunshine, and most importantly, a wholesome opportunity to show off the dancing and musical skills of the girls who attended her school.

What I neglected to add was this: Theodosia planned the event so that the young women wore flimsy gowns of virginal white, a blatant appeal to the young men invited to watch. After they marched to the ceremonial grounds, the nubile students picked up Maypole ribbons and danced and twirled rhythmically, winding in and out, around and around the pole. (And I thought pole dancing was a modern invention. Not so.)

The performance was both stunning in its visual impact and delightful in its display of artistry. More importantly, this pageantry never failed to stir the passions of the men seated in the audience. Amazing the effect a well-turned ankle, a slight sheen of perspiration, and a heaving bosom could have on a young man's fancies. In the weeks after the event, a number of students announced their engagements to prominent St. Louis scions.

Given such a successful track record, it was no surprise that when the St. Louis Arts Academy for Young Women merged with the Charles and Anne Lindbergh Academy (CALA), the new school decided to continue the May Day ceremony. More than a hundred years later, no matter how pagan and anachronistic the ceremony looks, it is a venerated and well-preserved St. Louis tradition. The romantic origins of the event make it a powerful recruiting tool. Most importantly, generations of CALA alumnae have given generously to the school, linking donations to the stipulation that the tradition continues.

As an astute student of marketing, I have to hand it to good old Theodosia. Her oil portrait depicted a stern-faced harpy with all the physical charms of a pit bull, but underneath that intimidating facade beat the heart of a true romantic. Mrs. Stephens understood who her audience was, and how to display the "merchandise" to best advantage. She must have been a real marketing genius to dream up a stunt like this.

My genius was to translate local events into sales opportunities for Time in a Bottle.

My other job was, to quote the *Saturday Night Fever* song, "Staying alive."

Ever since my husband, George, was murdered, his killer taunted both me and the police. The man who planned George's death was his best friend from high school and his business partner, a guy named Bill Ballard. By playing amateur sleuth, I helped the police finger Bill for the crime, but the creep managed to get away. Since then, I'd been the target of his threats.

Ugly postcards with threats showed up frequently in my mailbox. I received phone messages telling me I was a dead woman. Once, I found a fake fur effigy of my dog dowsed in what looked like blood and sprawled across the railing of my front porch.

For the most part, I ignored all this. I'm a survivor. I'm not about to let some jerk ruin my life.

But I'm not stupid or careless. I keep a watchful eye on my daughter, restricting her activities and checking up on her the way a nervous parent does.

Things got a lot easier when Detective Chad Detweiler and I started dating.

Scratch that.

Some portions of life got easier, and some were vastly more complicated. Ever since that Christmas night when he and his wife split up, we've spent most of our time together. We keep saying we're going to take it slow. (Okay, slow-LY, right?) Things are moving faster than Superman racing to Lois Lane's side.

He's not divorced. Not yet.

My best friend and former cleaning lady, Mert Chambers, tells me this is a very dangerous time. "You can't let yourself fall like the old ton of bricks for a man who ain't divorced. There's too much at risk for you."

"But you like Detweiler."

"Yep, but I *love* you. You're like a sister to me, and I'm telling you 'zactly what I'd tell one of them. Make him wait. You can't go wrong, and you're less likely to get hurt."

"Would you make him wait?" I raised an eyebrow.

"No, but I ain't you. I don't have a twelve-year-old daughter who lost her daddy and is looking for a replacement, neither."

Nor did Ben Novak go away happy. He was the guy I'd been dating—and briefly engaged to—before Detweiler was "free," so to speak.

"You're too sensitive to be involved with a cop. I give you six months of the carnage and depravity he'll bring home every day, and you'll be sick of it. Don't count me out, Kiki. I want to marry you. We were meant to be together."

Did I mention Detweiler's wife, Brenda, wasn't pleased? That was an understatement.

"Just because I threw him out didn't mean I didn't want him!" she screamed at me over the phone. "I told you to stay away from him, Kiki Lowenstein. What did you do? The minute he and I have a fight, you take up with him! You're a slut!"

Ouch.

Last but not least, my darling mother-in-law Sheila Lowenstein simply said, "You are nuts. Correction. You are insane and stupid. Ben can offer you and Anya a wonderful life. Detweiler's been married twice. He doesn't make a lot of money. And what a great job he has! Every day that he goes to work might be his last. Really, Kiki. I always thought you harbored a self-destructive streak, but you're really off the chart with this—this—low rent version of *Romeo and Juliet*."

My mother added her complaints to the Greek chorus. "A cop? Are you kidding? With your pedigree?"

See, Mom's family is what I call poor but pretentious. Actually, that's being unfair. I'm descended from a long line of important people. They steered the course of history, changed the fate of our nation, and left a legacy that endures today. Too bad they weren't very good with money.

You can't have everything.

As far as I was concerned, Detweiler was the best thing that ever happened to me. He was kind, considerate, loving, and protective. Very, very protective. When he heard about the shootings, he would probably go ballistic.

Oops. Bad choice of words.

TEN

WE PULLED UP IN the sally port of the government building where Robbie Holmes works. But no one could go anywhere until I fished around in Sheila's trunk and found an old pair of loafers for Mom to wear. She curled her lip and slid her feet into them with obvious distaste.

Sheila and I were barefoot. However, my phone had remained securely clipped to my waistband. Positively, absolutely amazing!

The policeman who had ridden along on his motorcycle called upstairs, and another man in uniform met us around back. He ushered us into Robbie Holmes's office. Robbie's secretary, La-Verna Torrez, offered us our choice of beverages. Mom sniffed and asked for a cup of Earl Grey. Hearing that they only had Lipton, she raised a hand to her forehead as though she was about to swoon and mumbled, "I suppose I will have to make do. I need to use your restroom." With that, she wandered off.

This whole scene was clearly an affectation. I never saw her drink tea in her life.

Sheila, Anya, and I settled for Diet Cokes, which LaVerna brought gladly. She also found Mom wandering the halls and led her back to where we were waiting.

As soon as the door closed, Mom had a conniption fit. I know that's redundant. "Conniption" means "a hysterical fit," but Southerners always call it a conniption fit, and that's what she had, since she had a regular fit twice over.

"How could you let this happen to me? What about my shoes? You'll need to buy me a new pair, Kiki! I think I'm going to have an asthma attack. Or a heart attack. I need to call Amanda. She'll be so worried. And Claudia. I need to talk to Claudia."

Who the heck is Claudia?

I decided I didn't care. "Mom, I'll call Amanda right now."

When I opened my phone, I saw numerous calls and texts that had come in during the crisis. Seems that almost everyone wanted to know that Anya and I were all right. Despite the gravity of the current situation, I smiled. I don't know what I've done to deserve so many wonderful friends, but I'm grateful to have them.

However, they would have to wait. I needed to update my sister. The self-same sibling who'd ignored all of my previous phone calls.

To my surprise, Amanda actually answered the phone on the first ring. Her voice shocked me into silence. But I quickly regained my senses. "Amanda, it's Kiki. There's been an unfortunate situation. Mom and Anya and I were shot at by a sniper."

"Is she—is Mom—is she dead?" wailed Amanda.

"No, no. She's fine."

"I am NOT!" screamed Mom. "I lost my shoes. I need to use the bathroom."

I cupped my hand over the phone. "Okay, she's a bit shook up, and she lost her shoes, but—"

"What?" screamed Amanda. "Are you telling me that you were shot at? By a sniper? She's only been visiting for two whole days!"

"Yes, well, as you can imagine, this was unexpected," I stuttered.

"Unexpected? No wonder St. Louis is the murder capital of the United States," said my sister.

"Um, it's not. Detroit is. We're number two. But we try harder."

"You have to be kidding me! How could this have happened? Huh? How could you let that happen to Mom? I should have known better than to let her visit you!" Amanda's voice moved from soprano to alto. "If I'd had any other option, I would have taken it!"

"Listen up, Amanda," I said, and then I tapped my mother on the shoulder. "Mom? You listen too, because I don't intend to repeat myself. Nobody did anything to Mom, understand? This was a horrible situation, but we're safe now. Nothing like this will happen again."

Robbie's office door swung open. The big man stood there, his face cold as a slab of granite. "Kiki, I'm not so sure about that. We need to talk."

ELEVEN

I GOT OFF THE phone really fast.

Mom stood up and started screaming at me. "See? See? This is all because of YOU!"

"Sit down, ma'am." Robbie's voice overflowed with authority. "When you are in this office, you will keep a civil tongue in your head."

That shut Mom right up.

"Police Chief Robbie Holmes, this is my mother, Lucia Montgomery," I said.

"So I gathered."

Mom groaned. "Kiki, you know better! One must always introduce a man to a woman, not the other way around. Where are your manners?"

"Probably back in the grass at CALA, I reckon." Proper etiquette being the least of my worries.

Sheila had taken Anya into her embrace, as best she could despite the chair arms between them. At the sight of her intended, my mother-in-law let go of my daughter and stretched her arms up to welcome Robbie. In return, he leaned down to give my mother-in-law a kiss on the lips. Instantly, Sheila's face shone with joy. I swear that man has a positively humanizing effect on her.

"You all right, sweetie?" Robbie asked Sheila. After she nodded, he asked, "And you, Anya, honey? Kiki? Are you okay?"

"Thanks to Kiki," said Sheila. "She figured out what was happening. First she made us duck under the folding chairs, then she grabbed Anya and got us all running toward the car before the crowd could trample us."

"Huh! How on earth can you thank Kiki?" my mother said, punctuating her comment with a loud huff. "She's the reason we had to run!"

"We don't know that for sure," Robbie said, pulling open his drawer and fishing out a handful of change. "Anya, honey, would you run down to the vending machines and get me one of those packages of cheese crackers with the peanut butter filling?"

My daughter moved slowly. Robbie handed over the change and gave Anya a quick hug. "That's my girl. Anyone else want a snack?"

I "ordered" M&Ms with peanuts, and Sheila asked for pretzels. Mom sniffed. "I'm far too upset to eat, but if there's any nice chocolate, I might try a bite."

This necessitated Anya making a short list and Robbie reminding her of the vending machine location. "If that one doesn't have everything, go try the one in the basement," he said.

Anya sighed. "I know you're trying to get me out of the room."

Robbie chuckled. "You are too smart, little darling. Too smart. Yes, I am. But I also want those crackers. How about it?"

She gave him an indulgent smile and headed for the machines.

TWELVE

AFTER HER FOOTSTEPS FADED, Sheila pushed the door closed. She turned and gave my mother a scalding look. "Robbie's right. There's no excuse for this sort of behavior. None. We've all been through a traumatic experience, Lucia, and your granddaughter is the person you should be concerned about. Not yourself. You are fine. For goodness sake, anyone would think you are more worried about a stupid pair of shoes than about your family."

Mom muttered darkly and asked where her tea was. "I have to use the bathroom."

"Anya can take you when she gets back," I said. I was relieved that Anya had left the room. There were questions that needed to be asked. "Robbie, how many people were hurt?"

He sighed. "Mrs. Fitzgerald was killed. Her son, Peter, suffered a gunshot wound. Five people suffered various injuries in the crush to get away. That's what we have right now."

"You're sure this had to do with my George's killer?" Sheila's face twisted with grief and rage. George had been her only child.

"No," Robbie sighed again. He leaned back in his big black desk chair and steepled his fingers. "Actually, I'm not sure of anything, except that you are a sight for sore eyes, darling. All I could think of was what'd I do if anything happened to you. It was not a happy thought."

"It doesn't make sense that it would be Bill Ballard," I said. "I mean, why involve all those other folks? If I'm the one he wants, he would only target me, right? The shots didn't hit that close to us. And the shooter had plenty of chances to get me in his crosshairs."

"Describe the scene to me." Robbie closed his eyes to listen.

I told him about arriving late and sitting on the outskirts of the crowd. "The viewfinder of Sheila's video camera has a really nice zoom. I saw this flower bloom on Edwina's chest. Of course, it wasn't a flower..." My throat closed up. I swallowed. "Robbie, that first shot must have hit her square in center mass."

"Center mass? What on earth does that mean?" asked my mother.

"That's what we teach law enforcement officials. We don't shoot to wound. If the situation is serious enough to require a shot being fired, you aim for center mass," said Robbie, using his index finger to draw a space between the shoulders and above the ribs. "One shot and they drop."

"Which would mean that the shooter knew what he or she was doing," I finished.

Robbie nodded. "Or got lucky."

I disagreed. "There must have been nearly two hundred people there. What are the chances of hitting one person center mass?"

"But Peter Fitzgerald suffered a wound to the thigh," Robbie reminded me.

"But no one else was wounded. I mean, what are the odds? Fish in a barrel, Robbie. The sniper could have picked off three more people easy."

"Easily," corrected my mother.

"How many shots did you hear?" Robbie asked all of us.

I turned to Sheila and Mom. "What did you count?"

They couldn't remember. I couldn't tell him. I knew it was more than four. "I'm sorry, Robbie. I know it's dumb not to know. I can tell you that they sounded like they came from that stand of trees."

He gave me another smile, this one wistful. "Hon, most people can't recall. There's something about being shot at that makes counting fly right out of your head. You did well to respond so quickly—and to get your daughter out of there. My men tell me there are girls still wandering around out there, sobbing and trying to figure out where their parents are. We've moved most of them into the building, but still ... "

"Can I help? I mean, I'd be happy to go to the school and sit with the girls, or even drive some of them home," I offered.

"No, it's best to let Mr. McMahan handle this. It's his job, not ours. We'll have our hands full with complaints that the incident even happened."

"Like I said, I was nearly killed!" Mom had recovered from her chastisement sufficiently to start complaining again.

"But you weren't," said Robbie. "However, Mrs. Fitzgerald is dead. Kiki, until I have more information, would you humor an old man and spend the night at Sheila's? I'll be over later. I know it will make it hard for you. It might put a crimp in your love life, but I think it's best."

I nodded.

Mom was slow on the uptake, but she caught his drift. "A crimp in her love life? Kiki, you aren't intimate with that cop, are you?"

Almost on cue, the door opened.

Detweiler stepped in. He was wearing a SWAT jacket and his customary Dockers. I jumped up and ran to his arms, comforted by the feel of his long and lean frame against mine. His Heineken bottle green eyes sparkled as he hugged me tightly. "Am I glad to see you," he said in a husky voice. Something stirred deep inside me, evoking both a memory and a promise.

Ignoring the onlookers, Detweiler kissed me soundly, lifting me off the floor. He didn't let go of me as he said, "Where's Anya? Down the hall? Good."

He closed the door. "Chief? Kiki? We have a problem."

THIRTEEN

"BILL BALLARD PUT OUT a contract on me?" I sounded like Minnie Mouse, my voice was that squeaky and high-pitched. I still held onto Detective Chad Detweiler or I would have toppled over. My head swam and my legs went back to rubber.

"Not exactly. Nothing so formal," Detweiler eased me into a chair while he knelt on the floor next to me. "One of our confidential informants heard a rumor that Bill Ballard's been bragging about—"

Detweiler stopped himself. He and Chief Holmes exchanged knowing looks.

I felt sick at my stomach.

"Getting even with you," Detweiler continued in a casual voice. "And he's looking for helpers."

"Arrest him!" Sheila shouted. "Drag him in, right now! He deserves the electric chair."

"Darling, that's hearsay. You can't arrest someone for hearsay," said Robbie, moving his chair to the side and reaching across his desk to take Sheila's hand.

"What about all the other stuff he's done?" I asked.

Detweiler pulled up a chair, turned it backwards and straddled it. "We're working on that."

"Working on that?" Now I sounded like Chip and Dale, the fabled chipmunks. "But … but he kidnapped me. You heard what he said! You heard him brag about shooting Roxanne!"

"I heard your side of the conversation," Detweiler said. "But I'm no longer an impartial witness. A sharp attorney would have that entire conversation ruled inadmissible."

"You have to be kidding me. He held a gun to my ribs!"

"Says you." Robbie was sympathetic, but firm.

"What? You think I'd make that up?" My face got hot.

"I know—we all know—that you didn't, but proving it in court is another thing entirely," said Detweiler. He held up fingers and ticked off points as he made them. "We don't have the gun that was used on Roxanne. We don't have physical evidence linking Bill Ballard to her murder. Basically, we're down to his word against yours in most instances. We do plan to arrest him and bring him in for questioning in regard to Mr. Lowenstein's death, and at the very least charge him with embezzling funds from Diamont Development."

"You can't let him get away with that!" Sheila said, with a wild expression of grief twisting her lovely features. "Robbie, he murdered my son! My only child!"

Robbie scooted his chair over beside Sheila and pulled her close. "I know, darling. I know. This is the most frustrating part of my job—when we know who did it and we're not sure we can convict them."

"But he killed my son! My strong, beautiful, wonderful son! The light of my life!" Sheila wailed as she leaned into Robbie. His huge hand patted her back, the way a mother might a baby. Big tears swelled in those faded blue eyes before spilling over to run down Sheila's face.

I willed myself not to make the situation more embarrassing by showing how shocked I was. I'd never seen Sheila cry over George. At his funeral, she stood stiff and still like a column of carved ice. When I blubbered while dropping a handful of dirt on the casket, she barely flinched as her offering splattered the dark mahogany.

I knew she mourned her son. At the *yahrzeit*, the one-year anniversary of George's death, we lit the memorial candle, and I struggled my way through the *Kaddish*. But Sheila's voice recited the prayer, praising God and accepting his dominion over us, without a hitch. I knew the purpose, that in the face of loss we want to rage at God, and I knew the *Kaddish* reminded us that God was the source of all good in life. How could we rage at the same creator who had brought this loved one into existence?

So I tried with all my might to follow her example. For the most part, I succeeded. But not always. When the tears leaked out, Sheila would silently offer me a linen handkerchief, but she never joined me in crying. No, never, not once, until today had I seen my mother-in-law cry.

Except today—and my heart ached in a new way, with a pain I didn't know I could feel for Sheila. We'd been through so much together. We'd gone from adversaries to wary opponents to reluctant colleagues and finally we'd reached this sweet spot. I could honestly call her my friend. In fact, in many ways, she had become my surrogate mother.

"I told you it was Kiki's fault." My biological mother lifted her chin high and looked very pleased with herself.

"Mom, how could you?" I buried my head in my hands.

"Mrs. Montgomery, your daughter is a victim. We do not blame the victim of a crime. She's done nothing, I repeat, nothing to bring this on herself. Shame on you for suggesting as much," Robbie wagged a finger at Mom. His voice brooked no debate, and I noticed Mom shrinking back in her chair.

"Sheila, darling, can I do anything for you?" he asked.

"No," she said in a voice so quiet that I strained to hear it. "Yes. Make him pay, Robbie. Make him pay."

Robbie hugged her, let her go and said, "Kiki, we aren't sure what Bill has planned. That's why we're thinking he might be behind the shooting today. In fact, he could even be the gunman."

"I don't think so. I can't see it," I said. "Doesn't feel right."

Detweiler drummed his fingers on his Dockers. "One of the officers on the scene noted that Mrs. Fitzgerald and Mrs. Lowenstein—" he nodded at Sheila "—were both wearing the same shade of blue. Could be a case of mistaken identity."

Only a man would confuse cornflower blue and periwinkle. A man who didn't scrapbook. I mean, they might as well have been wearing blue and orange. The colors are that different!

On the other hand, if the shooter was a man, maybe he didn't know the difference between cornflower blue and periwinkle either.

Mom snorted. "I thought so. I could have been hurt."

"It could still happen," said Sheila, with a meaningful glance toward me. "You aren't entirely in the clear."

But Mom didn't catch her drift.

I saw Detweiler's jaw clench. I knew that look. He was major league ticked off. He took those gorgeous golden-green eyes away from my mom and turned them on me. "You and Anya will have to be especially careful. Promise me you will."

I nodded. What else could I do?

FOURTEEN

We spent a restless Saturday evening at Sheila's house. Linnea, Sheila's maid, left sandwiches and salad for us in the refrigerator. In the crockpot simmered a tortilla soup that made me instantly hungry.

Even Mom dug into her meal without complaint. After she'd eaten, she sat at the table and made a big production out of taking an Ativan for her nerves.

Sheila asked Anya to show her grandmother to the only vacant guest room. When Anya returned with her gray kitten in her arms, she said, "Grandmére is sound asleep. I fed Seymour. I think he missed me."

With Mom down for the count, I decided to call my best friend Mert. But my cell phone was missing. I searched high and low. Finally I asked Anya and Sheila if they'd seen it.

"I think Grandmére had it. She tucked something into her pocket when we passed the front table," Anya said.

The front table was where I usually set my cell phone when I was at Sheila's house.

I tiptoed into the guest bedroom and past my snoring mother. On the bedside table sat my phone. I checked the last number called. A name came up that I didn't recognize: Beverly Glenn.

But no Claudia.

So who had Mom called? I sighed and dialed Mert's number.

"We're fine, Anya's a little shook up, but we're okay," I told her. The conversation was short because she was on her way out the door to go to dinner with her new beau Hank Redolf, a retired Marine sergeant. They were also going to be busy on Sunday, so we promised to catch up with each other sometime next week.

Linnea's tortilla soup

1 package of Tyson's prepared chicken, Southwestern style, cut
   into bite-sized pieces
1 jar of salsa (about 8 ounces of any brand)
1 can of tomatoes with Mexican spices
1 large onion, diced
1 can of yellow corn
1 can of black beans, drained
1 can of kidney beans, drained
1 32-ounce box of Swanson's Chicken bouillon
2 T. of cilantro paste such as Gourmet Garden brand
V-8 juice

   Mix all ingredients in a crockpot. Add enough V-8 juice and
water to fill. Stir and cook 4–6 hours on high. Serve with crushed
Doritos, sour cream, and chunks of avocado.

FIFTEEN

Sunday, May 2

AS WAS OUR ROUTINE, Anya and I ate pancakes and took Gracie for a long walk. To give Sheila and Robbie some alone time, I packed a picnic lunch of sandwiches and then Mom, Anya, and I went to the St. Louis Art Museum. Like the St. Louis Zoo, it's free, and fabulous. We wandered around for hours before grabbing a picnic table nearby and eating. I worked hard to steer the conversation clear of the sniper attack. I also tried my best to be solicitous of my mother.

That evening Sheila, Anya, and I curled up in front of the television. Anya stroked her sweet kitty, Seymour, whose purring soothed all of us. Gracie rested her head on my lap, which gave me comfort as well. By mutual agreement, we avoided talk about the shooting. But we couldn't escape it. The ten o'clock news led off with video from the sniper attack. I gawped at the screen. If I had any doubts that our nightmare was real, this cinched them. For a second, I sat frozen in the chair and had an out-of-body experience. Surely this hadn't happened to me. Surely we hadn't been shot at. Here in the comfort of Sheila's house, I could pretend we were like any other happy family.

Any other happy family targeted by a killer.

Sheila managed to hit the channel changer button quickly, but not quite fast enough.

We heard the headline, "Police are still investigating a shooting that left one woman dead and her son injured—"

Sheila switched the station to a rerun of *NCIS*.

"Time for bed." I nudged Anya. "You've got school tomorrow."

"Right," she said. "Maybe they should change the school colors from royal blue and gold to blood red and bullet gray."

I shuddered. "Hey, I feel like reading. How about you? What's that book you've been nose deep in?"

"*The Hunger Games*," she said. "It's about a society that forces kids to kill each other."

Oh, just ducky! What happened to Nancy Drew and that wimpy Ned she ran around with? Hmmm?

After Anya changed into her pajamas, snuggled under the sheets, and read for a while, I asked if she wanted me to rub her back. "Could you stay here, Mom? At least until I go to sleep? Seymour would like that, too."

I had answered all the phone and text messages from my friends with a quick text message of my own: *We're all right. Thanks for your concern.* Seems that everyone heard about the sniper, and they all wanted to know that me and mine were safe.

However, I simply didn't have the energy to engage in more detailed conversations. And now, my daughter was reverting to

childhood. So I had the perfect excuse to further avoid long dir-
courses on the tragedy.

Anya drifted off, clutching my hand. When I tried to withdraw
my fingers, she moaned and tightened her grip. I resigned myself
to balancing on a thin sliver of her bed and resting fitfully while
Seymour climbed to the highest point of her pillow and watched
over us, like the silent Sphinx guards the desert.

SIXTEEN

Monday, May 3

CALA's AUTOMATED CALLING SYSTEM rang my cell phone the next morning to inform me there would be a "late start," and that counselors would be on hand to talk to the students. Sheila offered to drop Anya off. Since she often drove my daughter to school, I felt okay with that. When there's been a tragedy, especially a loss of life, routine offers comfort. Not a lot, but some. You tell yourself that life will go on, and it does, and one day you forget what happened. Not for long. You remember it quickly enough, but for a blink in time, the hurt stops. That small respite gives you hope. You realize that one day, maybe in the distant future, the surcease from sorrow might actually outlast the pain. With that thin straw of optimism clutched in your hand, you think you can go on.

So you do.

I headed for Time in a Bottle, the little scrapbook store where I work. Admittedly, I was preoccupied and stressed, so I wasn't paying much attention when I approached the parking lot. Every one of my nerves was raw. I saw shadows in every corner, every car seemed to be following me, and the playful shadows cast by trees caused my heart to lurch with fear.

If Bill hired someone to hurt me, what would that person look like? Where might he or she attack me? What warning might they give? Detweiler had given me a copy of *The Gift of Fear* by Gavin de Becker. I was only halfway through, but I found the work fascinating. The author suggested that we tune in and trust ourselves because our unconscious minds would detect tiny inconsistencies that signaled threats faster than our rational minds could.

My unconscious mind shifted to high alert. My body switched itself to fight or flight mode. It wasn't just Bill Ballard who was making me tense. My own mother was standing on my last nerve, driving me nuts.

Last night on our way to Sheila's, Mom lit into me with both barrels blazing. Yep, Dear Old Mom, aka Lucia Drayton Montgomery Collins, was officially on a tear. (Even though they lived together until he died, Mom and Dad had officially divorced, so she'd resumed using her maiden surname of Montgomery, which she claimed was more elegant than Collins.) I sat there, hunched over in Sheila's back seat, and took it, hoping that if I didn't give her any resistance, she'd eventually wear down.

But I underestimated the impact of my mother's tirade on Anya.

Five minutes into my mother's harping, my daughter burst into tears. Sheila turned to wag an angry finger at Mom. "Lucia Montgomery, you say one more word and I will toss you out of this car and into the express lane of Highway 40. See if I don't. I've had it with you. Shut up! Right now!"

Wow. I'd never seen Sheila so angry. Or my mother so shocked. But Mom shut her mouth. We made the rest of the trip in blessed silence.

This morning Sheila, Anya, and I tiptoed around the house, happy to let Mom sleep.

"When is she going home?" Sheila asked.

"I haven't a clue. I hope it's soon."

"I'll pay for her flight."

"Actually, I think we could take up a collection," I said. I wasn't kidding. Everyone who had come in contact with my mother was eager to see her go.

I kissed Anya goodbye and hustled Gracie into my BMW. She wriggled with joy as she climbed in beside me and settled her rump in the passenger seat of my old convertible. My tension faded away as I traveled the familiar route to Time in a Bottle.

By the time I turned into the parking lot, I fairly hummed with anticipation. I planned to get caught up on my newest project, an ATC (Artist Trading Card) class. I was so lost in creative musing, so totally "in my head" and visualizing a new design, that I nearly overlooked the figure of a woman, bottoms up, face down in the grass.

Crud, I thought, as I jumped out of the car, leaving Gracie inside. *She must have fallen.*

"Are you all right?" I called out as I approached her.

"*Ja?*" The stranger sank back onto her heels and studied me. In one hand, she waved a pair of tiny embroidery scissors.

"Did you fall? May I help you get up?"

"*Nein.*"

I had watched enough reruns of *Hogan's Heroes* to translate her German into "No."

"Did you lose something?" That's me, Mrs. Helpful.

"Nein." She pushed a pair of glasses back on her nose. The frames were milky pink and the lenses were shaped like cats' eyes. Tiny trios of rhinestones sparkled in the outside corners. She struggled to her feet, her hands pushing away from me to show she didn't want assistance. "I am Margit Eichen. You must be Kiki."

She pronounced my first name, "Kick-ee."

I've been called worse.

"You are late," she added.

"Late?"

"For work."

I checked my cell phone. "It's only eight-oh-five."

"You are scheduled for eight o'clock."

With that she turned to the task at hand, squatting down on all fours so she could continue to clip the grass in the verge that ran between our sidewalk and the street. To my astonishment, she pulled a small ruler from a pocket. She not only trimmed the grass, she measured it first!

"I'm Kiki Lowenstein, and I'm part-owner of Time in a Bottle," I said. This time I stepped in closer, reached down and stuck my hand out, offering it to shake.

The woman stared up at me. "I know who you are. I am the new part-owner of Time in a Bottle."

My mouth flapped open. I didn't know what to say. An intense fury swept through me. Part-owner? What had Dodie done? She'd gone and added a co-owner without consulting me!

"I suggest you go inside. You are now ten minutes late," said Margit. "I hope this is not a habit for you."

Great. Just what I needed. Another harpy in my life. Now I was surrounded by ill-tempered, nasty older women: Sheila, Mom, and Margit.

I gnashed my teeth and stifled a scream. Enough! I'd had enough! How dare Dodie let this time- and measurement-obsessed woman invade my personal sanctuary! What could Dodie have been thinking? How could she add a new partner without running the idea past me first?

SEVENTEEN

TIME IN A BOTTLE might look like an ordinary storefront to passers-by, but to me, it's my home away from home.

Correction: Since my mom arrived, it's my only home. Mom has managed to turn my happy little domicile into one of Dante's Nine Circles of Hell. To be specific, I lived in "Wrath," because Mom was angry all the time.

So coming to Time in a Bottle this morning, well, it was balm to my soul.

But that had been ruined!

After surviving the sniper attack, dealing with my mother, and learning that a killer had put out a contract on me, I needed this haven more than ever. And here Dodie had brought in a new partner without consulting me! This was so unfair!

I stomped back to my car, retrieved Gracie, and stormed in through the back door.

Dodie sat behind her desk, nursing a big cup of tea. She's finished her chemo and radiation treatments for cancer of the larynx, which is good news. However, she has no appetite and she's tired a lot, which is bad news. The woman who was once compared to a wooly mammoth could double as a de-nuded stick figure these days. Usually, I fuss over her, try to encourage her to eat and keep drinking lots of liquids.

But not today. Today I was mad. Fighting mad.

"Kiki! I've been calling you all weekend! Is Anya all right? I've been following the sniper attack on the news. *Oy vey*, what a mess! I am glad to see you are unhurt. And Anya? She is all right as well?"

I nodded. Her concern took all the starch out of my panties. I snarled at her, "I sent a blanket text message saying we were upset but unharmed. Don't tell me you didn't get it."

"I'm not so good with technology yet," Dodie said as she came over to hug me. I accepted the gesture but stayed stiff as a piece of chip board. It is hard to be mad at someone who cares about you, but I kept a firm grasp on my indignation.

"We're all fine. Even Sheila and my mother. Not that you asked about them."

Dodie smirked. "Sheila is indestructible, and your mother is tough as shoe leather. You and I both know Sheila would walk through the D-Day invasion without getting wet feet. As for your mother, against stupidity God himself is helpless. The sniper never had a chance."

"We're lucky to be alive. Edwina Fitzgerald took a bullet in the chest. Died at the scene. Her son, Peter, was shot in the leg. There was a panic, but fortunately only five other people were injured. That sounds like a lot, but given the circumstances, it could have been much, much worse." As I talked, Dodie pulled an ice cold Diet Dr Pepper out of the refrigerator and handed it to me. The combination of her interest and her handing me my favorite tonic left me feeling silly about my upset.

"Edwina Fitzgerald," said Dodie. "May her memory be a blessing."

"You know—knew—her?"

"Yes. We were on an arts committee together years ago. Of course, she wouldn't have remembered me. I was just a committee member, and she was in charge. Edwina was Old St. Louis money. She enjoyed having people like me sign up to work, but she definitely had her own circle of friends for socializing."

"Fitzgerald. That's old St. Louis?"

"Her maiden name was Lichbaden."

"Lichbaden? Like the beer?"

"The same." I sipped my cola and gave that a think.

In the second half of the 1800s, four million Germans immigrated to the United States. Many of them settled in Missouri, finding its climate and soil much like that of their homeland. With all those Germans came the desire for a taste of home in the form of beer.

"Pabst, Busch, Schlitz, they all started together. Built their fortunes."

"The beer barons."

"Right. Edwina's great-great-great grandfather and his wife brought their family recipe with them when they came to America. Aldous Lichbaden bought hops and wheat from other local Germans. His wife, Gretchen, mixed the brew in their basement. They stored the brew in the caves under the city. About fifty years ago, Anheuser-Busch bought them out, but after the noncompete ended

Edwina's husband, Gergen, opened a microbrewery. They're back in the business again, this time with a new product and a new name."

"What does Peter do?" I knew quite a few of the parents at CALA, but not all of them. I could have pointed out Peter and his wife, Deanna, in a crowd, but other than that, they were ciphers to me.

"He works for Edwina. I believe his title is Vice President. I heard he had plans to expand the company. Start bottling that weird fermented tea."

"Kombucha?"

"Is that like Kumbaya? I hear that's a hit around the campfire," said Dodie.

"No. Kombucha is a fermented tea drink."

"Well, now he can do exactly as he wishes, after he buries his mother. Speaking of which, how are you getting along with yours?"

"Let's not go there," I said with a sigh. "Tell me about our new lawn service. You do realize that Margit is out there measuring the grass and cutting it."

Dodie laughed and took another swallow of her Dr. Brown's Cream Soda. She drank Dr. Brown and I drank Dr Pepper. We had a theme going. Or maybe we were both sick puppies. "I hoped to introduce you two formally, but Margit insisted on starting work earlier than I had anticipated. She's a widow, just like you. Her husband, Helmut, died last year. Margit doesn't know what to do with herself."

"What does she know about scrapbooking?"

"Nothing. Nothing at all. In fact, she thinks it's silly. Margit is a world-class knitter. If she had her way, this would be a yarn shop."

EIGHTEEN

"I LIKE YARN AS much as the next crafter, but if she doesn't appreciate papercrafting why did you let her buy Bama's share? I can't believe you didn't talk to me first. I thought that at least you'd let me meet the new partner before bringing her on. How can you tell if we're compatible?" I sputtered.

Once upon a time, I was Dodie's best customer. After my husband was killed, Dodie offered me a job, and I strove to become her best employee. Along the way, she offered me the chance to buy into Time in a Bottle and I happily accepted.

Dodie sighed. "This isn't a dating service, Sunshine. This is work. I brought her on board because of her talents. Margit is highly efficient and organized. She's also good with numbers." She paused, cleared her throat, coughed lightly, and sipped her cola.

Her distress brought me off my high horse. Her chemo and radiation for cancer of the larynx ended three months ago, but instead of looking better at the treatments' cessation, Dodie looked worse. She'd lost weight. Her color was off. Her energy level weighed in somewhere between sluggish and somnambulant. Several times in the past week, I caught her catnapping at her desk.

"So Margit's responsibilities will be...what?" I sat across from Dodie. Gracie flopped down on the floor next to me and rested her head in my lap. I stroked her velvety ears.

"Margit'll take over inventory control, ordering stock, paying vendors, and scheduling hours."

That's what I'd been afraid of. When I agreed to work for Dodie, we made an agreement that my child came first. At twelve, Anya isn't exactly a child anymore, but she still needs me. Dodie has been marvelously flexible. But Margit's insistence that I show up on the stroke of 8 a.m. worried me.

"Anya comes first in my life. Work runs a distant second."

"No problem, Sunshine."

"Margit better understand that, too."

Dodie sighed. "Margit will be a great addition, but you need to understand, I pay you to get along with people, not to quarrel with them. Look, I know you've had a rough weekend. I'm sorry about that. But we're all grownups here, Kiki. I expect you to act like one."

Tears welled in my eyes. Bama and I hadn't gotten along, for various reasons, and Dodie deserved some of the blame.

Clearly, she didn't agree. Or at the very least, she refused to acknowledge her part.

I checked my cell phone: 8:09, and already my day had been ruined. I pushed back my chair and led Gracie to her playpen. I couldn't even bring myself to respond to Dodie's salvo. It felt horribly, terribly unfair—and on top of my mother's cruel remarks, more than I could bear.

How quickly Dodie forgot all I'd done for her! While she'd been sick, I'd worked extra hours. When she had her first scare with cancer, I'd been super-supportive. Every time she needed me, I'd been right there for her.

I thought Dodie could benefit from a few lessons in managing people. Longing to tell her exactly that, I went through the motions of opening the store.

Jeopardy answer: Dodie Goldfader, Sheila Lowenstein, and Lucia Montgomery.

The question: Name three women convinced they have all the answers.

The gleesome trio shared one triumphant quality: Infallibility. Each believed she was right, unquestionably. I, on the other hand, was far too willing to believe I was wrong.

At the front door, I flipped over the OPEN sign. Yes, I turned it over early. As far as I was concerned, if some happy little scrapper jumped out of bed and made a beeline to our place, I was going to welcome her with open arms.

Dodie brought me the change drawer for the cash register. "This was certainly a May Day to remember. It's an ill wind that blows no good. Given the drama, I bet your album will be very popular. Maybe we should laser cut a page title. How about Mayday for May Day, eh?"

She smiled at her own pun. "Mayday" comes from the French *m'aider*, which means "I need help."

Dodie wiped her forehead with the back of her hand. "The school has already sent me an email. Lane Carlée, their new development director, wants you to do two memorial albums chronicling Edwina's life and her many contributions to CALA. One will go to the school for their archives and one will be a gift from the Alumni Association to Edwina's family. You saved the May Day album, didn't you?"

NINETEEN

A slow heat started at my neckline. "I was lucky to save myself and my family, Dodie. There wasn't time to grab the album."

"We need one made up ASAP. I'm sure people will want them. Especially now."

I wondered at her thinking. Usually Dodie is very careful, very circumspect about our store's image. "Really? I mean, it was a tragedy, Dodie. Remember? I was there. When does a shooting qualify as a Red Letter Day?"

She gestured away my concern. "At the very least, we need to have a May Day album kit available."

"Am I supposed to do this in my copious free time? You do realize I had thirty-plus hours of work in that May Day album. Now you want me to re-create that, plus two copies of a personalized memorial album. Will those hours be added to my store hours?"

Two could play Miss Meanie-Jeanie-Jelly-Beanie. Like Dodie, I counted on the revenue from selling May Day albums to CALA families. The initial concept through creation phase of any new project was the most time-consuming part. Once an album was extant, I could duplicate it *ad nauseam*, or even job out the duplication to other crafters. But the designing took all my concentration. And energy. And time.

I hoped I could remember what went into the May Day album.

I'd have to juggle re-creating that joyous piece of work with creating Edwina's solemn memorial book—and that meant partitioning my brain so I could work on two projects simultaneously. Both would need to be done quickly as the window of opportunity was tight.

Dodie's smile was tense, and I could tell that she was annoyed by my complaints. "I expect you to make it happen. I have always paid you for your work. Discuss scheduling issues with Margit. That reminds me. I know that your mother-in-law will want you to take time off for dress fittings and so on. I suggest you try to pin Sheila down so you can schedule the time in advance with Margit. Otherwise, your needs might create problems."

She turned slowly and shuffled off to her office. A part of me melted at the sight of her. She stooped over where she had once walked erect. Her hair had thinned. Her whole frame caved in on itself. I could tell she didn't feel well, because the Dodie of old would have never talked to me so curtly the way this new incarnation of my pal did. Even though she claimed she was back to normal, I could tell she wasn't her old self. The chemo and radiation treatments had definitely changed her personality, and not for the better.

I slapped a roll of pennies over the drawer dividers to break it. The coins flew up, bounced, and rolled across the floor.

The drawer would start a few cents short. That meant the day would end short as well. I looked over in the penny cup, with its cheerful "Need One? Take One. Have One? Leave One." sign. It was conspicuously absent. At last count, that cup contained at least twenty cents.

Great, just great. This was shaping up to be an all-around crummy day.

MARGIT'S TIPS FOR BEGINNING KNITTERS

Check out your local independent yarn store. Many of them offer classes just for beginners or sessions where you can bring your project and get help. Libraries also host knitting groups, so check around. Most veterans are more than happy to help you get started.

While it might seem like a waste of yarn to start by knitting a square or a simple project, consider these exercises as valuable preparation. Once you get the feel of needles in your hand, you'll be less likely to mess up your first real project.

A "how to knit" kit is a great way to get started. However, having someone teach you how to cast on is the easiest way to learn this important skill.

For your first real project, do invest in good yarn. After all, if you are going to put all this work and effort into your project, shouldn't it last a lifetime?

TWENTY

"Everything is peachy-keen, hunky-dory, super-fine, fantastic." I slammed a chair against the work table. "Ouch!" I caught my finger between the seat and the surface. Served me right. I'd been slamming stuff around all day and the damage was evident: lost pennies, spilled glitter, and now a mashed finger.

"Kiki Lowenstein, your nose grows longer by the minute." Clancy Whitehead laughed as I popped my finger into my mouth and sucked it. We shuffled more chairs into place. She had shown up twenty minutes early to help me get ready for our special crop. "Maybe you need to go home."

"Can't. I'm camping out at Sheila's."

"That's even better! She's got hired help. Let her maid coddle you. You've had a tough day. Put your feet up. Drink a glass of wine."

"I'd love to. My mother drank everything Sheila had in the house."

"How's her visit going?" Clancy set out the kits for the evening crop, plunking down one at each place.

"Not well."

"So your sister just called and said, 'Hey, pick up Mom from the airport'? She didn't even give you a choice in the matter?"

"Nope, in fact, Amanda didn't even talk to me, she just left a message on my phone."

"That was dicey," said Clancy. "What if you hadn't been available? I bet she listened when you told her you'd been shot at."

I nodded. "She listened long enough to hear what happened, and then she gave me a royal chewing-out for putting our mother in danger. Like I planned that! As for Mom, let's be kind and say she's been challenging. How's that for soft peddling what's really happening?"

Clancy laughed, but the sound lacked sparkle. Despite her gorgeous outfit—a striped Tommy Hilfiger blouse and a lightweight pin-striped blazer over a pair of neat denim slacks, Clancy looked tired these days.

I knew why. Her mother was having health problems. Clancy arranged a host of services to help out, including Meals on Wheels, a "panic" button connected to a 24-hour hotline, and a senior day care program. But Mrs. Clancy—my pal had taken her maiden name of "Clancy" as her first name because she hated being called "Druscilla"—fought her daughter every step of the way.

"I can guess what you're going through. My mother isn't her old self, either. Until recently, Mama was sharp as the proverbial tack. Now she phones me three and four times an hour and asks me what day it is. She wants me to move in with her," Clancy explained. "But I can't bring myself to do that. I'd give up all my freedom, and probably my sanity as well. We've never gotten along that well. I mean, I love Mama, and I want to do right by her, but we're very different in many ways."

"You have a brother, don't you? Why can't he help out?" I stopped distributing the ink pads for our session and I paused to watch Clancy's reaction.

Her whole body stiffened as though replaying a harsh blow. "Daniel says he's too busy with his law practice. His wife, Lora, never really got along well with Mama. I understand that. I know Mama felt Lora was an interloper and treated her as such."

"But she's his mother, too, right? He must be retirement age. Surely he can take time off and visit her. Or have her visit with them."

Clancy smiled, a weak watered-down version of her usual high-beams. "He says that since I'm divorced, I don't have any obligations. And he says it's too far for Mama to travel to his house, so I'm the logical choice of caregiver."

"Where does he live?"

"Kansas City."

Yikes. At worst that was a whole four hours away by car, counting lots of pit stops.

"How did your mother do on the flight here?" Clancy adjusted the placement of the name tags. She loved precision, but unlike many of that ilk, she never imposed her obsessions on other people.

"Fine, I guess. At least she didn't complain to me about the flight. And usually she would have. She seemed physically fine when Anya and I showed up at Lambert Field."

Lambert Field is the old name for the Lambert-St. Louis Airport, which was designed by Minoru Yamasaki, who also did the World Trade Center in New York. Clancy knew what I meant. I like calling it Lambert Field because it reminds me of the courageous St. Louis businessmen who financed Charles Lindbergh and his trans-Atlantic flight. Seems to me, it's awfully easy for us to forget the people who've made our lives as convenient and wonderful as they are today.

"But she was upset that I didn't get there earlier," I added.

Mom had been standing in the baggage claim area for all of, oh, five minutes, judging by the Arrivals board next to luggage claim. But five minutes had been too long, or so she thought. She caught sight of me and immediately started whining. "Do you know how long I've been waiting? Is this any way to make me feel welcome? I was so worried! I traveled all that way by myself, and no one was here to greet me!"

I apologized over and over, explaining that I'd just gotten Amanda's message, but Mom refused to be mollified.

Things had only gone downhill on a bobsled since then.

"So you still don't know why your mother suddenly decided to visit? Or how long she's here?"

TWENTY-ONE

"Nope." I stood up and rubbed my aching lower back. "My sister refuses to answer my calls. Except for the other day when we were being shot at by a sniper."

"I suppose that counts as progress," said Clancy. She's always looking at the bright side whereas I am a rainy cloud searching for a place to drizzle.

"Here." Reaching inside her pocket, Clancy handed me her own cell phone. "She won't recognize the number. It's from Illinois, remember?"

I nodded. Clancy was right. She lived across the river, so presumably Amanda would not recognize that I was phoning.

I dialed Amanda and she picked up immediately. "Don't hang up! Please! Could we just talk? For a minute?" I spoke fast.

A long silence ensued. Finally, "Your turn," was all Amanda said and she hung up.

I hit redial. The phone rang and rang.

Clancy sighed and put the cell phone back in her pocket. "What were the living arrangements before your sister lost her mind?"

"Mom used the money from the sale of her old house to help Amanda buy a house in Oro Valley, a Tucson suburb. In return, Amanda built out the garage, making it into an apartment for Mom. As far as I know, everything worked out fine, except that Mom started bugging me lately for money."

Clancy paused as she counted out the paper for our project. "Define 'bugging me lately for money.'"

I hadn't particularly wanted to share this, but I did need someone to talk to, and Clancy was good with people. She had a level head on her shoulders and a way of seeing things that made sense. "Mom has asked me to send her $400 a month. She says she needs it. But I don't have an extra $400 a month."

"Your mother still thinks you are rich, doesn't she?"

"I guess. But she might be coming around to the truth. Either that, or she's thinking I deserve an Academy Award."

"What category?" teased Clancy.

"Supporting actress. See, I support myself, my child, and my Great Dane. That ought to qualify, right?"

Clancy hooted with laughter. "Hasn't your mother noticed your low-rent lifestyle? Honestly, Kiki, you even reuse tea bags!"

"Mom refuses to believe I'm broke. I caught her pawing through my recycling, looking for proof of my legal address. I kid you not, Clancy. Mom even called Sheila to ask what I did with all the money I inherited from George."

"You have to be kidding," said Clancy. "I wish I could have overheard that conversation. I bet Sheila was less than pleased."

"You've got that right. She was downright annoyed. Told Mom it was none of her business. See, George's life insurance went to Sheila to repay a business loan. I never knew how indebted we were until he died and all the creditors started calling me." I closed my eyes and tried to blot out the memory. Even now, every time the phone rang, I felt sick, remembering the dunning calls we received. The situation had been so stressful, and I was so emotionally overwhelmed, that finally I started logging the calls into a little notebook that I hid under my mattress. I never wanted Anya to know how bad it had been.

"That must have been awful," said Clancy. "I am so sorry you went through that."

"It was a real nightmare. I sold everything we owned to pay off those debts. I only kept the BMW because it had no book value. Oh, and I hung onto my engagement ring so I could give it to Anya someday."

"I don't understand how your mother could possibly think you're wealthy. You buy your clothes at Goodwill or on sale at Target, you bring your lunch with you to work, you buy generic brands of everything. I mean, you're the original Miss Moneypenny-Pincher." Clancy finished distributing the paper and started collating and stapling together the handouts. Tonight our project featured Stamps by Judith! Her rubber stamps work together so a crafter can create custom images. They're oodles of fun.

Lately, we'd gone to a system of boxes and handouts to manage the supplies for our classes. The handouts gave instructions, step-by-step, and each portion of the project was broken down along with the necessary tools in boxes, numbered so that they went along with the instructions. So, if you were working on Step 1, and it called for you to make a hole, there was a hole punch in Box 1. If Step 1 also required a certain glue or brads or whatever, all that could be found in Box 1, too. The system allowed people to work at their own pace, while keeping small parts and tools organized.

"Get this—George's old partner is hatching plans to kill me."

"What?" Clancy startled and dropped an entire bottle of brads. We got on our hands and knees to pick up the small pieces. "You are kidding me," she said as we scrambled around under the tables. "Tell me you're joking around."

"I wish I were. Police Chief Holmes thinks the May Day sniper was after me."

"Bill's still at large, right?"

"That's right." A deep voice sounded over me, and I looked up into the face of Chad Detweiler.

"Det!" I squealed, jumped up, and threw my arms around him. "I'm so glad to see you!"

He laughed.

I could tell he was happy to see me, too. He hugged me tightly, and I responded by hugging him back for all I was worth. I took him by the hand and dragged him into the backroom. That didn't take much effort on my part, as he was my willing accomplice.

Once there, we kissed with the sort of fervor that makes your toes curl. We were busy like that when we heard an "ahem."

I turned to see Margit staring at us. We'd been blocking her pathway from the back sink to the store floor. Both her arms were loaded down with baked goods. "I was told that our customers like to eat," she said. "I made potato candy and German chocolate cake, plus a plain chocolate cake."

"Wow. The croppers are going to think they died and went to heaven. These smell terrific, Margit." My enthusiasm was sincere. I harbor a deep and abiding appreciation for food in all its various forms. Detweiler reached over and took one of the plates from my new co-worker, introducing himself as he did.

"I have heard about you," she said stiffly.

He carried the food out to the card table Clancy had decorated for this purpose. I introduced Margit to Clancy and then I grabbed Detweiler's hand. "I'm taking a quick break," I said before either woman could object.

Margit's potato candy

⅓ C. water

2 T. milk

½ tsp. salt

1 tsp. butter

2 T. mashed cooked potatoes or 2 T. instant potato granules

½ tsp. almond extract

1 lb. confectioners' sugar

1 (4 oz.) container of shredded coconut (1½ cups)

Put water, milk, and salt in two-quart saucepan and bring just to a boil. Remove from heat. Add butter and potato granules. With fork, beat until light and fluffy. Stir in almond extract. With spoon gradually beat in confectioners' sugar. Mixture will be liquid at first, then thicken. Beat until mixture holds shape. Mix in coconut. Drop by teaspoonful onto wax paper. Makes 1¾ lbs. or 38 pieces.

TWENTY-TWO

CLIPPING GRACIE TO HER leash, my boyfriend and I started on an around-the-block stroll designed to empty my big dog's tanks. Since Gracie adores Detweiler, it was a challenge to get her to walk rather than to lean against the hunky cop and gaze up at him fondly.

"We recovered Sheila's camera, like you suggested. There were five shots fired. We're still working on retrieving the bullet casings. You managed to capture the image of Edwina's hit on the video, and you responded to the shots."

"Which means what?"

"You turned toward the sound of the gunshots. The shooter was in the tree. We sent someone up there, and you nailed it, sweetie. The shooter left his gun in the tree. So we've got that."

"You can get fingerprints, right?"

He rubbed his chin. "I wish it worked in real life the way it does on TV. First of all, yes, we took prints. But they don't match the ones we have on file from Bill Ballard. He gave his prints when he went to work for a stock brokerage as an intern. We haven't heard from the FBI if the prints match anyone in their database. In fact, we probably won't know about that for a while."

The import of this struck me hard. "You're thinking it wasn't Bill who was the sniper? You agree with me that it doesn't feel right?"

Detweiler shook his head. "I'm not sure what to think. All I know is that Bill turned himself in this morning at seven a.m."

"What? You mean you had him in custody? But you just said he's still at large!"

Detweiler nodded, but his gesture lacked every sign of positivity. "Yeah. Have a seat in my office." He motioned toward a concrete block retaining wall circling a lawn.

Our shoulders touched, his hand captured mine, and we sat on the cold hard surface while Gracie rested her chin on the cop's thigh.

"I don't know how to tell you this, but Bill has retained counsel."

I struggled with what that might mean. "But he kidnapped me. He ran away. He shot at us. So if he's turned himself in—"

"He must think he's in the clear. Or that his lawyer will get him off."

"Who did he retain?"

"Jim Hagg."

Hagg was the go-to guy for folks in St. Louis who did the crime but evaded doing the time.

"Are you telling me Bill has been in custody and now he's back out on the streets?"

Detweiler sighed. "Right."

Despite the sun, I shivered.

Detweiler pulled me close to him, tucking me under his arm, as if to shelter me. "He had everything all arranged. His bail bondsman had the paperwork, and it was one of the fastest turnovers I've ever seen."

"But I thought you'd try to hold him for at least twenty-four hours. You need to see if he was the May Day sniper!"

"We have no evidence that he was involved."

"But … but your informant said—"

Detweiler waved my concerns away. "I know, I know. But we still don't have anything linking him to the crime. One of the biggest problems with our jail system is that creeps who get locked up meet other creeps. Bill might have met other criminals who were more than willing to shoot at you for him. The problem is proving that."

"Where does that leave me? I mean, are you telling me not to worry? Or are you suggesting that I continue to worry, but that now I worry about everyone, everywhere? Or should I not worry, because you know what you're doing? I'm confused."

"It means, you need to be careful, sweetheart. Anya needs to be warned. She has to stay aware of her surroundings. At least for a while. You both should be careful, Kiki. Meanwhile, Police Chief Holmes and I have been working on a plan."

TWENTY-THREE

I DIDN'T LIKE THEIR plan. Not one bit. First of all, it called for deception and acting skills. Secondly, it put a friend in danger. Third, it was a sure-fire way to make my best friend hate me forever.

As it turns out, the unlikeliest of duos had hatched this scheme: Police Chief Holmes and Johnny Chambers. Who'd have thunk it?

Johnny is the brother of Mert Chambers, my best friend, and he has a police record. He fell in with a bad group of friends just out of high school. He started drinking and got picked up for driving under the influence. Mert paid for an attorney, and Johnny started to straighten out his life. Then one night, Johnny met a few pals at a bar. They watched a Rams game, and since the Rams were then "the greatest show on turf," the friends decided to celebrate the success by getting totally wasted.

Not wanting to hazard another DUI, Johnny accepted a ride home with his buddies.

Turns out, they weren't going directly home. They planned to stop at a convenience store and rob it.

But Johnny didn't know that. He had passed out in the back seat. When he came to, one of the robbers shoved him out the passenger door and onto the pavement of the parking lot and tossed a gun after him. Johnny spent five years down in Potosi for armed robbery. Mert paid all his legal fees.

When Johnny was released, he started paying her back. He's really good with landscaping. He's been working for a grounds-keeping company, as well as freelancing at several houses around town, including doing yard work for my mother-in-law, Sheila. He ran into Police Chief Robbie Holmes while working at Sheila's.

Somehow Johnny and Robbie struck up a conversation. Somehow the subject turned to me and my problems, which Johnny knew in full.

Johnny and I had dated a few times before Detweiler and his wife separated. I have to admit, Johnny is a terrific kisser and the kind of "bad boy" that makes you wonder if being a "good girl" is worth the bother. But ultimately, my heart longed for Detweiler, and without me even telling Johnny, he knew our relationship wasn't going anywhere.

But still he's my friend and my best friend's brother. So Johnny had been privy to the sort of threats I was getting from Bill Ballard, the sort of havoc Bill caused in my life. He knew about Bill kidnapping me. About how Bill had either spent or run off with all of my husband's portion of their business. And finally, he knew about how Bill had been harassing me, sending threatening post-cards.

Like his sister, Mert, Johnny has an overly developed sense of fairness. Bill's bad behavior ticked Johnny off.

"Kiki's a good gal, and she don't deserve to live in fear. Nobody does," Johnny said to Police Chief Holmes. "Surely there's something I can do to help. Can't you use the fact I've served time to some advantage? I've got the right connections with the wrong sort of people."

Police Chief Holmes promised to think about it. He sort of back-burnered the idea until the sniper attack. The violent images juxtaposed against one of the city's more pastoral and honored rituals caused calls and letters to flood his office. Each day's letters to the editor in the *Post-Dispatch* brought more and more vitriolic responses to the tragedy.

The force of this blowback—and a tense meeting with the mayor—caused Robbie to reconsider all his options. Reminded of the politic maneuvering behind his appointment, Robbie decided to act forcefully and quickly. While "using" a criminal was a bad option, a desperate option, it was a better option than any other plan on the table.

He and Johnny met at a local diner and held a strategy session, or so Detweiler explained to me.

My guy pulled me closer, bent his head to talk to me in a low voice. "You need to have a very public fight with Johnny in front of a group of people. Has to be nasty business. Ugly stuff."

"I couldn't do that."

"Yes, you can."

"What would we fight about?"

"You should reject him. Hurt his feelings. Challenge his manhood. Tell him you aren't interested and you don't want him hanging around. Tell him he's not good enough for you. That you don't want to be seen with an ex-con."

"I would never say that! He's Mert's brother!"

"Right. That's exactly why Mert can't know about this being a setup."

"She'll be mad at me!"

"I imagine she will."

TWENTY-FOUR

"I CAN'T DO IT. Can't we just wait? Won't the prosecuting attorney press charges against Bill? You know what he told me. He confessed to murdering Roxanne."

"He's told his attorney that you staged that whole car-napping scene. That you were trying to get money out of him."

Stars swam in front of my eyes. I grabbed onto the concrete block erosion wall and tried to keep my balance. The neighborhood around our store is pretty transitional, but the residents try to keep up appearances. We'd made two turns around the block, so this was our usual stopping point for private chats. No one from the store could see or overhear our conversation.

Or my tears. Which started flowing hot and heavy.

Lately, I've been crying a lot. I guess I'm just being hormonal. This should have been a happy time in my life for a lot of reasons, one of which I chose to keep to myself for a little longer.

But there were plenty of public reasons to celebrate. Detweiler and I were enjoying each other's company, and we had a future ahead of us. But my mom's constant harping was wearing me down. So was my unease about the store. Even before Margit showed up, I had a hunch Dodie was going to choose a partner without consulting me. More and more, my boss acted without my input. She had my money. I was a part-owner, but I quickly came to realize that as a minority stockholder, I'd bought myself nothing but headaches. No voting privileges. No special rights or input. Just the slim chance of sharing in a yearly bonus that might or might not repay a portion of the investment I'd made.

I'd always thought of Dodie as a very fair person, but her high-handed decision-making style was eroding that opinion.

And Mom? Well, she'd never liked me. Ever. I remembered her picking at me and finding fault as I was growing up. I've heard some people say their mothers always "had their back." But my mother never treated me like she loved me. Or liked me. Or approved of me.

I knew why.

I just didn't want to think about it.

Mert had been more of a mother to me. Mert was the constant in my life. She would gladly go to bat for me, and as a matter of fact, she had on numerous occasions.

Now Detweiler was suggesting that I honk off my best friend.

He must have read my mind. "Kiki, Johnny is risking his life. He's putting himself on the line for you. I know it will be hard for you to have Mert mad, but the only people who know about this scheme are you, me, Police Chief Holmes, and Johnny. We might have to let Sheila in on this, just so she knows to stay vigilant, especially while you and Anya are at her house. I'll wait until Chief Holmes tells me to include her in our plans. But Mert can't know.

It's just too risky. It's entirely possible that she will still forgive you for saying something nasty about her brother. At the start, she has to believe you've quarreled. It has to be public, so that Johnny's actions make sense. He'll be safe to the degree that he's believable. Otherwise, Bill could turn on Johnny in a flash."

I sighed and wiped my eyes with my sleeve. He was right. If this plan was to work, Mert couldn't know. But he was wrong about the reasons. My friend had worked so hard to get her brother released from prison, and harder still to help him create a new life free from the currents of the underworld. This would put all that in jeopardy.

She would hate me for doing this.

"It's Johnny's choice," said Detweiler. "He suggested this to Chief Holmes. I guess he wants to make amends."

I could see that. Johnny and I often talked about retribution. We understood how guilt eats away at your joyfulness. I knew he wanted to feel he'd repaid society for "being stupid," as he put it.

"I better get back to the store." I picked up Gracie's leash.

Detweiler stopped me. "What's a good time for you to do this? We need to know so we can protect you. Obviously, it would be best for you to stay at Sheila's."

"Why?"

"Robbie will be there at night, there's a great alarm system, and we can easily observe the house. Your place in Webster Groves is too secluded."

"But if I stay at Sheila's won't that tip Bill off? He's bound to know something's up."

Detweiler rubbed his chin thoughtfully. "Does your house need any work done? Anything that Mr. Haversham has been putting off?"

"No, nothing. Wait—the roof! We lost a bunch of shingles during that last storm," I said.

"That'll work. I'll call Mr. Haversham and ask him for his help. Maybe he can get the work started immediately. Any ideas when and where you could pick a fight with Johnny?"

"There's a Fine Arts and Crafts Fair this weekend at Faust Park. We'll have a booth. Dodie asked Johnny to help us cart all our stuff there and set up. I guess that's as good a time as any. If we fight right after the fair opens, there should be plenty of people around."

"Faust covers two hundred acres," said Detweiler. "Who would see you? Won't folks be scattered all over? They'd be paying attention to the various booths and re-enactments. I'm not sure anyone would notice a quarrel over all the hubbub."

"Well, if he and I fought during the setup Wednesday night, the other vendors would be there. Our booths are located in a concentrated area, the prime space next to the building with the carousel inside."

"When exactly does the setup start?"

"Six p.m. on Wednesday. There's a V.I.P. preview that follows. Closing at eight. Let's get the kinks out, if there are any."

"Sounds like a plan."

Actually, it sounded like the perfect way to ruin another lovely spring evening.

TWENTY-FIVE

TRUE TO HER PLAN, Margit left as the local church bells rang noon. "I cannot work Monday—"

"Or Wednesday afternoons or Sundays," I repeated.

"*Ja,*" she smiled. "You have it right. I go to visit my mother at Oak Haven. We have delightful meals together, and she expects me. I must be there."

Oak Haven was a retirement home on the South Side. That was all I knew about the place. I made a mental note to Google it and see what I could learn. More information might help me to get to know Margit better. After all, I had known next to nothing about Bama, and that ignorance nearly cost both of us our lives.

Our Monday night croppers straggled in. Wendy Jo and Angela arrived early, eager to hear my version of the sniper attack. I got so weary of repeating the gruesome events that I decided I would type up the next crisis in my life, laminate it, and wear it around my neck as a signboard. But, deep down, their concern touched me, and I knew our scrappers weren't just asking because they were curious. They truly cared.

Rita Romano said, "Is Anya okay? All those girls must have been scared to death!"

A poor choice of words, that.

"I texted her at noon. She seemed fine. She texted me back that they discussed the shooting during advisory and during an assembly at chapel. A grief counselor held office hours. I think Anya planned to talk with the woman." I set down additional rubber stamps for the ATC cards we were making.

ATC means Artist Trading Cards, but everyone calls them ATC cards, which is redundant. Each one is a work of art on a 2½ by 3½ inch canvas. Back in 1996, a Zurich artist named M. Vänçi Stirnemann organized the first trading session of the cards as a way for people to meet face-to-face and share their creativity. Think of baseball cards, now swap out artistic designs for photos of designated hitters, and you'll get the picture. Literally.

Jennifer Moore joined us. Her daughter Nicci is Anya's best friend. "The advantages of a private school. There's money in the budget for a counselor. Gosh, am I ever glad that Nicci opted out of that silly ritual."

"What? Opted out? I thought it was mandatory." I spilled an entire container of blue glitter on the work table. Drat. That stuff loves static electricity. It's mega-hard to pick up.

"Used to be," said Lisa Burton, who set down her tote bag with all its pockets for papercrafting supplies. Lisa's daughter Sydney was a year ahead of Nicci and Anya. "That changed this year when a group of girls went to Elliott McMahan and protested."

"Um, not really," added Maggie Earheart, another CALA mom and a friend, who dragged along her Cropper Hopper, a rolling suitcase for scrappers. "It changed when someone from said 'group of girls' contacted an organization of feminists who threatened to hold a protest right outside the school's front door."

"They didn't stop there," said Jennifer. "Those feminists—of which I am a card-carrying member—contacted the ACLU. We were willing to take the school to court."

"Gee," I said, "I'm surprised at you, Jennifer. You being Old St. Louis and all."

She chuckled. Although she was one of the very, very prominent members of the Old Guard, she held very, very modern views.

"I didn't want them to drop the May Day celebration entirely. I just wanted girls to have choices, that's all," said Jennifer. "That's part of what education is all about. Expanding one's choices, right?"

Maggie shrugged. "The hubbub didn't leave Mr. McMahan with many choices. He can't afford to put an end to the May Day ceremony. Or rather, Lane Carlée can't afford to end it now that she's the new development director. Losing that money on her watch would be a career killer, and she's very gung-ho, or so I've heard."

"I don't understand," I said, and I didn't. "The May Day ceremony has to be expensive. They set up all those chairs and the platform. Rent a PA system. Buy flowers, hire a choreographer. Wouldn't the school save money by cancelling? I mean, if all the parents agreed to donate the money they spent on costumes, CALA would surely come out ahead."

"Ah, but think of all the revenue the school would lose," Jennifer helped me brush up the glitter with a fabric softener sheet, which cuts the static cling nicely.

"What revenue? No one pays for tickets to attend," I said.

Maggie grinned at me. "You are such a babe in the woods, Kiki. You are so naïve, so clueless."

Jennifer hugged me. "And that's what we love about you. You don't have a cynical bone in your body."

That series of clichés irked me, as it felt like my friends were in on a joke, but I wasn't. However, seeing as I was the *de facto* hostess of this crop, I plastered a pleasant smile on my face. "Then clue me in."

Clancy looked up from the card she was dipping in glitter. "I bet the alumnae donations were threatened, right? All those women who had participated in the ceremony in years gone by. To them, it's a sacred ritual. At least, I imagine it is."

I had forgotten that she once taught high school in Illinois. She knew the inner workings of the educational system better than I did.

"Bingo!" said Maggie. "The majority of endowments come from women, not men, because most women outlive their spouses. When one of the alumnae heard that May Day might be cancelled, she stormed into Mr. McMahan's office, checkbook in hand, and threatened to change her will."

"Wow," I said. "Who would do such a thing?"

Jennifer and Maggie exchanged looks.

"Who indeed?" said Maggie. "Who indeed."

TWENTY-SIX

JENNIFER HELD UP HER trading card. "This needs something, but I don't know what."

I puffed up with pride. When she first started crafting, Jennifer showed no sense of style. After nearly a year, that same fashion sense that dominated her tasteful wardrobe came through in her crafting. She could examine a piece and determine what it was lacking. That was the first step to bumping up her skill level.

"Try an embellishment here," I suggested.

"Can we see the album you're making for CALA?" asked Jennifer. "I bumped into Lane Carlée and she mentioned the school had commissioned one for the family and one for their archives."

I saw no harm in that. The album was to be on display in the school library, so it wasn't a secret. I ran to the back and grabbed the big book. After carefully clearing a space on the front counter, I opened my project.

"You do beautiful work." Jennifer flipped through the pages while Maggie peered over her shoulder.

"Peyton is a darling girl," said Maggie, using her index finger to point out the Fitzgerald girl. "But she's always been a bit of a tomboy. Hates girlie clothes. Dresses like a boy in Reeboks, Dockers, and golf shirts. Wears a Swatch."

"Did you have her in class?" I asked.

"I had her in fourth grade and again when I substituted for the freshman English teacher. Peyton is wonderful. Brilliant mind. But she's also determined to express her individuality. She can be a handful, but a good kid. I heard she's going to Princeton. I think she aced her SATs, and of course she'd be given preference to matriculate since she's a legacy."

"Her father or mother went?" I wondered.

"Heavens no," said Jennifer. "Her grandfather, Gergen, did. Her dad, poor Peter, barely graduated from CALA. I think he's dyslexic, or has another learning disorder, but back then, no one diagnosed the problem like they can today. He's a superb artist, but he was an awful student in the regular subjects. Deanna is nice enough. Her family is from the Lake."

That was St. Louis-speak for "Lake of the Ozarks," which was also code for "hillbilly."

That one remark—"Her family is from the Lake"—told me everything I needed to know. Jennifer never bad-mouthed other CALA parents, but her lackluster praise said volumes. It was clear that she didn't think much of Deanna.

I wondered why. Over the past two years, I've come to realize that Jennifer is whip-smart. At first glance, she looks like the typical Ladue Lady of Leisure, one of the many women in this tony suburb who swan around with nothing to do but practice calorie avoidance and shop. Since I've gotten to know her, I've learned she runs her family business, keeps her straying husband in line, adores her two children, and is incredibly observant. She would make a good poker player, I think.

As I mulled all this over, Jennifer must have sensed the weight of her disapproval, because she hastily added, "Deanna and Peter certainly are devoted to each other. They met when he was bouncing around, after he flunked out of Wash U. Her dad is one of those fishing guides who works the lakes in tourist season, hunts and traps in the winter for food. Her brother is a trapper, too. She was taking night classes to get her GED, and working as a waitress in a diner near U City, sleeping on a friend's sofa, when she met Peter. He would stop by for breakfast after a long night of partying. His black Porsche 911 made quite an impression on all the girls, as I recall. He drove it fast and he drove it hard."

Translation: Deanna was an uneducated country bumpkin who managed to snag a ne'er-do-well rich boy from a prominent St. Louis family. (Admittedly I was being harsh, but there was an undertone to Jennifer's description, and it said worlds more than mere words could convey. Honest to goodness, you needed a phrase translation handbook to understand the inner world of the St. Louis upper crust. I also knew that Wash U was short for Washington University, while U City was local slang for University City.)

"You'd never know she didn't come from money," said Maggie with a bit of wonderment in her voice. "She certainly dresses like a million bucks. Their house is over off of Litzsinger. One of those decorating magazines featured it on the cover and did a huge multi-page spread on the décor and the grounds. In fact, the Fitzgeralds only live a few blocks from your mother-in-law, Kiki."

I made a mental note to ask Sheila what she knew of Peter and Deanna.

"What was Edwina like? Maybe you all can help me with my research."

"Cut her and she'd bleed the CALA school colors. She was always one of the school's largest donors, and she wasn't shy about letting the staff know it," said Maggie. "Edwina gloried in the traditions. Once I stepped on the school seal because someone bumped into me. Edwina made me kiss it! I tried to dodge her, but she planted herself between me and the hallway. This happened on one of those forty-below-with-the-windchill days, so finally I gave in. My lips nearly froze to the marble! Later I was called into the headmaster's office because she reported me for lack of respect."

"Wow." That was all I could think to say.

"Yessirree, she was a real piece of work," Maggie shook her head, making her simple haircut swing this way and that. "She would call the school secretary and ask her to run errands for her."

"You are kidding!" My mouth dropped open.

"Wish I were. But I'm not," said Maggie in a sing-song voice. "I also heard that the development office had to run every piece of stationery past her because she usually found fault with the printing or the paper or whatever."

"She only wanted the best of everything. Nothing less was acceptable," said Jennifer. "That's why the family business did so well under her tenure. Edwina hunted down the best brewmeisters, the brightest advertising agencies, the most promising marketing talent. When she inherited the brewery, it was a mess. Gergen muddled along, but he barely managed to keep the place afloat. In less than a year after Gergen died, she transformed it. When she sold it, the contract worked to her favor, a real rarity in this economic downturn. She was smart enough not to sign anything that kept her out of the business long term. Now she's rebuilt everything, and she's renamed it Gergen Brands."

"Wait a sec. You said she hunted down the brightest advertising agencies. I thought Peter was the Vice President of Advertising." I remembered hearing his title mentioned in one of the news reports after the shooting.

Jennifer chuckled. "A title isn't a job, Kiki."

What in the heck did that mean?

Kiki's tips for improving your designs

1. Let your pieces ferment. Instead of hurrying through, build in time to step back and reflect on your work. If you are scrapbooking, pin up the layout where you can see it and leave it alone for a week. When you return to it, you'll recognize what's lacking.

2. Chart your eye path. Close your eyes, open them, and note where you look. From there where do your eyes want to go? There should be a strong pathway, often in a triangular shape.

3. Consider whether your piece is asymmetrical or evenly balanced. It has to be one or the other, so have you defined which it is?

4. Photocopy or photograph your work. Often a smaller image or another medium will help your eye determine what's missing.

5. Give it the squint test. Stand about six feet away. Squint. What pops out at you? What seems missing?

6. Make it temporary. Re-positional adhesive allows you to try before you commit permanently. If you have used a permanent adhesive, Undu, a solvent, can help you remove the offending item.

TWENTY-SEVEN

SHEILA MET ME AT her front door, grabbed me by the elbow, and dragged me down the walkway. The light from her security lamp at the back door showed how contorted her face was. "Linnea quit."

"What?" The wonderful, fabulous, totally unflappable Linnea had worked for the Lowensteins for more than thirty-five years. As far as I knew, quitting wasn't an option. She could die, but she could not turn in her resignation. No, no, no, no!

"You have to be kidding me," I said. "Is she sick or something? Have a terminal illness? Is one of her kids in trouble? This is temporary, isn't it?" I couldn't imagine Sheila functioning without the help of the rock-steady African-American maid.

"No, she scribbled out a letter of resignation on the back of an envelope she saved from the recycling. She said she couldn't wait to go home and type up something formal. She's dead serious."

"Did she read *The Help* and have an epiphany?"

"This is no time to be cute. I can't live without Linnea."

"When was the last time you gave her a raise?"

"Last month. She makes more money a year than you do."

That wasn't surprising. So did the pimple-faced boy flipping burgers at McDonald's. "What happened?"

"Not what. Who. Your mother."

I groaned. This was not wholly unexpected. My mother had a way of saying incredibly hurtful things to anyone who didn't meet her expectations. If she liked you, she loved you. If she didn't care for you, you were history on the losing side.

"How?"

"The final straw came when Lucia followed Linnea around and unmade all the beds."

"Let me guess: Linnea doesn't do hospital corners."

"What's with the hospital corners! Was your mother in a loony bin somewhere? I never heard of such nonsense. Since when did Martha Stewart send out minions?"

I rolled my eyes. "We used to be subject to hospital corner drills. Mom's mom was a nurse. Once Nana showed Mom the proper way—proper, that is, in a hospital setting—to make a bed, Mom became some sort of hospital corner devotee. A real fanatic. Complete with rituals and chanting. When it comes to bed making, she's always been positively obsessive."

"Well, good, because she's soon to be positively obsessive and homeless. She'll be making, or rather unmaking beds, down at the Salvation Army hotel. I'll toss her derriere out on the street and send her luggage flying after. I can't manage without Linnea. Especially not with my wedding coming up. I have too much to do, and Linnea is integral to the running of my household."

"I agree. Besides which, we all love her."

"Whereas your mother is barely tolerable."

"Yeah," I admitted. "That's a nice way of putting it."

"Your mother, your problem, you fix it," said Sheila.

I agreed with her assessment, so I got Gracie inside, stowed my purse, and went searching for Linnea. I found her in the pantry completing what looked suspiciously like a final inventory of canned goods.

"Linnea, can we talk?"

"You talk. I'm busy. I need to finish up and leave." She didn't even turn around to face me.

"Hey," I said. "Please. If you are going to quit, quit because you've had it with Sheila. Don't quit because of my mother. My mom is temporary. We're only here until the roof on my house gets fixed. Honest."

The coffee-colored woman showed no signs of relenting, so I brought out my big guns. "You'll break Anya's heart if you leave. It will totally crush her. Especially now after she lived through that sniper attack."

With those words, she turned to face me. The angry brown eyes softened, grew blurry. "I do love that child," said Linnea. "She's like one of my own. I fixed her warm milk with vanilla in it to help her calm down, poor lamb."

"What would we do without you? Especially Anya? Without you, she'd starve to death. Please don't leave. For Anya's sake, I'm begging you. I'll talk to my mom."

"You think that'll do any good?" Linnea raised an eyebrow at me. I noticed she also took her calloused hands out of her pockets where they'd been jammed along with her pencil and pad.

"Not one bit. But I owe it to you to try. I'll also take Mom with me as much as I can. Keep her out of your hair."

Linnea sighed. "I guess you better show me how to make hospital corners. The Good Lord tells us not to be stiff-necked with pride. I'll do what I gotta do for that girl of yours."

"Ours," I corrected Linnea. "That girl of ours."

TWENTY-EIGHT

Tuesday, May 4

"Take her with you. Or take me. Better yet, let's send your mother back to your house in Webster Groves. Bill Ballard can perform a civic service by shooting her," said Sheila the next morning. "It would be a *mitzvah*."

Mitzvah is Hebrew for "blessing."

"I'll see if I can get Mom to come to the store with me." I finished my toast, rinsed the plate, and put it in the dishwasher. Linnea had rescinded her letter of resignation, but after a quick pow-wow in the laundry room, Sheila and I concluded this was a good time for Linnea to take a week off. With pay.

This morning, I'd fixed myself a piece of dry toast and a cup of weak tea. I offered to make eggs for Sheila and Robbie, but thankfully they declined. My stomach was in an uproar. I worried whether I could cook without racing to the powder room, but I was game to try. As it was, when I opened the refrigerator for the butter, the smell of leftover tuna fish salad made me heave.

Luckily for me, Anya contented herself with a bowl of cereal.

"You okay, honey?" I asked.

"I guess."

"Have any bad dreams?"

"No. I think the milk Linnea made me helped a lot."

"It probably did. Mom? How about coming to work with me? I could use your help."

She peered up at me from an over-stuffed chair in front of Sheila's flat screen TV. "I don't want to miss Katie Couric. I like her."

"There's a television in our office. Don't you want to see where I work? What I do?"

"We drove past it. Squatty little building in a ratty neighborhood."

That was true. "Yep. But it's what's inside that's really special."

"I'm comfortable here. I hate to get up." She had appropriated that particular chair as her own. When she wasn't sitting there, she put a book or her purse on the cushion to save her seat.

"All the people I work with are dying to meet you." I threw in this white lie as a sweetener. They weren't dying to meet her, but they did regularly die of laughter at some of her more famous antics, such as tearing apart an album I made for her so that she could use the pieces to make her own version. That particular album cost me $300 in supplies and took weeks to make. When she mailed me a photo of how she'd chopped up the photos, I nearly wept. I could have sent her duplicates for less than $10, if she'd only asked. Instead, she'd butchered wonderful original family pictures.

"I guess they are interested in me. That makes sense. I'm sure you can use my help."

She hoisted herself from the chair and wobbled before taking a step. I rushed to her side. "You all right?"

"I get woozy sometimes if I've been sitting too long. I need to use the bathroom before we go."

The color of her skin was grayish, and her hand felt clammy in mine. I re-doubled my determination to call Amanda. Maybe Mom needed to see a doctor here. If so, I would need her medical records.

Maybe if I called Amanda from the store phone, she'd answer.

Maybe pigs would fly, and Lambert Field would add a couple new runways devotedly only to porkers.

Anything was possible. Possible but not likely.

TWENTY-NINE

To MY SURPRISE, MOM and Dodie got along like identical twins accidently separated at birth. They seemed to genuinely enjoy each other's company. Mom regaled Dodie with stories about her days as a chorus girl in off-Broadway musicals. Her one big claim to fame was that William Warfield heard her sing and said, "You have a bright future ahead of yourself, young lady. You just need a lucky break."

Dodie heard this fable and was impressed. "When Old Man River says you've got talent, you are indeed on your way!"

Unfortunately, Mom got a bad break instead. She had fallen in love with a stage door Johnny, my dad, and when he asked her to marry him, she consented. They eloped two days after she met Mr. Warfield. "I threw my promising career right out the window along with my overnight bag. I was willing to make the sacrifice. You see, I'd always wanted a family of my own."

Why? I wondered. *You never seemed happy to be our mother. You didn't enjoy being at home. You didn't like cooking or cleaning or caring for us.*

Of course, it did mean she'd have all of us to boss around, and a plausible reason not to continue facing the rejection and discipline that was a natural part of show business. A family was an all-purpose, no questions asked, type of excuse that transformed Mom's lack of ambition into sainthood.

Dodie, bless her heart, seemed fascinated by my mother's stories. She listened with appreciation, and even asked questions. It seemed my mother had found her audience in one of the lost tribes of Israel. That made Mom happy. Dodie seemed content as well. The two of them hung out in Dodie's office and watched television together. This allowed Dodie to be here, but stay off her feet, and Mom to be here, but stay out from under my feet.

Margit approved of my mother's visit. Her round face beamed like a full moon at me. "This is good. Bringing your *mutti* along is good. You are a good daughter, Kickee."

Since Gracie was a rescued purebred and not a "mutt," I figured Margit was talking about my mom.

At one time in my life, I lived for praise. Fortunately, I'm growing past that. Praise is like a shine on your shoes. It only matters if the leather underneath is solid. Oh, praise looks good, it's flashy, but substance wins over fluff any day in my book.

"Mom, I need your help." I set her down at a table smack-dab in the middle of the store and showed her how to assemble kits. Before long, she had the task down pat, continuing a running commentary on her life to all and sundry as she divvied up supplies.

"You know, I taught Kiki everything she knows about scrap-booking," said Mom. "Yes, I was ahead of my time."

To say that this amazed and astonished our customers would be an understatement. "Shock and awe" prevailed in our store. I briefly considered amending her story, but Dodie put a hand on my shoulder. "She is happy. What difference does it make? If you don't want to get old, hang yourself when you are young."

Bolstered by that cheery Yiddish aphorism, I climbed into my car and headed for CALA.

I walked the marble hallways to a frosty glass door with gold lettering: Lane Carlée, MFA, AFP. With her shoulder-length cloud of soft blonde curls and big eyes, Lane could double as an angel in a Christmas pageant. Lane adjusted her black velvet headband, looked me over carefully, and offered me a seat. Her desk took up every inch of space. How they got it into that tiny office, I couldn't even imagine. Actually, I could imagine. Some poor *schmo* must have disassembled it and reassembled it piece by piece.

"May I offer you a cup of tea?" said Lane. "I understand you were there at our May Day celebration. As you might imagine, all of us here at CALA are still in shock over the tragedy. Mr. McMahan suggested that we order a memorial album that we could display, and I emailed Mrs. Goldfader immediately. We'd like two copies, one for the family and one for our library here at CALA. We're hoping that a tribute to Mrs. Fitzgerald's life might go a long way toward expressing our grief. Edwina Fitzgerald supported this school and our mission in countless ways. She insisted that her grandchildren follow family tradition and attend here. Just as CALA has been a tradition in your family as well."

"Miss Carlée—"

"Lane," she corrected me.

"Forgive me if I'm being rude, but what on earth is that?" I pointed to an unusual vase, about fifteen inches tall with a pebbled brown surface. A thick white starfish hung off the top, near the mouth, and a row of seashells added a further ornamentation.

It was, by far, the ugliest desk accessory I had ever seen. Adding to the general weirdness was an obviously fake bouquet of pink silk lilies.

"A dead armadillo," said Lane with a smile. "Or at least part of the dead 'dillo. Isn't it fabulous?"

"Uh…" I stalled for time.

"I won it at an auction. The money went to the Boynton Beach City Library, I'm happy to say. A wonderful place. I love to read, don't you? An author made it out of roadkill."

"Let me guess. Carl Hiaasen?"

"No, I think his characters eat road kill. This author just believes in recycling."

"Recycling?"

"Yes, she saw the dead armadillo on the side of a road in Florida and couldn't resist."

I swallowed. "I think I'll take that cup of tea, please."

When she left her office to get the beverage, I sneaked over and examined the vase more carefully. A faint smell, a bit like flesh and dirt, emanated from the big brown Tootsie Roll shaped tube.

"It's a wonderful reminder to eat fiber every day, isn't it?" chirped Lane.

"I was thinking that it looks like a tarted-up piece of poop."

Lane laughed. "Kiki, you are a breath of fresh air. Although we are meeting under sad circumstances, I'm glad to get to know you."

"Likewise," I said with a grin. "After seeing this and knowing the money went for a good cause, I'm going to keep my eyes out while I'm driving. Maybe I can find you a turtle shell to use as a candy bowl."

We both laughed.

"When do you need the album?" I picked up the packet she handed me.

"Naturally, we'd love to present one of the albums to the family at the funeral."

"That's tomorrow."

"Right. At three p.m. Surely this won't take you long."

"Lane, I am a scrapbook artist. My work has appeared in a variety of publications, both domestic and international. To do justice to a job like this, I'll need at least a week. Maybe two."

She blanched.

"You see, I also work full-time at the store, and I have other projects."

Lane nodded. "Of course. I guess you can tell that I don't know much about scrapbooking. You came highly recommended. Elliott McMahan told me you were the only person for the job. I just didn't realize it would be so involved."

"I want this to truly reflect the Fitzgerald family's devotion to CALA," I said, "and I know you do, too. I'll do my best to get at least one of the albums done in time for the funeral, but I'm not making any promises."

"That's a great compromise. I'm sure you'll do a lovely job, although I must admit, I'm not exactly sure how these will be different from the commonplace photo albums." Her smile dimmed a bit. "I trust I can count on you to be, um, sensitive. As you well know, every family has its secrets and its skeletons in the closet."

I blushed, thinking about my husband and the circumstances of his death.

"Don't worry. A public tribute like this is the place for the Fitzgeralds to shine. I'll make sure that's the focus."

With that, I took my leave. But I did wonder, what was she warning me away from?

THIRTY

IN THE HALLWAY, I sank onto a bench, opened the packet, and glanced over the photos. Skimpy pickings. Certainly, they didn't offer me much to work with. Most of the photos included Edwina as a part of large groups. Strictly grip and grin. What I needed were candid shots, photos of her and her family, closeups.

I also needed background materials for basic journaling. "Journaling" is a term that scrapbookers have appropriated. It refers to the verbiage that accompanies photos. In fact, it's the journaling that transforms a photo album into a memory album. A photo album is merely a collection of pictures. Lane Carlée was one of the many who weren't aware of the difference.

A memory album tells a story. Combining photos and narrative, the creator builds a monument, a biography or documentary of a subject or an event. A photo album, if lost by the owner, tells you little. Without an accompanying narrative, it's nothing more than a dry collection of images. A memory album tells you everything— who the people were, what they valued, and why you should care.

This manila envelope proved insufficient for my purposes.

I headed for the Alumni Office and my old friend, Ruth Glazer.

"Kiki! Wait 'til you see the new photos I have of my grandbabies!"

Ruth greeted me like the long-lost friend that I was. I worked with her to construct her first scrapbook album many months ago. That hooked her. She shopped regularly in our store, always taking time to share her newest photos with me.

That's the way it is with scrapbookers. Since most of us focus on our families, all our scrapping peeps learn a lot about each of us, our backgrounds, and our clans. Granted, sometimes I wish I knew a little less. There are days when I chaff under the burden hearing every detail about every cotton-picking grandbaby. But listening to Ruth's joy reminded me that God willing, someday, I might be a grandmother, too. That was surely worth smiling about.

"What brings you here, Kiki? An assignment?" Ruth asked.

I explained about the albums for Edwina Fitzgerald's family and CALA.

"My goodness. You certainly don't have much time, do you? How about if I help you pull the files that are pertinent?"

Normally, the file room was off-limits. It was the repository for all of CALA's history, complete with photos of students, records, and applications. I first gained access when I started working on the alumni newsletter. Having proved I could be trusted, the file room became a wonderful resource. Word of my albums slowly made its way through the CALA social set. Having me do an album for a family was quickly becoming a status symbol, much like having an expensive family portrait taken each year. Actually,

CALA should not have given me such freedom. But as one mother said, "When you're part of the CALA family, you are part of the family." If the expensive tuition did nothing else, it guaranteed you a place at the table.

Ruth led the way, pulling open drawers and searching for photos and articles that had previously appeared in the school newsletter.

"You will probably want to supplement what you find here with photos from their family albums, if they have any."

I agreed. "I don't know Deanna. Do you? I'm thinking that calling her right now will seem rude. I mean, everyone reacts differently to a loss."

"I served on several committees with her. She's an involved parent. How about if I call her and smooth the way?"

"I'd be grateful for that," I said. "Tell me about Edwina Fitzgerald. That will help me determine the style of albums. If Edwina was a color, what color would she have been?"

"Royal blue and gold. She adored CALA. She frequently wore the school colors."

Ruth took a quick glance around, walked to the door, and shut it, closing us in the small room. "Like a lot of our parents, Mrs. Fitzgerald was a Type A personality. We joke about how there are parents who only notice you when they need you or want something. Otherwise, they look right past you. Mrs. Fitzgerald was like that. She would call on a Saturday and demand that a piece of trash be removed from the edge of the grounds. She actually asked me to pick up her dry cleaning on several occasions."

"You have to be joking!"

"No. She told me to have it ready for her because she was coming by the school for a meeting with Mr. McMahan. Mrs. Fitzgerald treated us like her personal staff."

"How about the rest of her family? Peter's recovering from that shot in his leg, I guess. Did they also act so imperious?"

"No. Poor Peter."

"Gee, 'Poor Peter' seems to be that guy's nickname!"

"It was."

THIRTY-ONE

MRS. GLAZER CONTINUED, "THAT young man had such talent as an artist. You've seen the mural that connects the second floor to the new gym? He did that in his sophomore year. But Mrs. Fitzgerald refused to let him major in art. He even dropped out of college and tried to put himself through school to get an art degree, but by then Deanna was pregnant. Eventually, he acceded to his mother's demands."

"Which were?"

"That he work for the family business."

"He must have done pretty well for himself. He was a vice president."

"As I understand it, Mrs. Fitzgerald kept a tight rein on Peter. He would propose a campaign, she would agree to it, and halfway through, she'd yank the schedule. Or make a change. Or cancel the programs."

I rocked back on my heels. I'd been digging in a bottom drawer. "Wow. That must have been ..." I couldn't think of the right word.

"Unsettling? Demoralizing? Infantilizing? All of the above. I heard that Peter finally gave up. After twenty years of trying, he resigned himself to sitting in a big office, playing solitaire, and taking long lunches." Her voice dropped to a whisper. "And drinking. I think he tried to drown his disappointment."

"Why didn't he quit? Leave the job and get another?"

"He couldn't afford to. Without a degree or a track record, where could he go? No one would hire him at his level of income. No, he was stuck. A bird in a golden cage. He had nowhere to go but down, and it would be a drastic lifestyle change."

She smiled. "Besides, I imagine that Peter and Deanna were trying to hang in there, as the kids say. Edwina had promised he'd become the CEO when she retired. Then he could work on his art all day long and have people run the company and report to him. It was a rotten career path, but he'd been traveling it so long that they really didn't have any other options."

People without money envy people with money, but those without have nowhere to go but up. Those with money have nowhere to go but down. On the way up, people offer you a hand. On the way down, they offer you the boot. Minimum wage jobs are a dime a dozen, but only a tiny percentage make the big bucks. So if you lose that high-earning job, you can go a long time without any hope of replacement. If you don't have savings, if you can't or won't downscale, you are sunk.

I know all this because I went from a cushy life where I never had to worry about bills to pinching pennies so hard that Lincoln yells, "Run!" when he sees me coming. I'm not discounting the problems of the poor, but sad to say, I've seen the other side. We'd all like to believe that money solves problems. It does. It also creates them.

Mrs. Glazer helped me fill a shallow box with photos and clippings. In return, I handed her a discount card. "You are saving me time and helping me make a good impression."

"I couldn't take this," she said.

"Why not? It's a gift from one friend to the other. We give them to our best customers. You certainly qualify for that."

She gave me a hug and fairly skipped away.

I couldn't wait to dig into that box. Working on the album would completely occupy my mind. Since the turnaround time was slim, I would need to tackle it right away and probably keep at it through the evening. The project would provide a perfect reason to ignore my mother and her harping.

Just what the doctor ordered!

THIRTY-TWO

SHEILA SWUNG BY AND picked up Mom and me after Anya's school let out at two-thirty. While I didn't relish including my mother in our fittings for wedding finery, I couldn't see any other option. I didn't think it fair to Dodie to leave Mom with my boss at the store.

Anya squirmed in the back seat as I climbed in beside her, but my kid quickly made room for me. Mom took the front passenger seat and kept up a constant prattle, a full report of her day, including all the people who enjoyed making her acquaintance.

"Kiki, most of them did not know I was a professional in the entertainment industry. I can't imagine how you neglected to mention me."

Probably because I'd been searching for something nice to say and words failed me. Or possibly I said nothing because I didn't want to break down and cry. Choose either option.

Mom continued with, "I explained to the customers that I am the true expert in scrapbooking."

"Have you been published?" asked Anya.

I clamped my mouth shut and stared out the windshield. Oh, my golly. My daughter was a quick study.

"Of course not. You see, I was scrapbooking before it became trendy. Your mother is a Johnny-come-lately to the craft."

"Mom, what did you do today?" Anya reached over and squeezed my hand three times.

"I—"

"Piddling stuff. Time wasters. She stocked shelves. She cut out pieces for kits. Then she took a long break," my mother said, speaking on my behalf.

"I—"

"I can't imagine what took her so long. She said she went to pick up photos. That surely couldn't have taken more than fifteen minutes, but she was gone for an hour and a half. Honestly, I'm surprised she didn't get fired," said Mom, tut-tutting in disgust.

"I—"

"Fortunately I helped out. Dodie found me invaluable. I even waited on customers," Mom smiled with pleasure.

I'd heard about that "waiting on customers." My mother misread a price tag and told a customer that an album was $5 when it was $50, but luckily for us, the woman loved our store, so she was content with a discount and an apology when Dodie rang up her purchase.

"As a matter of fact, I worked so hard that I'm exhausted. Please drop me off at the house. I need to put my feet up."

"With pleasure," said Sheila.

She meant it.

THIRTY-THREE

"You've gained weight." Sheila shook her head in disgust. "I can see that zipper straining from here."

"I guess I have."

"No problem. We have plenty of room to let the side seams out," said the alterations woman at Cassidy's Bridal Boutique. With a quick slash of her razor, she afforded me breathing room.

"Not if she keeps packing on the pounds," said Sheila.

"As I am wont to do," I added.

"For goodness sake, Kiki. Get a grip. I can't have a bridesmaid looking like a beached whale."

"That wouldn't be a problem if the dress wasn't gray," I said. "If it were a bright color, I would look like an overinflated balloon."

"Pewter. A classic shade." Sheila sniffed. "Perhaps not the most flattering shade for you, but Betsy Ridour is my oldest friend, so naturally she's my matron of honor."

The cobalt blue that Betsy was destined to wear would have looked stunning on me. But this was Sheila's party, her big day, and I had decided when she asked me to be a part of the wedding that I would go along with whatever she wanted. More importantly, I would do it with a smile plastered on my face. If she wanted me to wear a corset, ruffles, and bows and tiptoe down the aisle like Cinderella going to the ball, that's what I would do. I owed her this much. The fact that she had included me at all in the wedding party was an honor. It marked an important shift in our relationship, and I cherished the thought behind the gesture, even if it meant signing on for all sorts of stones cast in my general direction.

"Isn't the future Mrs. Holmes radiant?" The saleswoman posed a rhetorical question designed to tactfully shift attention from my weight gain to Sheila's beautiful gown. The pale blue brought out the silver in her hair and the denim blue of her eyes.

"Mrs. Holmes?" Anya scrunched her face. "Who is that?"

"Me, of course. That will be my name after I marry Robbie," said Sheila, turning slowly to admire herself in the three-way mirror.

Anya lifted her arms so the alterations woman could adjust the fit around her bust. A couple of months ago, Sheila took Anya shopping for her first real bra. My baby was growing up. How often did we mothers say that? That was the way of life. We prayed our children along every step of their lives but watched the blessing of their growth with astonishment.

"You'll change your name? From Lowenstein? That means Mom and I will be the only Lowensteins. But what if Mom marries

Detweiler? Then … then I'll be all alone." Her voice quivered as did her lower lip.

"Marry Detweiler? I hope not." Sheila snorted.

"Honey, we don't know what the future will bring." I tried to comfort my daughter, but adorned as she was in straight pins, Anya rivaled a hedgehog. Finally, I simply patted her shoulder.

"Yes, we do. Gran will marry Robbie. You will marry Detweiler. I will be the only Lowenstein in town, and everyone will have forgotten my real dad. No one will know who my parents are. I'll be like those kids at school whose parents move on after a divorce. I'll be all by myself. The only Lowenstein in the entire school. Maybe even in the whole town!" Bright crescents of silver tears rested on her lower lashes. She was one tick away from sobbing, and I knew it.

"For pity's sake." Sheila closed her eyes in an attempt to block out the scene. "This is a happy moment, Anya. You are gaining a grandfather, a wonderful man who loves you."

Sheila was never curt with Anya, so the tone of her voice sent a chill through me. Anya stiffened under my hand. I feared my mother was rubbing off on all of us. We were treating each other with the sort of brusque disregard that was the hallmark of her life.

"Robbie already has nine grandkids. Nine! I'm just the tenth little Indian," said Anya, as the tears sprang from her eyes. "I'm nobody. I don't have a dad! I'm the next best thing to an orphan!"

Her class was reading Agatha Christie. While I wholeheartedly approved of the teacher's choice of literature, I wondered if Anya realized she'd referenced one of the most classic murder mysteries of all time. Murder had been no stranger in our lives, what with George's death and the aftermath.

And now, my kid had seen fatal shots fired by a sniper. She'd witnessed the raw fear that moved a crowd to stampede. What she didn't know—what she couldn't know because I couldn't tell her—was that her father's killer had put a contract out on her mother.

Suddenly, a sense of panic overwhelmed me. If I were to die, where would Anya go? Would she be accepted by Robbie? Would he and Sheila raise her as their own? I'd made plans for Sheila to be her guardian. But that was before Sheila became engaged to Robbie. I hadn't thought to revisit my decision with them both.

And I needed to.

This wasn't the sort of life I'd envisioned when I brought a child into this world. Before I could stop myself, I started crying, too.

THIRTY-FOUR

"Thanks for the memories," snarled Sheila as she dropped me off back at the store. "We're off to have fun with your mother."

"Not my fault," I muttered as I slammed the heavy door on the Mercedes extra hard. "I'll get back to your house as soon as possible. I need to drop by the Fitzgeralds' house."

I paused. "Look, Sheila, I'm sorry. I don't know what came over me. Really, I apologize. I wanted this to be a happy event for you."

She sighed. "I know. Look, I shouldn't have snapped at Anya."

We both glanced over at my daughter who was curled up in the back seat sound asleep. She'd cried buckets, dissolved into hiccups, dried her tears, eaten frozen custard from Ted Drewes, and conked out on us.

"We're all overtired and overwrought," I said. "This sniper incident was bad enough, but my mother adds to the strain."

Sheila nodded. "Even though I don't like the woman, she is your mother, and I respect that. I know Robbie wants you at my place. I think I can guess why."

I didn't respond because I didn't know how much he wanted her to know.

"Please share my condolences with Peter and Deanna. Edwina was a hard woman, but she contributed a lot to the CALA community," Sheila said. From her that was high praise. Sheila loved CALA. My name wasn't on the donor's list, but hers certainly was.

"I'll try to get back to your place as soon as possible," I said.

"And I'll try not to wring your mother's neck before you arrive. If you do walk in and catch me choking her, take your time dialing nine-one-one."

With that, Sheila roared off into the sunset.

THIRTY-FIVE

AFTER REPAIRING MY MAKEUP, I grabbed several sample albums, the envelope of photos, and drove over to Peter and Deanna Fitzgerald's home. A long paved driveway, lined with impatiens in various colors, led me to a secluded portico and a honking big structure. I figured the house's square footage at five thousand, but later learned it was actually ten thousand square feet if you counted the guest house and the full basement.

A man opened the door. His weather-beaten skin showed the sort of leathery texture from years of being in the outdoors. His neatly ironed plaid shirt and faded jeans were tidy, but his scuffed work boots had seen better days.

"Hi. I'm Kiki Lowenstein. I believe Mrs. Fitzgerald is expecting me."

"This is a bad time for visitors." He blocked the doorway, his tired eyes measuring me and finding me no challenge.

"Yes, and I'm sorry to disturb the household." I didn't yield an inch. "As I said, she's expecting me."

"You can wait here," he showed me into the foyer.

Because of my former life and Sheila's longstanding involvement in the arts community and charities, I've been a guest in a lot of houses in Ladue. But none of those places seemed as purposefully designed and decorated to intimidate as this one. The cavernous marble entryway magnified every sound. Over my head dangled an enormous gold and crystal chandelier. In the center of the space sat a round walnut table, buffed to a high polish to reflect a tall ceramic vase full of fragrant fresh freesia, star lilies, birds of paradise, and palms.

"Deanna says come on back," said my greeter. He led the way along a wide hallway with carpeting so thick and plush that I nearly toppled over as my shoes sank into it. Deanna was seated in the middle of a sitting room, staring into a formal fireplace where a crackling fire burned. She barely looked up when I came in.

"Hello, Deanna," I said and she nodded toward me. "Please accept my condolences. I am so sorry for your loss. My mother-in-law, Sheila, asked me to convey her sympathies as well."

She responded by turning away.

"How's Peter?" I asked.

"He's in pain," she said without looking at me.

"I didn't catch your name," I said to my minder. I stuck out my hand in a most aggressive manner before he could move away from me.

As punishment, he gave my fingers the sort of squeeze designed to make me cry out. But I didn't. "Derrick Roper. I'm Deanna's brother."

"Did you come down for the May Day ceremony?" I managed through gritted teeth. "I don't remember seeing you there. Of course, everything is a blur now."

"Got here a few days before," he said, and then he stopped. "Is this a social call?"

Maybe I was born mean, but I took a seat even though I hadn't been offered one. I sank back into a large chintz wingback chair. I competed with two overstuffed pillows, festooned with yards and yards of silk braid and tassels.

Derrick Roper moved over to stand behind his sister, with one big hand on her shoulder. Meanwhile, Deanna turned to stare at me, seeming as silent and judgmental as that carved statue of Lincoln inside his monument. Her huge diamond splashed rainbows across the walls.

"I'll try not to take long, but as Lane Carlée probably told you, CALA wants me to make a memorial album commemorating your late mother-in-law's life."

Derrick coughed softly into his hand.

Deanna's face stayed expressionless.

"The school gave me access to their archives, but I don't have any candid pictures of Mrs. Fitzgerald," I said. "I hoped to get one or two as well as a few family portraits."

"How come?" asked Derrick. "How come you can't use what they give you?"

"I'm sure those will work fine," said Deanna.

This was a tussle of wills. Logic suggested they were mourning and I should bow to their wishes. But I was tired of giving in to other people. Besides, I wasn't about to return to Lane Carlée and explain I had no materials to work with. Not after I'd gone out of my way to convince her that I knew what I was doing.

"No, it won't be fine. I need family photos, candid shots of you all interacting as a family. The school commissioned this as their way of saying 'thank you' to your family."

"That school—" started Derrick, but his sister cut him off.

"That's totally unnecessary. My mother-in-law did what she did because she loves—loved—CALA more than anything else in her life."

Did I detect a note of bitterness? Yessirree, I sure did.

"I know. I heard she was very generous to the school, and we all appreciate it."

Her face flickered, the way a candle blinks in the wind.

"Look, I realize this is a difficult time for you," I continued. "I know you've been through a lot. If you have family albums, just let me borrow those. I'll copy the photos I need, and return everything intact. Then I won't bother you anymore."

Deanna considered this. A muscle flickered in her jaw. "You are Sheila Lowenstein's daughter-in-law?"

"Yes."

"How is she as a mother-in-law? Is she nice to you? Does she accept you?"

This strange question took me aback. "Um, she's very good to my daughter. She and I get along fine."

"Really?" Deanna raised an eyebrow. "She's a perfectionist. Mrs. Fitzgerald was, too. People like them can be hard. You can't please them."

Her syntax hinted at her rural roots. She pronounced "can't" like "cain't."

I nodded. "You're right. It can be—trying."

"Does she help you out? With money and all?" Derrick's eyes pinned me down like I was a butterfly on a bulletin board.

"On occasion." Was it that obvious? Did I look that shabby? The weather still cycled rapidly from chilly to warm and back again. After checking the forecast today and learning it would be coolish, I put on a brown skirt I'd found at Goodwill, a cream knit sweater, and a large beaded necklace that I'd made myself. Brown tights and low shoes completed my outfit.

In contrast, the slub silk of Deanna's black dress screamed expensive designer.

What prompted Deanna's question? Had she heard how Sheila paid for Anya's tuition, books, and clothes? Sheila often shared more than I thought prudent. Certainly, she didn't seem to consider what might embarrass me. Her focus was on how she looked. Not my feelings.

I amended my answer. "A lot, actually. Sheila helps me a lot."

"You get paid for this?" asked Derrick. "This playing with pictures?"

He pronounced the word "pit-churs."

"Yes," I said. "This is my job. I'm a single mom."

Deanna came to a decision. "Can you make up large photos of Mrs. Fitzgerald? I mean for tomorrow, to display at the funeral home? I'll pay you."

"Of course." Lane had asked me to meet her at the funeral home with the memorial albums so she could present one to the Fitzgerald family right after the service. I would have to arrive a little earlier than I'd planned to set up the photos, but that wasn't a big deal. Besides, I could use the money. So I added, "I've done this before, and I know just what to do. You'll be very pleased with the result."

"Derrick, take her to Peter's office. Get her the albums."

I followed him into a masculine room with a big desk and walnut paneling. To cover my awkwardness, I tried to make conversation. "How's Peter handling the loss of his mother?"

"What do you expect? He's sad, of course." Derrick grabbed a handful of leather-bound albums and held them out for me.

"Of course." *Who are we fooling?* I thought to myself.

THIRTY-SIX

I spent the rest of the afternoon touching up photos, design-ing, and creating Edwina's memorial album. Since we stocked al-bums in all the local school colors, I selected a royal blue and gold leather binder. Next I started on the interior design work.

Every fifteen minutes, Margit would come and stare over my shoulder. She would mutter to herself in a discouraged tone. At one point, Margit clucked her tongue. "What a *Schlamassel.*"

Whatever.

Nietzsche said, "One must have chaos within one's self to give birth to a dancing star." I know from experience that negative thinking can douse the spark of creativity. I kept playing, letting the child within me explore different combinations, until finally, I happened upon one that worked beautifully.

We carried a calla lily image that I stamped, hand-colored, and duplicated onto nice paper. To add dimension, I twisted paper coffee filters into the shape of the flowers. When glued to the stamped and colored images, these created 3-D blossoms.

I also selected a shield shape, representative of the CALA school shield, and made multiple journaling boxes from it.

Finally, I devised a border. After sewing a gathering stitch down the middle of a wide piece of royal blue ribbon, I drew it taut. This yielded a puckered satin ruffle that worked perfectly for the bottom of the pages.

To pull these items together, I matted the photos of Edwina and family on a subtle royal blue print, and then on gold paper. My background paper was a royal blue and gold print. The resulting base pages were both classic in their simplicity and yet complex enough to hold your attention.

"*Wunderbar!*" Margit said, startling me. I had been so wrapped up in my work that I hadn't noticed her peering over my shoulder. "*Das beste, was man sich nur denken kann.*"

"In English, please." I stepped away from my work table to study the title page. I always add a title page to the front of any album. Besides listing the contents in order, it also details why the album was made, who commissioned it, and finally it documents me as the creator and gives the date finished. Without that elementary information, no one knows the vantage point of the assemblage, and yes, we all see the world differently so that's important.

"That means 'the best one could possibly imagine.' That's what you have done. It's simply *wunderbar.*" She clasped her hands to her chest, her round face aglow with delight. "Dodie told me you had a talent. I could not see it. I wondered if she was mistaken. Now I know she was quite correct. This thing you do, with paper and trinkets, it is quite nice. This woman is dead, is she not? What a tribute to her. Her family will cherish this."

"That's the general idea. These other photos will be on display at the funeral tomorrow. They'll serve as a reminder of her life."

"Tomorrow? What time?"

"I need to drop this off tomorrow around two-thirty. I'm scheduled to work all afternoon, so you'll have to switch shifts with me."

"*Nein*, I told Dodie, I must have Monday afternoons, Wednesday afternoons off. Sunday also."

Brother. Why was I the only person who had to be flexible? Huh?

"Hey, I'm not asking for myself. The client requested that I set up the photos, and Lane over at CALA asked me to bring these albums to her before the memorial service. Dodie told me to make this happen. Surely, you can switch with me just this once."

"Absolutely not!" Margit gave her head such a violent shake that her glasses slipped down her nose. She smacked her fist on the desk top. "I was very clear on this. I will not work on Monday or Wednesday afternoon or on Sunday."

Yeah, yeah, yeah. Blah, blah, blah. I was just too tired to care.

THIRTY-SEVEN

By THE TIME I pulled into Sheila's driveway, my head pounded like a scrapbooker setting eyelets with a hammer. I dragged my sorry self up the walkway, through the back door, and into the kitchen. Gracie rose from her bed, a soft cushion that Linnea had insisted she have.

The sounds from the TV in Sheila's room drifted down through the ceiling. I figured that she and Robbie were having a private moment. I hoped they were. Between their upcoming wedding, the sniper attack, and my darling mother's visit, my mother-in-law and her intended were coping with a lot of stress. But they made a good couple. Robbie exuded a manly steadiness, and Sheila provided a generous helping of zing. They complemented each other. More and more I noticed how they turned to each other for support.

I envied them. To me, the best part of being married is knowing that someone is there for you. Even though George and I had our problems, I could always depend on him. He was always in my corner. He never spoke ill of me in public, he took my side, and he listened to my opinion. With a few notable exceptions, we treated each other with great courtesy. Perhaps because we weren't in love, we didn't fall out of love. We were partners in almost every aspect of our lives.

My stomach rumbled. I needed food. There were cups, plates, dinnerware, and glasses on every surface. Pots and pans littered the granite countertop. Empty cans tilted precariously in the recycling bin and tattled that dinner tonight had been soup. An empty bag of Payday candy bars sat in the sink. Those must have been Mom's snacks, because she loves Paydays.

I missed Linnea. She would have left the kitchen spotless and a meal for me warming in the oven. She would have made me a fresh batch of Snickerdoodles, too.

The refrigerator shelves held nothing but a carton of cottage cheese. I grabbed that, opened a can of peaches, and ate the impromptu fruit salad for dinner. As the nourishment flowed through my system, my energy rebounded. I began to feel almost human again.

I text-messaged Clancy, "Need help tomorrow afternoon at store. Can u come at noon?"

Halfway through loading the dishwasher, I felt my phone vibrating. "See you then. C."

Slinging my backpack over one shoulder, I trudged up the stairs with Gracie following closely behind me. After a quick shower, I settled onto the big, comfortable bed and glanced through the Fitzgerald family albums Deanna had loaned me.

Like most albums, the pictures followed a chronological order. Someone had taken the time and care to slip photos into photo corners. That was good, because it would make removing photos easier.

I stared at old baby photos with names and dates under them. Two sour-faced people held a baby in a white christening dress that draped over the woman's arms. Beneath them, a thin script labeled the photo as, "Edwina Rose Lichbaden," and offered her date of birth. Later shots of Edwina showed her arm-in-arm with her CALA chums. In one picture, she wielded a field hockey stick while wearing a fearsome expression of concentration on her face. In another, she wore the traditional white bridal gown that senior girls wear for the May Day celebration. Even though the foxing blurred the image, I saw the pearls and gems covered the bodice. Belatedly I realized she was holding the huge bouquet given to one special girl, the Queen of the May Day celebration.

A few pages later on the occasion of her own wedding, she wore a simple silk gown with tiers of lace. Sad to say, it seemed somehow anti-climatic.

Another album held photos of Edwina's husband, Gergen Fitzgerald. While this volume was considerably thinner, it still chronicled his life. Gergen must have come from a modest background. There were no pony rides, no fancy clothes, no formal events. But he did appear quite dapper wearing an Army uniform.

So Edwina fell for a man in the service. With that in mind, the timeframe of photos of the couple made more sense to me.

Peter's birth occasioned another scrapbook. Formal photos were interspersed with candid shots. Evidently Peter had a sister, Elsa, a beautiful girl with the round face and almond eyes that signal Down syndrome. Elsa appeared briefly on pages, but around the age of five, she vanished.

The thinnest album told Deanna's life story. School pictures were the only formal photos here. When Deanna turned eleven, her grandparents bought her a Brownie camera for her birthday, or so the scrawl below a photo of Deanna with a lopsided cake explained. From that day on, boxy photos with white deckle edges dominated the pages of her album.

I flipped through pictures of Deanna with her dog, a mixed breed of beagle and chow; Deanna fishing with Derrick; Deanna and her family standing proudly beside a young Derrick in uniform holding a medal; Deanna and her mother in their Easter finery; and Deanna with her father and brother standing over an eight-point buck.

When I couldn't keep my eyes open any longer, I carefully stacked all the albums at the side of my bed. I fell asleep dreaming up layouts that featured four candid photos of Edwina, including the radiant picture of her as the May Day Queen. It would be a fitting, if ironic, tribute to what had clearly been the one great love of her life: CALA.

THIRTY-EIGHT

Wednesday, May 5

SHEILA WOKE ME AT six by rapping on my door. I stumbled out of
bed and tried to remember where I was. I tripped over Gracie and
apologized for stepping on her paw.

"Yes?"

"Today is National Take Your Mother to Work day."

"It is?"

"Yes. Either you take your mother with you to work today or I
will kill her." Sheila leaned against my door jam and held her fluffy
white bathrobe clutched closed. A tremor in one eyelid caused it to
jump around weirdly. With a twitchy eye and no makeup, she sure
didn't look like the Sheila we all knew and feared.

"What happened? What'd she do now?"

She shook her head and walked into my room. "You don't want
to hear about it."

"Oh, yes, I do."

"She put Anya's cat in the microwave."

"What!"

"We had that vet appointment for Seymour's six-month check up. I put the cat carrier on the kitchen counter. Anya and I went looking for Seymour. Your mother sang out, 'I've got him,' and by the time we made it into the kitchen, Lucia was stuffing Seymour into the microwave oven. She turned and told us, 'That should make it easier for you to take him to the vet.' Fortunately, Seymour is okay."

I groaned. The gray and white tabby had won all of our hearts. His tiny pink nose would tickle your ear as you sat watching TV. He and Gracie had become the best of buddies, and often Seymour slept curled up between the Great Dane's big front paws.

"She's also been incredibly mean toward Anya. Picking on her. Finding fault with her hair, her nails, her clothes."

I sank down onto the bed and tried to fend off unhappy memories. Sheila joined me. "Was it like this for you when you were a kid?"

"No cats were harmed during my childhood."

"She must have Alzheimer's. Or another form of dementia. You need to get her medical records together, get her an appointment with a specialist, and have her diagnosed. Maybe there's a program that can help."

"There is. Euthanasia."

"Right. Until then, we can't leave her here alone. It's too dangerous. I can't babysit her. Today I meet with the floral designer to go over plans for how I want the tables decorated for our wedding dinner at the Ritz."

"Yes, of course." I nodded. No use whining to Sheila that Amanda still refused to take my calls. I'd have to break through my sister's wall of silence. I just wasn't sure how.

"I'm going to Edwina's funeral. I can take her along. That should keep Mom occupied."

"Better keep your mom on a short leash. Lucia could get into plenty of mischief at the service. You'll be there representing the store, and everyone from CALA will be attending. Your mother has to be on her best behavior."

THIRTY-NINE

I SET MOM TO counting sheets of paper while I worked at our computer station scanning and enlarging the photos of Edwina Fitzgerald to display at the funeral. I also scanned Fitzgerald family photos and newspaper clippings for the memorial album. A few of them I color-corrected, and on one I repaired a small rip.

"I knocked over my coffee," Mom said.

The strong smell of vanilla in the air surprised me. I swallowed hard and tried not to retch. I reached into my pocket and grabbed a Saltine. Chewing it settled my stomach.

Sure enough, her floral polyester skirt bore a spreading stain from her vanilla latte. I hopped up from my work and raced to the work table. A stack of paper floated on a sea of brown java. I grabbed the top layer of paper and moved it, but the liquid ruined hundreds of sheets.

I mopped up the mess and helped Mom blot her skirt. Luckily it was floral, so the coffee didn't show.

"Mom, remember how I asked you not to put your coffee on the table?"

"Phoo," she waved a hand at me. "That paper is fine. It's still in one piece."

"Our customers won't like the coffee stains. They want to buy paper in perfect condition."

"Who cares about them?"

I gave up. I came up with a new task for her, dividing beads into Ziploc bags. The beads came in large containers of one thousand, but scrapbookers never needed that many, so we parcel the beads into lots of twenty. At least Mom couldn't ruin the beads.

Margit showed up a few minutes before nine. "I brought strudel. Plum kuchen. I cut a big piece of the strudel and gave it to your mother."

"That's very kind of you. Thanks so much. I couldn't get her to eat any breakfast, although she did have coffee. Well, a little coffee at least."

"You are a lucky girl to have her with you."

I wanted to feel lucky. But I didn't.

"She and I will be going to Edwina Fitzgerald's funeral today. I'll need to leave at two-thirty. Clancy is coming in at noon to take my place."

"Good. My schedule is *unangetastet.*"

"Right." I had no idea what she was saying. I believe she was telling me that she was inflexible. Sure looked that way to me. Nothing in her stance said, "Hey, let's roll with it."

"Um, we had a small accident this morning. My mother spilled her coffee on a pile of paper."

Margit pushed her glasses up on her nose. Today she wore a lilac polyester pantsuit with a cream blouse underneath. Although neat as a pin—and I've never understood how pins can be tidy or messy—she seemed frozen in time, as though she once had a vibrant life and it had since passed her by, leaving her with a dated haircut and a closet full of polyester. Sad to think how the polyester—in all its ugliness—would outlast all of us. That didn't seem fair.

"Accidents happen. Your mother helps out, *ja*? So this is not important."

"No, it's not. However, you might want to deduct those from our inventory and reorder. I might be able to put it in the blender and use it for our handmade paper class. I'm not sure, but I'll try."

Margit appraised me thoughtfully. "That is smart. Very smart."

I handed her a sheet of charges for the Fitzgerald photos. "I've divided the charges two ways. One set is for the album that CALA commissioned, so CALA would pay for those as part of the total cost of the album. The other set covers the enlargements for the funeral. We should charge the family for the enlargements, as per Deanna, the daughter-in-law."

"You are very thorough. Good. I see you also included the addresses for billing. Very good."

I handed her another sheet. "Here are the supply costs for both sets. You'll notice that I mounted the enlargements on foam core board and added easel backs so they would stand up. I can't quite figure out how much glue I used, but I've included a mention of that since it is a supply that we provided. This way we can track our exact costs versus the income made from these special projects."

"*Ja,*" Margit adjusted her spectacles to peer through the bifocal lenses. "Is that important?"

"If we aren't making a profit on these special jobs either we need to charge more or quit doing them. It's easy to have the cost of supplies sneak up on us."

Margit studied me over the frame of her glasses. "That is right. It is good you thought of that. You can really use the paper to make that other thing?"

"I don't see why not. All you do is take paper and fabric and blend it, pour the mix through a screen and dry it. I've been dying to offer a class in papermaking, and this might give me a good excuse."

That's what I said, but I really felt like saying, "Hello! I'm not as dumb or worthless as you thought. I'm actually very responsible and resourceful." But I didn't. I didn't need to prove myself to Margit. Dodie was the person who couldn't see how much I cared about this business. And I was tired of trying to prove myself to her.

FORTY

THE HOURS TRUDGED BY. If everything went as planned, this evening I would pick a fight with my best friend's brother.

I tried hard not to think about it.

Instead, I kept my hands busy. In a weird way, Mom helped because she needed constant attention. First she spilled two baggies of beads on the floor. I crawled around on my hands and knees trying to recover them, worrying that a customer would slip and fall. Next she locked herself in the bathroom. While she carried on, yelling and banging on the door, Margit handed me a paper clip to open the lock. Last, but not least, I caught Mom feeding Gracie big hunks of strudel.

"Mom, Great Danes have very, very delicate digestive systems. She can't have that."

"She likes it!"

"Yes, she does. But she'll get sick."

"Phooey." Mom waved a dismissive hand at me.

I tried another tack. "Mom, here's the real reason: I want to eat more of the strudel. Don't give it to the dog!"

That worked. I made Mom another cup of coffee. She, Margit, and I took a long break and finished most of the plum kuchen. (I put aside a piece for Clancy.) Before Margit left, I extracted a promise from her to bring me a copy of the recipe. "My friend Bridget from Tai Chi shared it with me," explained Margit. "Because her kuchen is the best."

"Tai Chi?" I said. "You do Tai Chi?"

"Yes," Margit smiled. "Is very good for the mind and the body. You must come try it some time with me."

I promised I would. Once again, at the stroke of noon, Margit hurried out of the store. That left Mom and me. I found a lot of small jobs to keep Mom busy. She continued to have one problem after another that kept me hopping.

Between crises, I dialed Amanda's number. Clancy clocked in and saw what I was doing. "Why don't you text-message your sister?"

Duh. Why hadn't I thought of that?

I text-messaged Amanda about Mom putting Seymour in the microwave and added: "I think we need a medical opinion of her mental state. Please advise who her local doctor is. I need Mom's records."

A few minutes later, my phone vibrated in my pocket. The screen said: "Will call you later."

Progress!

BRIDGET'S GERMAN PLUM KUCHEN WITH STREUSEL

Plum Kuchen

1½ C. flour

1 tsp. baking powder

¾ stick butter

¾ C. sugar

1 egg

2–3 lb. Italian plums, halved

Sugar and cinnamon to taste

(1 T. sugar and ½ tsp. cinnamon)

Grease a springform pan and heat oven to 350° F. Sift flour and baking powder, set aside.

Cream butter and sugar, add egg and mix. Add the sifted flour with baking powder and mix until well combined.

Pour into greased pan and top with plums. Sprinkle with combined sugar/cinnamon, top everything with streusel.

Bake at 350° F for 1–1½ hours.

Streusel

½ stick butter

¼ C. sugar

½ C. flour

Mix together till crumbly.

Note: If plums are omitted, add cinnamon to streusel.

FORTY-ONE

I INTRODUCED MYSELF AND my mother to Mr. Berry, the funeral director at Killian and Berry. He led us to the viewing area, a large room set up with rows and rows of chairs.

"An open casket," said Mom loudly. "That's positively barbaric."

"Shhh," I warned her.

A walnut coffin with shining brass handles took pride of place on a raised platform. Floral tributes covered most of the stage, forcing me to rearrange the sprays carefully so the photos would show.

Mom walked right up to the casket where Edwina's craggy profile rose from the snow white fabric like Mount Rushmore. I moved quickly, swallowing hard because the scent of lilies nearly overpowered me. Or maybe it was the sickening sweet fragrance of formaldehyde.

I struggled not to retch.

My mother viewed the body in the casket and offered a steady stream of yakking. "Look at her lying there! She's just a big piece of dead meat."

"Please keep your voice down," I cautioned Mom, tugging at her arm. "That's not nice."

A couple dressed in black took their seats. Another woman in navy wandered along the aisles, searching for the perfect spot.

"When I'm dead, I want you to be absolutely positive I'm dead and then close the coffin lid tight. I don't want people parading around and staring at me. Making comments on how I look. When I can't defend myself. That's awful."

"Mom, shhhhh. Someone might overhear." Outside the door footsteps echoed and a murmur of voices began to swell. The door opened and a clutch of folks dressed like blackbirds straggled in.

"Was she that ugly in real life?" Mom asked Mr. Berry.

"Ma'am," said the unamused funeral director. "You don't know what we had to work with."

"This is how she looked in real life." I pointed to the enlarged photo of Edwina.

"Not much to recommend her. Was she rich? Must have been, because she sure wasn't much to look at."

"Um, have you seen a woman named Lane Carlée?" I asked Mr. Berry.

"No, why?"

"I have this album that she wanted to display," I said as I held up the Edwina Fitzgerald memorial book. I really needed to do more work on it, but since I'd promised Lane I'd bring it, I'd kept my word. It didn't have nearly enough pages to suit me, but at least it was a start.

"I strongly discourage that," said Mr. Berry. "As you can see, we have a plethora of floral tributes. We're expecting a large crowd. If mourners congregate up front, it would be problematic."

Not for Edwina, I thought. *She's past all this.*

"If Ms. Carlée has a problem with me because the book isn't on display, will you tell her what you just told me?" I asked.

"Of course," said Mr. Berry.

I tucked the album into a large shoulder bag and ushered Mom to a seat at the rear of the room as more and more mourners trickled in. The crowd grew, the doors opened, and in came Derrick Roper pushing Peter in a wheelchair. Deanna walked behind them, holding tightly to the arm of a young woman I recognized from the photos as Peyton, their daughter.

"Why didn't that dead woman get a facelift? That's what I want to know," Mom's whisper carried. "She's got more skin than one of those Shar Pei dogs."

People turned to stare.

"Let's go outside. I bet they have refreshments in the hall." I tugged Mom by the arm.

"I'm fine. In fact, all that strudel is giving me gas."

I could tell. So could the people near us. I noticed a few of them fanning themselves frantically.

"Mom, let's go outside and mingle."

"Why didn't you say so?"

FORTY-TWO

"OF COURSE, EVERYONE NOTICED my talent. And my good looks. People assumed I was a beauty pageant winner." Mom backed two unsuspecting mourners into a corner. Both women were either (a) fascinated or (b) too stunned to walk away. As she talked, Mom waved a half-eaten cookie she'd swiped from the next funeral over. Masticated crumbs fell out of her mouth and rolled down the front of her blouse. I closed my eyes. I couldn't bear to watch any more of this. But I couldn't stick my fingers in my ears, so I heard her say, "As you might guess, I had more than my share of admirers."

The service wasn't supposed to start for another fifteen minutes. Folks paying their respects continued to arrive. I looked around for Lane Carlée but didn't see her. While Mom prattled, I eavesdropped on other conversations.

"We're flat out of options. We should have made the change while we still could," said a man in a pin-striped suit as he rubbed the back of his neck. "This couldn't have happened at a worse time."

"She didn't plan to die," said a nervous-looking man wearing a blue tie.

"None of us do," said Pin-Striped Suit.

Isn't that the truth? I thought to myself. A *one-way ticket with no ETA.*

"See these legs?" I glanced over in time to see my mother hiking her skirt. Quick as a snap, she grabbed the hand of an elderly man and guided his palm to her upper thigh. "Feel this! Hard as a rock! That's all those years of dancing!"

"My, my," he said.

"Mom!" I hissed. "What are you doing?"

I yanked her hem down to a modest level. "It's almost curtain time. Let's move along."

"I was a chorus girl!" she trilled over her shoulder to the stunned onlookers. "And I still have gorgeous legs! Want to see them?"

"Not now." I took her by the arm. She smacked at me, but I dodged her slap and slipped my arm around her waist. I wanted to wait for Lane, but my mother was quickly getting out of control. I had one option and one option only: "Come on, Mom."

"I want Claudia!" wailed my mother. "I miss her!"

"Time to go, Mom." I steered her toward the blinking red EXIT sign.

"Claudia? Where is Claudia?" howled my mother.

Who the heck is Claudia?

And where the heck was Lane Carlée?

FORTY-THREE

IT WAS TOUGH TO tear Mom away from her awestruck audience. Finally, one of the funeral assistants must have noticed my distress because he sent Mr. Killian my way.

"I don't believe I've met this charming young lady," Mr. Killian crooned to my mother. "Are you new in town?"

Mom responded with a girlish giggle.

Mr. William Killian was smooth, very smooth. Cary Grant had nothing on him. He pulled Mom's hand through his arm, patted it gently, and led her toward the parking lot. They chatted merrily the whole time. Actually the sight of the two white heads tipped toward each other tickled me.

After he helped her buckle herself in, he gently closed the passenger side door. "*Adieu*, dear lady! Until we meet again."

He straightened, tucked in his tie, and smiled at me.

"Your mother must have been a great beauty ... once. We are all of us fading, not so much dying as simply evaporating into the greater cosmos. Our bodies are betraying us."

I thanked him for his help.

"Any time. Although this is my business, I am not immune to grief. I pray I never shall be, either."

"But my mom didn't know Mrs. Fitzgerald."

"No, but your mother realizes what is ahead. That's the difference between us old farts and the teenagers. They think they'll never die, and we know death is just around the corner. Their lack of knowledge leaves them giddy. Our surfeit of knowledge makes us sad." With a courtly salute, he bid me farewell.

Mom fell asleep on the ride back from the funeral home. I cranked back the passenger seat, and she continued to snore loudly. When I pulled up at CALA, I cracked the windows, parked in the shade, locked the doors, and left Mom to her slumber while I ran inside.

Okay. I confess: I'd had about all of my mother that I could take. I secretly hoped someone would steal the car with her in it, but that was unlikely. CALA's parking lot is full of new BMWs, Land Rovers, Mercedes coupes, Escalades, and Mazda Miatas. And those are the kids' cars. No one at CALA would be caught dead in my old beater.

Teachers had their own parents to deal with, presumably. They would have noticed my snoring mother and thought, "I've got one just like that at home."

"Excuse me," I said to the receptionist at the main desk. "I was supposed to meet Lane Carlée at Edwina Fitzgerald's funeral. But I didn't see her."

"She called in sick this morning. Lane gets nasty migraines. You can't imagine how sick they make her," said the receptionist.

I decided since I was there, I'd return the alumnae materials to Ruth Glazer. I ran back out to the car, checked to see that Mom was still asleep and comfortable, grabbed the materials, and ran back into the building and down the hall to the Alumni Office.

"What happened to Elsa?" I asked.

"Elsa? Elsa who?" Ruth looked confused.

"Peter Fitzgerald's younger sister. The one with Down Syndrome. She appeared in a few early pictures, but that was all."

"Goodness, I'd forgotten all about her. Mind you, this was very hush-hush. I never knew he had a sister until one day when poor Peter started crying in class. They were reading *Where the Red Fern Grows*, I think. Miss Mitchell took him out in the hall. That's where I saw him. I was an English teacher then, so my classroom was nearby. He told Sandra Mitchell how just that morning at breakfast two men showed up and took Elsa away. He was sure he would never see her again."

"Doctors?"

"Two men in white coats. Probably they were orderlies. All I know is that he was terrified. Absolutely beside himself. The poor boy was a nervous wreck."

"How frightening it must have been, to see your sister taken away!"

Ruth nodded. "He was shivering and crying, poor boy. His mother told him to finish his oatmeal. His father had already gone to work. Neither of the orderlies would answer any of his questions and his sister was shrieking with fear."

"I realize they used to advise families to send children away, but still, it must have been heartbreaking for him to lose his little sister!"

Ruth nodded and played with her tea bag, mashing it with her spoon. "Until the mid-1960s, experts counseled parents to institutionalize their Down Syndrome children before they bonded with them. It was Gergen who wanted to bring Elsa home. He had hired a special nurse to care for her. But Edwina was embarrassed. She viewed their daughter as a personal failure, I guess. I never heard her speak of the child. Not once."

"Is it Down Syndrome or Down's Syndrome?"

"In the '60s, it became properly known as Down Syndrome since the possessive implied ownership by Dr. John Langdon Haydon Down."

"So did Elsa ever come home?"

Ruth shook her head sadly and coughed a little, the way you do when you can't find your voice. "A fire swept through the institution, and Elsa and twelve other children perished. Neither Gergen nor Peter ever forgave Edwina. Later it came out that one of the boys in the home was a firebug. He loved playing with matches, and he set the fire accidently. They were all improperly supervised. The boy perished, too, of course. This was before sprinkler systems."

"Oh, my gosh. That must have broken Peter's and Gergen's hearts."

She sighed. "Actually, Peter was incredibly angry. He turned violent. Punched his locker door in so badly it had to be replaced. Broke a bone in his right hand. Told his guidance counselor he wanted to change his last name. After that, he acted out in class. Spent a lot of time in detention. Poor Peter."

I agreed. "Poor, poor Peter."

FORTY-FOUR

Mom woke up when I opened the driver's side door.

"I need to tinkle." I took her back inside the school. After a long wait, she came out of the ladies' room and said, "I couldn't go."

I drove to my mother-in-law's home, helped my mom out of the car, and walked her upstairs. She sat on the toilet.

"I still can't go," said Mom, staring down at herself.

It was hard to reconcile the woman who was once so private with this sagging, elderly person sitting on a porcelain throne and showing no signs of embarrassment because the bathroom door was open.

"What do you mean?"

"I have to go, but I can't."

"I'll run some warm water in the sink. Why don't you reach over and put your hand in it?" I'd used this trick when I was potty-training Anya.

It worked, but I could tell by the abbreviated splashing that she hadn't released much urine. Mom accepted my help to get up from her seated position. I braced myself for her weight, but she was light as a kite on a windy spring day. Beneath my fingers, her bones were sharp and her musculature was meager.

Who was this woman masquerading as my mother?

Was her need to visit the bathroom frequently an affectation? A bid for attention? Or a sign of a physical problem?

The import hit me: I didn't know much about her health. I'd text-messaged Amanda for Mom's records because I worried about Alzheimer's, but now I considered how important it might be to have a complete set of her records.

"I hate these hose," said my mother, plucking at the nylon.

"Why don't you do like all the fashion magazines suggest and go without?"

"They do? All right. I'll try it." Mom struggled to step out of her panty hose.

I moved to the laundry basket; it was totally empty. "Mom? Don't you have any dirty clothes?"

She waved an airy hand of dismissal at me. "I wear things twice."

That accounted for the smell of dirty hair and old perspiration that followed her around. I rummaged through her suitcase and her closet and collected an armful of garments.

"I'll take care of these for you."

She shrugged. "I'm tired. I think I'll take a nap."

As I was sorting Mom's things in the laundry room, the front door opened. Sheila and Anya walked through, chatting merrily. The two of them giggled over a joke. Sheila had picked Anya up from school and then they'd gone to Bread Co. for a healthy snack. I could smell the roast turkey and the whole wheat bread.

"Homework, first," I heard Sheila remind Anya. "You know the rules."

Indeed, she did know the rules. They were the same in Sheila's house as in ours. Sheila had become my co-parent, caring for Anya in a responsible, thoughtful way. Our disagreements about child raising had been few and far between. Sheila always backed me up when I put my foot down or told Anya, "No."

I turned to Sheila for help, relied on her for insight, and generally took her advice. In return, the void in Sheila's life (the one caused by George's premature death) was partially filled by her time with Anya and with me. An unlikely trinity, the three of us pulled together to be a functional family unit.

"Kiki?" Sheila popped her head in the laundry room. "Have you eaten? I bought extra at Bread Co. If you start that load, I'll dry and fold it for you."

"That would be great."

Blue liquid laundry detergent spilled over the clothes in a design like cracked marbles. As I watched it, I marveled at the complicated strands of connection that turn strangers into families. No one would have blamed Sheila if she had ignored me or if I had turned my back on her after George died. But instead of turning away from each other, we had slowly turned toward each other.

In a strange sad way, the death of the man Sheila and I both loved forced us to really see each other. To take a long, hard look. By unspoken mutual consent, and in his absence, each of us set about to discover for ourselves the qualities George had seen—and loved—in us.

Odd. If he had lived, he would have always stood between us, the filter for our relationship. He would have always been the peacemaker and the conduit. His love/approval would have been a prize we both coveted. Without him to win or lose, we were on our own. We were forced to deal honestly with each other.

O, Lord, I am grateful that my daughter has at least one grandparent who can encourage and love her, I thought as I hit the ON button and heard the water flood into the washer. *Is it too late for us to have a good relationship with my mother as well? I'm not asking for love. I'd settle for mutual respect. Is that too much to ask?*

FORTY-FIVE

ROBBIE HOLMES CAME HOME early. Sheila had phoned him and picked up his favorite roast beef panini from Bread Co. He dug in with the sort of gusto that announced he hadn't eaten all day. Anya elected to take her food into the great room where she and Seymour could watch the latest installment of *American Idol*.

"I dropped by the alumni office at CALA today to return the information I borrowed about the Fitzgerald family," I said. I hoped my tone sounded desultory, not like I had a mission in mind. Which I did. "You know, everybody calls that guy the same thing. Poor Peter. I mean, it's practically his nickname, isn't it?"

Sheila shrugged and swallowed a spoonful of minestrone soup. "I guess."

"Did you know him, Sheila? I mean, do you know him? Or did you know Edwina?"

Robbie kept his eyes on his plate as he chewed slowly and thoughtfully.

"Well enough, I guess." Sheila blew on her soup.

"What does that mean?" It wasn't like Sheila to be coy.

"We both belong to Bellerive Country Club. We served on CALA committees together. Harry served on the Lichbaden board of directors."

"Really? That's interesting."

"Why?" Sheila frowned at me. "Harry worked with a lot of boards. He had a talent for that sort of thing."

My turn to shrug. "I've heard that the board wasn't all that happy with Peter's performance. Just scuttlebutt. Nothing solid."

"What difference would that make? Look, are you suggesting he shot his mother and then shot himself in the leg? Really, Kiki. That's far-fetched even for someone with a vivid imagination," said Sheila. Her voice turned huffy, as she added, "Leave the police work to Robbie. That's his bailiwick, not yours."

Robbie put down his sandwich. "We've heard the rumors about his impending demotion, Kiki. But as Sheila says, he certainly couldn't have shot himself in the leg. I mean, you were there. It was physically impossible for him to be the shooter."

I agreed. "I guess I've been thinking about his relationship with his mother. I don't think anyone could call Edwina warm and fuzzy. Or nurturing."

"Huh," Sheila snorted. "Especially after she broke her son's hand."

"What?" Robbie and I echoed in chorus.

"Of course, she didn't break his hand *personally* … she paid a creep to do it," Sheila said.

"Honey, that's gossip. We heard about it down at the station. But that's just hearsay, and I'm surprised you'd repeat it." Robbie took a swig of his root beer.

Sheila sat back and crossed her arms over her chest. "I do not repeat gossip. Robbie, you know better."

"But that can't possibly be true, can it? I mean, what mother breaks her own son's hand?"

"A desperate woman whose son has won a full-ride scholarship to art school in Chicago," replied Sheila. "A frustrated woman who has planned her whole life around her son succeeding her in the family business. A woman pushed over the edge. And I know it's true because I was in the ladies' room when she admitted as much to Ditsy Keenor."

I knew Ditsy. She lived up to (or down to, depending on your logic) her nickname. Her given name was actually Dorothy, but Ditsy was a complete nut-case, probably because she drank like a fish. (Do fish actually drink? If so, do they pee? Inquiring minds want to know.)

Two times in the past year, we'd called cabs for Ditsy when she showed up pie-eyed at our crops. Scissors and craft knives in the hands of a drunk do not inspire confidence.

Ditsy was a notorious blabbermouth who kept up a running commentary on everything she knew, thought she knew, and didn't know but thought she knew.

As if reading my mind, Sheila added, "Ditsy followed Edwina into the ladies'. I was already there in a stall. I heard Ditsy ask Edwina point-blank if she'd hired those two thugs who mugged Peter and smashed his hand in a car door."

"What did she say?" asked Robbie, picking apart a piece of lettuce on his plate.

"Edwina said to Ditsy—and I quote—'I would do anything to secure my son's future. That goes double for making sure our business stays in the family.' Then Edwina got this really nasty tone in her voice and she said, 'Ditsy, no one would ever believe I hurt my own child. But here's the honest truth: It's better that he cry now than I cry later. We all do what we have to so our children lead successful lives. I haven't done anything you wouldn't have done if you were in the same situation.'"

"You watch," Sheila said. "There will be times ahead when you are forced to make decisions. Horrible, painful decisions. You'll do what you need to do. You'll do things that Anya won't like and won't understand. You'll do whatever is necessary and be willing to take the blame, because you know what's best for your child."

"Or think you do," Robbie said, pushing his plate away and leaving the table.

FORTY-SIX

I WANTED TO TAKE the rest of the day off, but I couldn't. I had to load up supplies and take them to Faust Park, because I had my *faux* fight with Johnny to look forward to. Because Margit was so incredibly inflexible, and Dodie had a doctor's appointment, Clancy was working the late afternoon/evening shift alone, except for Gracie, my dog.

The Great Dane started a high-pitched whine the minute I walked through the back door. Instead of going docilely from her playpen to the back door for a potty break, she bee-lined around me and into the sales area.

"Gracie, no!" I yelled, racing after her. She knew the sales floor was off-limits. I'd never seen my dog make a dash into that forbidden territory.

Clancy sat at the work table, her head in her hands. Even before she glanced up, I could tell she'd been crying. Gracie whined and stuck her nose against Clancy's face. Clancy reached up and petted her. The Great Dane looked from her to me and whimpered. "Good old Gracie," she said, dabbing at her eyes, "you are such a sweetheart."

"What's wrong? Are you sick? Hurt?"

"I'm okay. I have to leave. I've been calling you."

"Oh my gosh. I am so sorry, Clancy. I forgot to turn my ringer back on after I visited the funeral home."

"It's not your fault. You didn't know I'd need you." Clancy dug in her purse for her keys. "It's Mom. She fell. A neighbor found her on the floor. We think she broke her hip. Maybe her arm, too. No telling how long she was lying there. I've got to go—"

"You sure you're okay to drive? We can close the store if necessary and I'll take you there."

"No. Please do not close the store. The one thing I don't need is more guilt. My brother has already called me twice and he's furious. He's telling me that this wouldn't have happened if I wasn't so selfish."

I didn't want to get into what I thought about that, so I gave her a hug, which she accepted stiffly, and sent her on her way.

Mert dropped in a short time later to help me load up supplies for our Art Fair booth. She had changed out of her work uniform of black slacks and white blouse, and into a skinny pair of jeans and a bright orange low-cut top. Her eyes sparkled as she told me about her recent date with Hank. I admit that I only half-listened. I loved Mert. She'd been my best friend for nearly ten years. We've always found plenty to talk about. We didn't have any secrets from each other until now.

"You're awful quiet," she said before she launched into another volley of "Hank says" and "Hank thinks."

Keeping my mouth shut entirely seemed the safest course of action. I desperately wanted to tell her about the plot to snare Bill. I wanted to hear what she thought of it. I wanted to see her righteous anger at the man who killed my husband.

But I also knew that Mert would be furious if she learned how Bill put out a contract on my life. She might even take justice—in the form of a frying pan—into her own hands.

So I sat silent as a sack of dirty laundry in her candy-apple-red Chevy S10 truck.

We found a good spot in the parking lot at Faust Park. Mert and I worked steadily to load boxes onto a cart. Johnny arrived late on his new motorcycle. Once we had all the boxes of merchandise out of the truck, he said, "Sis, why don't you move your Chevy to the far end of the lot? That way other folks can use these closer spaces for loading, too."

That left us alone. Just Johnny and me.

"I'm scared," I admitted.

"Ain't nothing going to happen to you, babe."

"No, I mean scared about my relationship with your sister. If you and I fight, she'll feel miserable. She's the best friend I've ever had."

"She'll be safer if we pull this off."

"Excuse me? What do you mean?"

"Bill hasn't just threatened you, Kiki. He's going after other people in your life, too."

"What? He's done something to Mert? She hasn't told me anything!"

"She gets nasty postcards. Hang-up calls. Kid stuff. But last week, her truck windshield got broken."

"She told me that was a rock."

"Yeah, a rock someone tossed," he snickered.

"How about Sheila?"

"Since Robbie moved in, it's all good."

"But before?"

Johnny shrugged. "Someone poured gasoline on her lawn and lit it. Postcards with threats. Hang-ups. Her garage door got jimmied open. A dead rat was nailed to the back wall of her house. That's how come Robbie moved in."

I couldn't believe what I was hearing. I knew none of this. None.

"Bill's been bragging about taking a lot of folks down a peg. That's why he shot up the May Day shindig," Johnny said.

"He said that? I mean, he bragged about shooting Edwina Fitzgerald at the May Day ceremony?"

Johnny shook his head. "Not exactly. See, he's been telling guys that he means to make you pay, and he wants to settle a few scores with other people here in town. He says he's got help, so I figure he hired someone. Who else could it be behind that attack? He's a graduate of CALA, right? His kids go there."

"Went there. Past tense. After he car-napped me, his wife took the kids and moved to Los Angeles."

"These were his stomping grounds. He knows his way around. Any offender will tell you that it's easier to pull off a job when you know your surroundings. Besides, it's not like you're a world traveler. You're here. He's here. He's going to take his best shot at you."

I shivered. I hoped Johnny was speaking metaphorically. Somehow I doubted it.

FORTY-SEVEN

Other vendors arrived at the retail area. Johnny set up our tables, fitted the pieces of our display that he'd built. A colorful sign with a glass jar full of watch faces welcomed visitors to our booth. Peg board walls facilitated displaying merchandise. A fold-out shelving unit showed off more goodies.

Mert racked hanging goods while I organized table displays. There was a lot to do, more than I remembered, and hauling boxes made for sweaty work. A part of me started to get ticked off, thinking about how Dodie didn't trust me to share big decisions, like taking on a new partner, but she sure didn't mind tasking me with a huge responsibility like setting up our entire booth for this event.

Maybe I was overtired, but the harder and longer Mert and I worked, the more irritated I got. Why was I busting my butt for Dodie? She sure didn't think much of me. Why was I out here sweating and grunting and overseeing Mert's efforts, while Dodie rested at home? She had a funny way of ignoring the responsibilities she'd shifted my way while still treating me like I knew nothing about the business.

I was hungry, angry, lonely, and tired. A volatile combination to be sure.

So when Johnny came up from behind me and gave me a big open-mouth kiss, the wrong kind of fireworks went off inside my head.

I pushed him away. "Stop it."

"But I've been working so hard, and you look so cute all hot and bothered like this." He put a hand behind my neck and kissed me. I tried to squirm free, but I couldn't. His grip was too powerful.

Before I could think, before I could apply reason, I panicked. Suddenly, I was a helpless child again, a child forced to endure her father's "affection." Johnny's mouth covered mine and I gagged.

My mind shut down. I forgot who I was, what I'd been through, and the progress I made in becoming an adult. Johnny's whiskers, rough at the end of the day, sandpapered my face the way Daddy's had. Johnny's hands, insistent behind my head, pressured me into submission. Mert looked away in embarrassment, and that served to trigger a memory of Mom turning the other way.

The child inside me cried for help. All this happened in the nanoseconds that it takes for neurons and synapses to fire in the brain. Johnny's forced kiss took me to a place I'd escaped from, and I fought being dragged back there the way a swimmer resists having her head held under water.

An atavistic impulse gave me a sudden surge of strength. I brought my knee up hard, slamming it into Johnny's groin. As he went down, I gave him a slap to the side of the head so hard that the skin on my palm stung. As he sank to the dirt, he sputtered, "Cop lover."

The haze of my vision clouded. I kicked him in the gut, and I would have done it again, but Mert grabbed me.

She and I wrestled. "Stop it! Jest stop it! Kiki? Johnny? Have you both gone nuts?"

"Get your hands off me." I wrenched away from her. In my peripheral vision, I noted the crowd, a group of curious onlookers, some amused, most horrified.

I leaned over and screamed at Johnny, "You no-good bum. Stay away from me! You got it? Keep away!"

"Calm down," said Mert.

But I'd lost my head. I was well and truly crazed. Her admonition to "calm down" had exactly the opposite effect on me.

"Don't you tell me what to do!" I screamed. "Get out of my sight! Beat it! And take your bum of a brother with you!"

FORTY-EIGHT

Thursday, May 6

"GOOD WORK. YOUR QUARREL with Johnny and Mert was certainly convincing," Robbie winked at me from over his coffee cup. With Linnea gone and Sheila being hopeless in the kitchen, KP duty fell to Robbie. I sipped the tea he brewed for me and nibbled at my toast. My reflection in the bathroom mirror sported big dark circles under both eyes. I hadn't gotten much sleep. I kept reviewing what happened at Faust Park and praying Mert would forgive me. Someday. Maybe.

"Plenty of onlookers, plenty of drama," he added.

"Right."

"Having Detweiler come pick you up. Nice touch."

"Yep." I hadn't had a choice. I needed a ride home. Sheila was meeting the string quartet she'd hired for her wedding. After Detweiler dropped me off, I noticed I'd missed a phone call from my sister Amanda. I'd turned off my ringer so it wouldn't interrupt my "fight" with Johnny, and in the chilly aftermath, I'd neglected to turn it back on.

All in all, it ranked as one of the worst evenings of my life.

Robbie sipped his coffee and continued, "Mert being out of the way is a plus. If she knew what Johnny planned—"

"She would kill me and spoil Bill's fun."

Last night while lying in my bed, I went over and over the plan that Robbie and Johnny had concocted. For the first time, I realized how much of a risk Johnny was taking. One of the conditions of parole is nonassociation with criminals. This cockamamie plot put Johnny back in the thick of the wrong sort of people.

"How did you get permission from his P.O. to pull this off?"

"That was tough. Johnny's been a model citizen. To make this happen, he's hanging out with guys one step away from being arrested. But the stakes went up dramatically with the sniper attack."

"Got it. After an important citizen died, the P.O. decided to throw Johnny under the bus."

"The parole officer owed me a favor. You were in danger. So was Sheila. And Anya." Robbie pushed his coffee cup away. "We're family now. That's how this works."

Actually, we were not family. Not yet. The wedding was three weeks away, but I got his point. I couldn't help thinking that before Robbie and I "were family," Johnny and Mert had been my family.

Family. Such a fluid concept. Handy, too. An all-purpose excuse.

An hour later, I cradled another cup of tea at the Grantwood Diner. Detweiler's amazing green eyes smiled at me. "Boy, when you play a part, you aim for an Academy Award, don't you?" His long legs stretched under the table. We'd gotten our food—in my case, the tea and a toasted bagel—and moved to a red Naugahyde booth in the back for privacy's sake.

I tried to smile at him, but my effort proved weak. I pressed my fingertips to my eyes to stop the imminent flow of tears. "I hated it. I thought it would be hard, but it was worse than hard. Why didn't anyone tell me that Bill threatened Mert? And Sheila?"

"Did you need more on your plate?"

"No."

"Look, our C.I. says Bill's flashing cash for anyone who will bring you to a warehouse so he can teach you manners."

"That's not enough to pick him up and put him in jail?"

"A confidential informant's testimony doesn't hold much weight in court."

That made sense.

"I brought a gift for you."

I'd noticed the red gift bag but pretended not to. I love gifts. I figured he knew how hard it'd been for me last night, and he picked up an iced cookie for me. Lately, he'd made a habit of stopping by bakeries and bringing me a pastry. I hadn't been eating much, and I'd had trouble keeping food down.

The tissue paper crinkled beneath my fingers. At the bottom of the paper bag, I found a box. On the lid was a photo of a gun.

"It's a Kel-Tec .308. Here are the bullets." He pulled a small box from his jacket pocket and rattled it at me. "Remember, never pull or display your gun unless you are willing to use it."

"Huh?"

"Once a creep sees your gun, his natural response is to shoot you first."

"That makes sense. Why the Kel-Tec?"

We'd been to the shooting range, more for sport than serious lessons. Or so I had thought. I hate to admit it, but blasting the heck out of a target labeled "Bill" always put me in a good mood. To Detweiler's surprise, and mine, I turned out to be a pretty good shot. But I never expected our outings to be preparation. I knew that Detweiler's life depended on his gun, but mine didn't.

Or did it?

"It's lightweight. You can put it in your purse. It'll fit in your glove compartment."

So that was why he'd encouraged me to get my concealed carry permit. At the time, it seemed like a bunch of useless rigmarole. But Detweiler had been planning ahead. The question was, why?

"I really need this?" I picked up the box and slid it into my purse.

"I hope not." He leaned over and kissed me, his lips soft on mine. "I sure hope not."

I stared at him, feeling that completeness, that sense that I'd found what I'd been searching for. "I want this mess behind me." I leaned across the table and kissed him back. When we were through, he captured my hand in both of his.

"I know you will. People think you're this piece of fluff, but you aren't. That's why no one will suspect you are carrying. I only hope—"

A loud crash caused us both to lift our heads.

FORTY-NINE

"GET AWAY FROM HIM! He's my husband!" Brenda Detweiler shrieked.

I ducked as she took a swing at me. Her fist went wide. Her body followed. Her hands slammed the table and stopped her from smacking her face down into my tea cup.

Detweiler stood up and hauled her by the collar to an upright position. "Brenda, that's enough."

She lunged toward me, took another swing as she neared my face. "I told you to keep away from him. I warned you."

"It's over, Brenda. Sign the papers," Detweiler said, pulling her off to one side. I've never seen his eyes so flat and hard.

"It's not over until I want it to be. You're not dumping me for her!" Brenda poked her finger into his chest. "You married me. You'll die with me."

Heads swiveled to stare. A man wearing a cheap tie and well-worn button-down shirt hurried to our table. He twisted his hands nervously. "Folks, let's simmer down."

"Shut up!" Brenda screamed at him and yanked herself free from Detweiler's grip. "Mind your own business."

"Excuse me, but this is my business, Miss. I'm the manager here. If you have a quarrel, please take it outside. You are bothering the other patrons." He gestured to the onlookers. Actually, they looked more fascinated than bothered. Brenda was putting on a fine floorshow.

"You're making a spectacle of yourself," added the manager, belatedly.

"You think? I'm just getting started. Watch this." Brenda grabbed my mug and smashed it against the table. Tea splattered me, the table, and the floor. Porcelain pieces flew everywhere. Brenda grabbed the chunk attached to the handle and waved it at the manager like it was a gun. "Back off, Jack. And I mean now."

The manager's eyes grew bigger than a blue-plate special. He yelled toward the kitchen. "Help! Someone dial nine-one-one!"

Detweiler opened his jacket and flashed his badge. "Don't bother. I've got it." With a quick movement, he grabbed Brenda's arm and twisted it behind her back. "Stop it now, or I'll cuff you."

He crab-walked her toward the exit.

"Oh, yeah? This is all HER fault," shouted Brenda, jerking her head toward me. "Kiki Lowenstein is a home-wrecker! She broke up our marriage!"

I wanted to sink through the floor. Since that was a scientific impossibility, I decided to settle for a speedy exit of my own. Blotting tea off my clothes, I tried to clean up the mess. I dug around in my purse and tucked a crumpled five dollar bill under my water glass. Now all I needed was to locate my car keys.

Brenda kept yelling as Detweiler moved her toward the main entrance.

"It's over, people. We're coming around with coffee on the house," the manager said.

I thought the drama was over.

I was wrong.

When I couldn't locate my keys, I pulled the Kel-Tec out of my purse.

That was a mistake.

"Gun!" screamed a customer next to me. "She's got a gun!"

I thought Brenda had returned. I assumed she was packing heat.

I grabbed my new toy and scrambled under the table. With my purse held tightly against my chest, I hid there. All around me, chairs overturned. Feet scrambled. Legs ran past. Screams filled the air.

I leaned my head against the seat of the booth. I was so very, very tired. I hadn't been sleeping well. I closed my eyes. Sirens blared in the distance. I opened my eyes and counted wads of gum stuck to the underside of the table. They hung like multicolored rubbery stalactites.

The noise of scraping chairs continued, as more legs swirled this way and that. I decided to snuggle down and get comfortable.

My eyes grew heavy.

When the Grantwood cops showed up to arrest me, I was sound asleep.

FIFTY

"YOU ARE LATE." MARGIT crossed her arms across her chest, wrinkling her lime green polyester pantsuit. "How will you manage to get everything done? We have stock coming in."

"Them's the breaks," I muttered walking past her toward the sales floor. "Actually, I'm a time management whiz kid. I've managed to start a riot, get arrested, and make bail, yet still show up before our first customer walks in."

"You think you are amusing, but you are not." Margit followed on my heels.

Actually, I hadn't made bail. Once I got hold of Detweiler, the whole matter was dropped.

I turned over the OPEN sign. I started counting the cash drawer. Maybe it was my imagination, but ever since my ride in the police car, my skin had been crawling. Picking at my hair, I plucked out a round, fat bug. I promptly squashed it between my fingernails. Was it a tick? A flea? Or ... ugh ... head lice?

"*Ja*, the schedule says—" she waved a paper at me "—you come in at eight. To run this store properly—"

"I know what the schedule says. To run this store properly, we need to act like a team. Did you prep any kits? Did you start the handouts for tomorrow's crops? Did you divide up the supplies for tomorrow's make-and-takes? Did you work on the May Day album? Hmm? Did you?"

I continued, "You didn't, did you? You don't know how, do you? I can make a schedule. I've put in orders. But you know nothing about scrapbooking or papercrafting. Nothing. Let me translate for you. That's *nichts*. In Spanish, it's *nada*. In English, that's zip, zilch, zero. So unless you can do it all, I suggest you put a sock in it. Because I'm doing the very best I can and my being late is NOT MY FAULT."

After hearing Robbie compliment me for ruining the most important friendship of my adult life, after being assaulted by Brenda Detweiler, and after riding in a police car because the officers thought I pulled a gun in a crowded restaurant, I was in no mood for lectures from a living, breathing, complaining Hummel statue dressed in a gaudy, unnatural shade of lime.

My back hurt, my boobs felt like they'd been used as punching bags, my eyes twitched with exhaustion, and my stomach roiled. Added to those miseries was a creepy-crawly feeling, no doubt caused by vermin hitchhikers from the back seat of the patrol car.

"Put a sock in it?" she stared at me, her goggle-eyes swimming in convex lenses.

"*Ja, Maul zu!*"

Margit's body quivered. "You speak German?"

"Nope. I speak Internet." My high school chemistry teacher also taught German. When our class acted rowdy, he shook a stern finger over us and intoned "zip it" in his adopted language. To be sure of the pronunciation, I'd looked up the phrase thinking it might come in handy. And it had.

The older woman's body sagged, her shoulders rolled inward and an air of defeat pressed mightily on her.

In response, I felt shame and I burst into tears. *She pushed me. She made me angry. But I don't want this sort of relationship with her. I want us to get along.*

Margit's jaw drooped as I sobbed uncontrollably. I wanted my old life back. I wanted to repair my friendship with Mert. I wanted Brenda Detweiler and Bill Ballard out of my hair. And I wanted my mother ... to go home!

"I apologize," I said between hiccups. "I'm not feeling well. Forgive me. I am sorry I arrived late. I was unavoidably detained." With that, I moved past her and started collecting supplies for another May Day album.

FIFTY-ONE

I PHONED CALA AND asked to speak to Lane Carlée. The receptionist told me she was out sick. While I felt bad for Lane, I breathed a sigh of relief because I wanted to do a little more work on the Edwina Fitzgerald album. I knew it was foolish; I'd done enough already. But I really wanted it to show off my talents since the finished product would be on display at CALA.

I hand-colored more embellishments and while they dried, I turned my attention to the May Day album. By noon, I had the May Day background pages assembled, but I was still a long way from finished when Dodie phoned. "Sunshine, I need a break. Can you come spell me? The crowd here at Faust isn't large, but it's steady. I've been on my feet all morning."

"Of course. I'm on my way." Crying had done wonders for my disposition, clearing my mood like a pelting summer rain.

"Grab lunch for me, would you? One of those chicken pecan salads from Wendy's? And a large ice tea. My throat." She stopped.

"Gladly." I knew it was tough for her to say she was hurting.

"Can Margit handle the store?" A note of doubt crept into Dodie's voice.

"You hired her. Can she?"

Dodie chuckled. "You're making me pay, aren't you?"

I told her goodbye and walked into the backroom. Margit sat behind the big desk, punching buttons and tallying up numbers on the old adding machine that Dodie refused to replace. I watched the tape spit out a total before I rapped on the doorframe. "Dodie needs me at Faust Park. You'll have to handle the sales floor here."

"I—I don't," she caught herself. Adjusting her glasses, she stared at me in a manner almost accusatory. "You haven't shown me how to run the cash register."

"Gee, I would have thought you'd want to learn that first thing. Dodie didn't show you?"

She colored. "*Ja.* But I…"

For a long moment, I let her flounder. It did my heart good to see Miss Priss try to admit she didn't know something.

I'm not a mean person by nature. Usually, I'm the first to bend over backward until I'm doing a series of one-handed flips. But Margit had rubbed me wrong. Bama had too. Neither paid me the sort of respect I felt I deserved. Both seemed more ready to deliver criticism than give me credit. With Bama, I'd rolled over and bared my jugular vein in submission. That proved disastrous, so I decided to take a new approach. There was just one problem: I couldn't find a good middle ground. I wanted to be assertive but not pushy, confident but not cruel, and instead I was coming off nasty.

Watching Margit's face crumble with embarrassment, I felt awful. Sure, she slapped down arrogance like it was a winning hand at the poker table. Sure, she hassled me about arriving late. But I didn't want a repeat of my situation with Bama. Some of that particular hassle had been Bama's fault, but I could accept my portion of the blame.

"Come on. I'll show you."

Margit proved a worthy student. I praised her as she mastered the most basic steps to ringing up an order. Fishing around under the drawer, I found the instruction manual. "I've marked the pertinent passages with a highlighter. Call me if you have questions. Or problems."

"Clancy comes in at three. It's on the schedule."

I nodded. "I hope so. Her mother took a tumble yesterday."

"Is she all right? The mother?"

"I don't know. I tried to call Clancy last night. She didn't answer. Clancy's very reliable. If she couldn't come in, she would have called by now."

"She is a good daughter." Margit confirmed, more to herself than to me.

"Yes. Clancy's a good friend and a good worker, too. But this business with her mother, well, it's hard."

"We must honor our mother and our father. The Bible tells us we must. This is one of God's own commandments."

"I know." I struggled to make sense of the law. Did honor include getting walked on? Did it mean that I should honor every one of her requests? Did it mean I should never criticize Mom or disagree with her? Never complain about her to my friends?

Or was it enough to love her, to want the best for her, and still take care of my own needs? Was it honoring her when I told a little white lie rather than hurt her feelings or get crossways with her? Was it honor that caused me to try to win her favor? That forced me to keep in contact with her even when she hurt my feelings?

I tried to treat my mother with respect. But did I give her "great respect and admiration" as the dictionary defined the word "honor"? I admired her for her achievements. She pursued a career back when most women were content to marry and live through their children. She raised my sisters and me almost single-handedly. But I didn't admire her self-centeredness, her insatiable desire to hog the limelight, her unbridled need to take credit for every accomplishment that Catherine, Amanda, and I eeked out of life. Nor did I admire the way she demanded that her needs trump all of ours.

I hated the way she had allowed our father to abuse us. When I thought back to the circumstances leading to Catherine's departure...

I couldn't go there.

FIFTY-TWO

As if summoned by my musings, my phone rang and I recognized the number. "Mom?"

"I want to go shopping."

I couldn't take her. Neither could Sheila. I knew my mother-in-law was spending the entire day working with her caterer, Leon Coleman, a person clearly destined for sainthood, if his African Methodist Episcopalian Church approved the promotion. So far, Sheila had changed her entire menu three times. She demanded to see Leon's recipes and handed him her own "improved" versions. When she tried to cut back the number of items being served, his fingers pushed his reading glasses up the bridge of his broad nose. Looking suspiciously like Morgan Freeman, he said, "Jews don't set no skimpy tables."

Sheila capitulated. It might not have been the scolding. It might have been because Leon Coleman was Linnea's second cousin. We all wanted her back. Soon. As in yesterday.

"Mom, I can't take you to the mall. Not this afternoon."

She whined like a toddler who'd tossed all his toys out of his playpen. "I'm bored. You can't expect me to sit around all day with nothing to do."

"Why don't you watch TV?"

"I have. I've been watching the shopping channel. I saw a chest of drawers that I like. And two dresses. But they say there's a problem with my credit card."

Uh-oh. That doesn't sound good.

She prattled on. "Claudia called. She misses me. She wants to see me. I want to see Claudia. When can I go home?"

Again with the Claudia stuff. I had no idea who Claudia was, but I understood having a problem with her credit card and that was definitely not good.

"Hang on. I'll come pick you up."

"Hurry," she moaned. "I'm not sure how long I can last."

FIFTY-THREE

On my way to Sheila's I dialed Amanda. When she answered on the first ring, I was so shocked I couldn't manage a proper greeting. Instead, I sat too long at a green light only to be honked at by the car behind me and its driver who glared at me as he zoomed past.

"Hello?" my sister repeated.

The words came out in a rush. "Don't hang up. It's about Mom. Is she sick? I mean, she keeps having to use the restroom. What's up with her credit cards? Why does she keep asking for Claudia. Who's Claudia?"

Amanda sighed. "Hello to you, too. I don't have much time to talk. I'm getting my nails done."

Wow, I thought, *that sounds like pure heaven to me!*

"Look," Amanda continued, "I honestly don't know if Mom is sick or not. She's always been a frequent pee-er. That's not unusual for a woman her age."

"Okay," I took that onboard. "But what's the story with her credit card? Who's Claudia? Mom demands to see her."

"That's a long story."

I pulled off to one side. I knew Dodie needed her lunch. I knew Mom was waiting impatiently for me. I also knew my sister. Amanda could be the slowest talker in the world when she chose to be. Hurrying her along would not help. I needed to hang in there and let her tell the story at her own pace.

She didn't say anything.

"Amanda? Amanda, are you there? Look, you don't have to handle all this alone. You get mad at me because I don't help. Give me a chance. Talk to me. What's up?"

In a halting voice, she said, "Do you remember Mrs. McMurray? The red-haired lady two houses over? I think her first name is Rena. Her daughter hired a helper by the name of Claudia Turrow. A couple of times, Claudia brought Mom books that Mrs. McMurray had finished reading and wanted to share. She also invited Mom over to visit Mrs. McMurray. Once or twice she even took both the women out for lunch."

That didn't sound like a problem. In fact, it sounded rather nice. I wondered why Amanda sounded upset. I kept quiet.

"Last month Mrs. McMurray started having serious health problems. She went to her doctor. Her cancer has come back, and the treatments aren't working. They've called in hospice. Claudia's last day is next Friday, a week from tomorrow."

"So this Claudia person is nice to Mom? That's a good thing, right?"

"It would be. But I don't trust her. Kiki, there's something weird about her. Makes my skin crawl to be around her."

FIFTY-FOUR

I SAT THERE FOR a minute and watched cars go by. "What do you think is going on?"

"Claudia is looking for her next job. She's been telling Mom how much she admires her. Mom's been saying weird stuff like, 'Claudia loves me. She's says I'm the mother she never had.'"

Either Claudia had been orphaned at an early age or she'd been raised by a pack of feral wolves.

Amanda continued, "I want to talk to Mrs. McMurray's daughter and get the straight scoop, but as you can guess, the timing isn't right. Poor old Mrs. McMurray is on death's doorstep."

"There's more to this, isn't there?" I could feel it.

"Last time I visited, I noticed that a few of Mrs. McMurray's possessions were missing. An ivory mirror and brush. A signed lithograph by Erté. A small bronze statue that I think was a Remington."

"Mom doesn't have much to lose."

"No, but what she does have should stay in the family. Even if Mrs. McMurray gave those objects to Claudia, the woman had no business accepting them. Not when Mrs. McMurray wasn't thinking clearly." Amanda huffed and puffed like the Big Bad Wolf in the fairy tale. "I suspect that Claudia is latching onto Mom because she's looking for a full-time job as a caregiver."

"But Mom doesn't need full-time care. She lives with you."

"Not exactly. Mom has her own part of the house, her own apartment. I work all day. I have my own life. So, yes, we share the same address, but I'm not around 24/7 to babysit our mother." Amanda sounded snippy, but I decided not to take offense.

I'd never seen the house in Arizona, never been invited there. I guess she'd made assumptions about my life and I'd made assumptions about hers, in that ignorantly judgmental way that people do. So we'd nurtured our hurts and thought the worst of each other. Sibling rivalry doesn't end at childhood. Instead, it smolders and flares up like a brush fire throughout your life.

"I'm sorry if I sounded offensive," I said sincerely. "Mom's lucky to have you so close by."

"Yeah? That's not what Claudia has convinced her. Claudia has told Mom I ignore her. She's convinced Mom that she deserves better, that I'm a negligent, thankless child. I found a note she sent Mom suggesting that my ingratitude was sharper than a serpent's tooth."

Nothing like using the Bible to divide and conquer, to sow animosity and pain. I could only imagine all the angels wincing. How did God put up with us? What a miserable lot we were.

Amanda sighed, "Mom's convinced she can't live without Claudia. Wait till you hear what that woman charges for her caregiver services." My sister named a figure easily three times my current wages.

"And she's not even a nurse?"

"Nope. She's a companion. That's it, that's all."

"That's why you sent Mom to me?"

"It's one reason. Another is that I just had a physical and my blood pressure is off the charts. The doctor suggested I take a break. And yeah, I figured if Mom disappeared, she couldn't hire Claudia. If she couldn't hire Claudia, Claudia would move on. Problem solved."

Simple and elegant. I had to admire Amanda. She'd thought this through.

"Good work, Amanda."

"Not so fast. We aren't out of the woods yet. Claudia has a contract until the end of the next week, and she's very, very sneaky. One of Mom's friends called me to say that Claudia was pressuring her for your phone number. I've already made Mom's cell phone disappear. I don't know if you can live without yours, but you might want to be careful about answering calls from strange numbers."

I thought about that. I remembered the name on my cell . . . Beverly Somebody. Could that have been Claudia? Or a wrong number?

I put on my blinker, checked for oncoming traffic, and pulled back onto the street. "You were always a lot sneakier than I was. I admire that about you, leetle seester." It was my pet name for her.

"Thank you, big seester."

I grinned for the first time in several days. Despite all the stuff going wrong in my life, I felt great. I had my sister back!

FIFTY-FIVE

Mom stood on the curb outside Sheila's house, chomping on the proverbial bit and raring to go. She danced around like a horse headed back to the barn.

"I want to go to that mall. The one with the fancy stores and the piano in the center court."

"We're heading somewhere much more special." I backed out of the driveway carefully. "Put your seat belt on."

She needed help with that. My mom, a woman known for her physical flexibility, couldn't twist far enough to capture the end with the buckle.

Who is this woman? She's not the mother I grew up with. She's not limber, or mentally sharp. She's more like a child than a woman in her mid-seventies.

"This is a special event. I know how much you like history. We're visiting a historic landmark, and there's a butterfly house on the grounds."

She squinched up her mouth, pinching it tighter than a miser's purse. "But I wanted to get a new pair of shoes. You ruined mine. You owe me a pair."

"Yes, but we can go to the mall tomorrow or the next day. I'm taking you to a special event that only occurs once a year and it's this weekend." I hesitated. Should I go over the top? I sneaked a quick glance at Mom and saw the mulish set of her face. So I added, "I've been bragging about you to the other vendors. They are all dying to meet you. Besides, I thought we could grab lunch."

She sat in the car while I grabbed my wallet and got our food. When I came back, my cell phone was sitting on the console. I didn't recall leaving it there, but I was too hungry to worry over it and Mom began to attack her food as if she were a starving animal. This was wholly at odds with the woman who had raised me. That parent had insisted on impeccable manners.

At Faust Park, Dodie greeted Mom warmly, took her salad gratefully, and told me about what she'd sold. When Mom toddled off to look over our neighbor's booth, Dodie gave me a broad grin. "After I finish eating, I'll take her for a stroll and show her the 1920 carousel."

"Carousel?" Mom's ears perked up and she came back over to us. I bought her a bag of kettle corn and all of us munched happily on the sweet snack.

"The carousel is inside that special building. It has sixty hand-carved animals. They're absolutely beautiful," said Dodie. My boss turned her attention toward me. "Kiki, do you know if Clancy showed up to relieve Margit? I don't think she's comfortable with the cash register yet."

"I gave Margit a quick tutorial. I told her to call me if she had any problems."

"I appreciate that, Sunshine. Really I do." Dodie's eyes lit up with the sort of spark I hadn't seen in awhile, at least not since she'd been taking chemo and radiation therapy for cancer of the larynx. "It's good to hear you two are getting off on the right foot."

Suddenly, our booth began to sway and tremble. The back wall buckled outwards. This wouldn't be St. Louis's first earthquake, or it's last . . . but then I realized that the tremor was only affecting our little domicile.

"What on earth?" I leapt to my feet and grabbed at the back wall, but my fingers missed their grip. All three of us watched in horror as it crashed down, taking hundreds of dollars of merchandise along.

Standing to one side of the mess was a laughing Brenda Detweiler. "How do you like that? Homewrecker!"

But I didn't have time to react to her, because I was busy trying to steady the left and right walls. Without the back side bracing them, they listed dangerously toward the center. I raced to the left, and Dodie stood up and steadied the right. Brenda ran to Dodie's side and pushed against the wobbling structure.

"Stop it! Get away!" Dodie swatted at her. "Somebody help! Help!"

"Mom, run!" I held up my side of the structure with one arm as I frantically gestured to my mother to clear out. But she stood there in the center, mesmerized by the activity around her.

"Mom, please move. I'm begging you. This could fall. I don't want you to get hurt."

"Stop it, Brenda! Quit it!" Dodie's raspy voice soared over creaks and moans of the rocking structure. Shrink-wrapped packages fell to the dirt as Brenda's rhythmic shoving motion loosened the hooks holding them.

"Brenda?" I straddled the left wall to brace it. "Knock it off. Let's talk, okay? Just you and me? No need to involve Dodie or my mother."

"Done talking," she said followed by a mighty "ooph."

With my free hand I reached into my pocket and hit the speed dial for Detweiler.

But Brenda moved faster than I did. She slapped my phone out of my hand. "I told you to stay away from my husband! You slut! I told you you'd be sorry! I'm on to you, Kiki Lowenstein!" She reached over and grabbed a handful of my hair.

"Ow!" I yelled.

"Hey, lady. Knock it off." A passerby pulled on Brenda's sweatshirt. His tug caused her to lose her grip on me.

Two men came to my aid, lending their shoulders to support the booth wall, and a third, a beefy guy who could have been a professional wrestler, raised his huge arms to steady Dodie's side. "Cut it out," Big Man said to Brenda.

In response, Brenda bobbed and weaved. She ducked under the framework and lifted one side of our display table. The cash register slid off the surface, hit the ground, and bounced along, jingling merrily. The drawer flew open and money fluttered up and around like a legion of green butterflies chasing copper and silver coins.

"Stop that!" A security guard came over at a trot.

Dodging the mess she'd made, Brenda raced off into the crowd.

FIFTY-SIX

It took longer for us to make a police report and reorganize the booth than it had to set it up originally. Our merchandise littered the grassy aisle and scattered over into other booths. Dodie and I scrambled to pick up metal pegs, shrink-wrapped packages, tools, supplies, and money. Mom helped by sorting the dollar bills and coins as we retrieved them.

The cash register refused to work.

"Thirty-six dollars and twenty-five cents short," said Dodie punctuating the loss from our drawer with a long and sorrowful sigh. "But that's nothing compared to the bill for getting this thing fixed."

We both knew the encounter had cost more than that. While we were putzing around with the booth, we lost out on the opportunity to engage potential customers. Visitors to the art fair gave us a wide berth, noting that our wares were in disarray. We tried to maintain a cheery attitude, but the destruction hurt.

Maybe I should apologize. But why? This wasn't my fault! I had done nothing to provoke Brenda Detweiler's ire. She had thrown her husband out, causing the final breach of their marital contract—and this was after he'd supported her while she was going through drug rehab. Now she wanted Chad Detweiler back, but harassing me wasn't the way to his heart. Somewhere along the line, she'd failed to take responsibility for her own behavior. I was loathe to apologize to Dodie because that seemed to me to signal that, indeed, I was to blame, just like Brenda had suggested.

The heightened drama around our booth's near-collapse suited Mom's sense of theatre. She flitted around "helping" us and chatting with the astonished passers-by about that "crazy woman" who attacked her daughter. I marveled at my mother's ability to turn every situation into a platform for her to talk about her favorite subject: Lucia Montgomery. While I rehung our page kits, Mom told attendees about her career on stage. "Jealousy! That's what this was all about. I put up with more than my share of it throughout my career. So many of the other chorus girls wished they had my talent," she said as she patted her hair into place.

For once I was happy she could weave fanciful tales. Her ongoing commentary kept her busy while Dodie and I worked. Mom positioned herself in the middle of our booth and held court, while we straightened out the mess.

Several page kits and packages of patterned paper were ruined beyond saving. Dodie and I conferred, ultimately deciding to label a cardboard box "damaged goods" and starting the painful process of marking these down.

I was bent over a page kit trying to flatten the crumpled embellishments when I heard a voice sing out, "Luci! Darling, Luci! I've been looking all over for you!"

I straightened in time to see a woman set down two suitcases and start running toward my mother. The two hugged and kissed and cooed over each other. The newcomer had a frizzled head of over-processed bleached hair. Her kisses left pink lipstick imprints on my mother's cheek.

Dodie shot me a quizzical look. I shrugged, mouthing, "Beats me."

"Um, I'm Kiki Lowenstein." I extended my hand toward the newcomer.

"Of course you are," Bleached Blondie said, handling my digits as if trying to avoid a contagious disease.

"I'm sorry," I said. "I didn't catch your name."

"Why, Kiki, don't you know who this is? I've been telling you about her. I've missed her so much!" Mom slipped a proprietary arm around the woman's waist. The two shared a giggle.

Bleached Blondie gave me a half-smile and narrowed her eyes. "Claudia. Claudia Turrow."

FIFTY-SEVEN

"OKAY, LET'S CALL IT a day," I sang out, eager to leave our booth. In my experience, there are days that can't be salvaged. Instead, it's best to end them early, to call it quits and retreat, with hope for a good night's sleep and the promise of a clean slate on the morrow. Forget knitting up the raveled sleeve of care. Toss the old mess and start anew.

"Come on, Claudia," said Mom. After roaming the grounds and sampling the other exhibits, Mom and her BFF commandeered the only two chairs we had in the booth, never offering to share or spell me. I stood for the next four hours, greeting shoppers and writing out sales tickets by hand. While I worked, they gossiped and giggled.

"Claudia, where can I drop you off?" I said as we walked toward my car.

"She's staying with me." Mom swung an arm around her friend's shoulders.

"That would work if you had your own place, but since Linnea left,"—*after you drove her away by insulting the poor woman*— "Sheila's stuck doing all the housework. I'm sure we can find a nice hotel for Claudia."

"Oh, no. I'm here for Luci. I couldn't possibly leave her. She needs me. I don't mind sharing a room with her. I'll even sleep on a sofa if I have to. Or on the floor." Claudia's thin grin smacked of self-satisfaction. "We could even share a bed."

Ugh. Icky gross.

"I'm so sorry, but that won't work." I smiled and in return received a frosty glare.

The glint in Claudia's eyes told me this was a standoff, but I wasn't giving in. "Where can I drop you? There's a lovely Drury Inn right down the street."

"She can stay in my room," Mom said. "I don't know why you are being so rude. Ever since that man shot at you—"

"What? Oh, my darling Luci! Were you there? Are you all right?" Claudia threw both arms around my mother.

Right on cue, Mom burst into sobs.

Claudia continued over my mother's caterwauling. "What if something had happened to you? I can't bear to think about it. It must have been awful! My poor dear, brave, Luci!"

"You can't imagine. I was so scared! Bullets flying. People yelling. I lost my shoes!" Mom sobbed like a lost toddler. I stood off to the side, an interloper, watching this strange woman with the fresh-fried Day-Glo hair as she patted my mother's back and murmured, "There, there. You poor baby."

FIFTY-EIGHT

THE RIDE TO SHEILA'S never seemed so long. Claudia and Mother huddled together in the back seat, whispering and exchanging secrets. After I parked the car, Claudia helped Mom out. "Kiki, I'll need my bags," Claudia sang out to me as she led my mother into Sheila's house.

I fumed but decided I had no choice but to play the role of bell captain.

"I'm starving," said my mother, while watching me struggle to carry her two suitcases into the house. I'd just crossed the threshold when Claudia let go of Sheila's heavy front door. It walloped me a good one, bruising my elbows.

"So am I," said Claudia. "In fact, I'm famished. They don't feed you on the plane. I was in such a hurry to see you that I didn't stop to eat after we landed." She paused and looked around. "Nice place you've got here. I guess I'd better change if we're going out to eat."

I bit my tongue. "We won't be eating out."

"But I'm hungry!" Mom's voice climbed a notch higher. "So is Claudia."

My own stomach rumbled. Gracie looked at me and whimpered, so I let her outside and put down kibble. Both women stared at me expectantly. I'd been on my feet all day, but they climbed onto Sheila's kitchen stools, propped their elbows on the counter, and started yakking.

I gave in. Sheila kept a well-stocked pantry, so I found a can of tuna fish, another of peas, a can of cream of mushroom soup, and a box of macaroni and cheese. I didn't ask if they liked tuna noodle casserole. I simply put the water on the stove to boil and went upstairs to change out of my work clothes. My waistband dug into my skin, leaving an angry red mark. Peeling out of the slacks and blouse, I slipped into a hot shower. That buggy feeling from my ride in the squad car was still with me. Soaping up felt good. In fact, I toyed with the idea of staying under the water until it turned cold, but in the end, I figured my mother would come hunting for me.

When I got back to the kitchen, I saw that Mom and Claudia had moved from the kitchen stools to the plush overstuffed sofa in Sheila's living room. Claudia maintained a clear view of the kitchen from her seat.

"Don't you have anything we could nibble on? Cheese and crackers? Some brie perhaps? Or a hunk of Wensleydale? A glass of wine? I'd like a nice merlot," Claudia called to me. "Luci would like one, too. Please make sure it's a good bottle. Cheap wine gives us both a headache."

While I rummaged in Sheila's cupboard and refrigerator, I comforted myself by playing the "good news/bad news" game. The good news was that I knew exactly where Claudia was. She hadn't moved in with Mom, so she didn't have access to Mom's family treasures, such as they were. Or to Mom's meager bank account. The bad news was that I now was dealing with both Mom and Claudia, or to be more precise, I was now relegated to the role of household help for two imperious—and hungry—divas.

If I'd had more energy, I might have stiffened my backbone. If I hadn't been worrying about Bill Ballard, I might have shooed Claudia away and told her to stay away. Admittedly, Claudia had a calming effect on Mom, and right now was a bad time for me to cope with one of Mom's meltdowns. We had too much at risk.

First I'd deal with Bill Ballard, then I'd handle Ms. Claudia Turrow.

FIFTY-NINE

WHILE I PUT TOGETHER a plate of cheese and crackers, I phoned Robbie Holmes to tell him about the havoc Brenda had wreaked on our booth. "Robbie, I'm worried that she's following me. What if she gets in the middle of this thing with Bill?"

Robbie sighed. "Look, I'd like to help, but you girls will have to settle this quarrel yourselves."

I couldn't believe what he was saying. He made it sound like a high school spat over who we sat next to in the cafeteria.

"You do know that Brenda's dad is an important politician over in Illinois, don't you?" Robbie asked.

No, I didn't.

"He's all over Chad's parents about the divorce. I guess he's really steamed."

Great. Could things get any better? I wasn't even officially involved with their son and the Detweilers already had reason to dislike me.

"Just … just deal with it, Kiki," Robbie said. "We're close to wrapping this up. Bill and Johnny made contact last night. Bill actually went looking for Johnny because he heard about the spat you had at Faust Park. Lucky for us, Johnny's been hanging out at the same bar every night, so he was easy enough for Bill to find."

He paused and spoke in a low tone, "Bill wants Johnny to 'grab' you from the store."

"What do I need to do?"

"Nothing. It's best that you be surprised. Johnny will pretend to kidnap you, probably on a night when you work late. He'll drive you to a designated spot under a viaduct, and swap you out for a female officer who is about your size."

"But how about Johnny? Will he be safe? I mean, what if Bill pulls a gun on him?" I knew that as a condition of parole, Johnny couldn't have a firearm in his possession.

"Johnny knew the risks going in. Look, there's a GPS tracking device under Johnny's truck and under his sister Mert's truck as well. Even if Johnny switches out vehicles, we'll be monitoring his route. We should be able to protect him."

Should be able to protect him? That sounded awfully iffy to me. I could just imagine Mert discovering she'd been bugged. She'd be furious. She hated the Patriot Act, or the "Spy on Your Friends" Act, as she called it.

"We set a similar trap for the South County rapist. Learned a lot from that operation. Caught the guy. Sent him away. He's serving three consecutive lifetimes."

Thinking about all the ways that Robbie's trap could go wrong sent shivers down my spine.

Claudia stuck her head in the kitchen and interrupted my conversation. "I was wondering what was taking you so long. Your mom's really hungry. We're both thirsty."

I told Robbie goodbye and turned to face Claudia. "We're all out of wine."

"Really? I should think that anyone living in a nice place like this would have a bottle or two stashed away," she walked over to the cutlery drawer and fingered Sheila's silver. "Nice place you've got here."

So Claudia thought this was my home. *Hmmm.*

"Well, I'll go keep Luci company. I hope you don't take long. Your mother's hungry."

I put a circle of brie on a plate, spooned apricot jam over the top, sprinkled it with sliced almonds, and stuck everything in the microwave for about sixty seconds. I poured two glasses of iced tea and put everything on one of Sheila's handsome walnut trays. Balancing the food carefully, I carried it out to the low table where Claudia and Mom were sitting.

Neither woman thanked me. Claudia smirked up at me and said, "I thought maybe you got lost or something."

I bit my tongue.

Back in the kitchen, I grabbed my cell phone. Before I could think about what I was doing, I called Mert. After all, she was my "go to" friend, my confidant.

Just as quickly, I realized what I was doing and pressed "End Call." I stared at the silent phone. I sure missed talking with her. Over the years, I'd grown to rely on her wisdom and her straightforward common sense. She, more than anyone, had taught me to stand up for myself.

I wanted to talk to my friend, but I couldn't. I wanted to call Detweiler, but I couldn't. I thought about Dodie...and Clancy... and realized I was in this alone.

As I chopped onions and celery for dinner, I played Dr. Phil's logic in my head. If I forced Claudia to leave now, Amanda might have to deal with the woman later on Mom's home turf. If I let Claudia hang around, she could be Mom's play buddy. She would keep Mom occupied.

That was good.

Really good.

I couldn't take the chance of Mom getting involved in our scheme to trap Bill Ballard.

Sheila and Anya pulled into the drive, so I raced out to meet them and to explain who Claudia was. I finished with, "It's best that we don't make a big production about the fact that this is Sheila's house. At least for a while. I don't want Claudia to feel uncomfortable. I think Mom likes having a friend around. Anya, can you play along?"

"Sure," said my daughter.

My mother-in-law rolled her eyes. "Anything to keep your mother out of my hair."

"You okay, sweetheart?" I gave Anya a hug.

"Yeah, whatever," she said as she started walking toward the house.

SIXTY

Friday, May 7

"JUST YOU AND ME, babe," I rubbed Gracie's ears, as we walked into the empty store. At nine o'clock, I phoned CALA and learned that Lane was still under the weather. That meant I had the entire weekend to finish up the Edwina Fitzgerald album. I spent the morning getting ready for our Friday night crop.

At noon, Margit started her shift. "How you doing with the cash register?" I asked.

"You are a good teacher, Kick-ee." She rewarded me with a happy smile. "I cooked sauerbraten last night. I always make too much, so I brought enough to share."

I took one bite of the plate she offered me and my taste buds danced a happy jig. "Wow! This is great! And these potatoes, they're just scrumptious. What's this in the green beans?"

"Spaetzle. German dumplings." Margit's face glowed. "I sprinkled it with dried parsley, too." She made herself a plate and we sat happily, side by side, eating.

"Why did you want to own part of a scrapbook store? I mean, you don't scrapbook, do you? You're obviously a great cook, but do you like crafts?"

"*Ja*, I like knitting and crochet. I make cards. I'll show you." She reached into an oilcloth bag and extracted a plastic folder. From this, she withdrew colorful, magical cards, the likes of which I'd never seen before.

"What do you call this?"

"It is iris eye folding. You begin with an aperture, then you fill the space with pieces of paper that overlap in a pleasing pattern. It began in Holland, using the brightly colored lining of envelopes."

I turned the cards over and over in my hands. "These are fabulous, and I mean it. Could you teach a class in this?"

We put our heads together and designed a project for that very evening. Clancy called a couple of times to report her sales at Faust Park and ask for more merchandise. I put together a box of products to take to our booth. "How's your mother?" I asked.

"Right now, she's still in the hospital. It's awful, Kiki, really bad."

"You mean her break? Was it her arm or her leg or both?"

"The broken arm will heal. Luckily her ankle is only sprained."

"That's not too bad, is it? I mean, it could have been a lot worse."

Clancy said nothing for a beat, then blurted, "The doctor says her equilibrium is compromised. So is her mobility. She can't move back into her own home. And she's insisting on living with me!"

I felt Clancy's pain. Her voice, usually so cultured and precise, was blurred with emotion. "I'm so upset that I can't talk about it now. How's it going for you? Dodie told me about Brenda trashing our booth."

"Yeah, that was pretty bad."

"Dodie thinks you should get a restraining order."

"Um, I'll consider it." But I wouldn't. I didn't want to make the situation worse than it was.

After I hung up, I turned around to find Margit staring at me thoughtfully. I could tell by the look on her face that she'd been listening in. "If you don't get back to trouble, trouble will have kittens," she said.

"Is that an old German saying?"

"*Nein*. It's something my husband used to say when he was in sales. *Ja*, some problems go away, but others, you have to escort them out of your life."

MARGIT'S IRIS EYE FOLDING PROJECT

This is the perfect way to use up strips of paper or paper with patterns that are no longer appealing. Margit suggests you start with a negative space (a hole) shaped like a square or a diamond. When you add in the strips, place them in opposite corners and work to fill the center. By the way, real iris eye folding does involve folding paper, but layering strips is just as cute and as much fun.

1. Punch or cut a simple shape out of the center of a piece of cardstock, leaving a border of at least two inches all around the hole. Tip: Use a die cut machine or an "anywhere" punch to make this aperture.
2. Cut strips of paper no more than ½ inch wide and 12 inches long.
3. Starting at the outside edges, layer strips of paper, overlapping each strip until you have filled in the space. As you lay down a strip, tape the edges down on the backside. Tip: Move from outside corners inward. You are building a pattern with the strips of paper.
4. Tape all the strips down on the back. Trim as necessary.

SIXTY-ONE

I PLANNED TO RUN home only long enough to light the Shabbas candles with Sheila and Anya. I also expected Mom to join us as we prayed. Despite the fact I'd been raised Episcopalian, my mother always showed a keen interest in other religions. She particularly felt reverence toward Judaism, in part because our family priest bragged about his own Jewish son-in-law, "He's a better Christian than most who claim the title. The Jews are, after all, God's Chosen people."

I left my car in the driveway and raced in through the front door. Sheila and Anya stood at the dining room table. The silver candlesticks glowed in the waning sunlight. As always, Sheila's house was fragrant with the smell of baking challah. A still-hot loaf took pride of place on a special plate in the center. A decanter of merlot sat to one side, along with two glasses of wine and a glass of grape juice for Anya. Mom was nowhere in sight.

"I'll get Mom," I offered.

"Don't bother," said Sheila.

"What?"

"She's not coming," said Anya, in that sort of bored voice that teens do so well.

"Is she not feeling well?"

"She's fine." Sheila's tightly crossed arms matched the tense expression on her face. "Except for dropping a bottle of pills all over the floor."

"What?"

"Your mother's hands shake. Claudia explained she couldn't possibly get down on her hands and knees because she has a bad back. So I've been all over the floor chasing down pills."

"Yeah, Mom, Claudia wouldn't even help!" said Anya in a stage whisper. "And you know that Gran's knees bother her."

"I'm sorry, Sheila. Really I am."

"Not your fault. Let's get on with our Sabbath," said Sheila, handing a match to Anya.

We thanked God for the light, for fruit of the vine, and for bread. Gracie sat obediently at Anya's side, knowing that she, too, would receive a portion of the challah to ensure a blessed week. Anya gave a piece to the dog and promptly disappeared up the stairs, giving her bedroom door a mighty slam shut.

"What's going on?" I followed Sheila into the kitchen. At the counter there, my mother and Claudia helped themselves to the roast chicken and vegetables that were the usual Lowenstein Friday meal. In fact, they'd more than helped themselves. I noticed most of the chicken was gone, and only a few vegetables remained. Clearly, Claudia and Mom had started eating before we'd lit the candles.

"Hey, why didn't you join us?" I asked as I stabbed a fork in a slender slice of white meat and scraped around for the last of the carrots. I assumed that Sheila had another chicken in the oven. There certainly wasn't enough here for Robbie. "Mom, you always enjoy lighting the candles."

"Oh, that," she said with a wave of her hand.

I couldn't believe my ears. "Say what?"

"What do you call your God?" asked Claudia.

"Jehovah? God? Lord? Actually, many observant Jews don't call him by name. He is too powerful, and his name is too holy."

"Pfff." Claudia snorted. "Blasphemy."

I nearly hit the ceiling. Here she was, a guest in someone else's home, and she was calling our religion blasphemy. I glanced quickly over my shoulder. Sheila stood in the doorway. Her eyes twin pools of icy blue anger.

"Excuse me?" I stared at Claudia.

"My pastor told us about people like you. You believe in—"

I reached my limit. "Claudia, I don't need you to tell me what I believe in. You don't know what I believe in. Please remember, you are a guest in this home."

"Huh," said Claudia. "I know exactly what you believe. I've seen how you treat your mother."

SIXTY-TWO

THE FRIDAY NIGHT CROPPERS started arriving shortly before I finished our preparations. Usually, I would panic (a little) because it's hard to finish readying the tables, greeting people, organizing the food, and waiting on customers. But Margit had printed up coupons, covered the work tables with fresh white butcher paper, set out all the chairs, and generally had everything ready to go.

She'd assembled small kits with the paper for the iris eye folding project. I could tell she was both nervous and excited about sharing her talents with our scrapbookers.

"You'll be fine," I told her. "They are lovely women, and they are always eager to try new techniques. This one is just fabulous."

"Thank you for your help with everything," Margit said.

"You are welcome. Hey, would you do me a favor? I'm glad to help you learn about scrapbooking, and I'm also happy to help you teach classes. Could you show me how our bookkeeping works? If I could learn more about our ordering systems, and our accounts payable, maybe I could do a better job of planning and promoting."

"What do you mean?"

"If we have paper or supplies that aren't moving, I can take that into consideration as I come up with projects. I mean, I already do, in that I look around and see what's on the shelves."

"But if you knew about our discounts and the promotions that the manufacturers offer, you could do more, *ja*?"

"They offer promotions?"

She nodded, her bowl-shaped hair swinging back and forth. "Sometimes if you buy this, you get another product at a discount. Or if you buy more of this before a certain date, they'll send you a special bonus."

"Gosh, I definitely could help us hit those goals. Our page kits sell really well. If I knew we needed to move a certain type of paper, I could make up the page kits with that particular product."

For the next ten minutes, Margit and I brainstormed more efficient ways to create "turn," which she explained means the number of times your inventory turns over. The faster your turn is, the more money you make. If merchandise sits on the shelf for six months, your capital is tied up for six months—and you can't make as much profit as you would if your merchandise turned over every six weeks.

Margit counseled me to "think of inventory turn as a payday. Would you rather get money for every week you work? Or for every month? Providing that you always make the same or an equal amount of money?"

"Weekly. If I always get the same amount—in this case roughly the same percentage of sales profit—I'd rather be paid fifty-two times a year instead of twelve times."

"*Ja.* You understand it now, Kick-ee." Her face was bright pink with pleasure. "It should be a good night?"

I nodded. Crop nights didn't bring in tons of money. We charged a nominal fee for our crops, and we gave away a lot in terms of coupons with discounts, supplies that accompanied the new techniques we taught, and so on. But every cropper bought more consumables: paper, adhesives, embellishments. Each new scrapbooker wound up trying at least one or two tools and that often resulted in a purchase. Best of all, over the years we had built a community. We kept this community, this group of scrapbookers, excited and interested in the hobby. In return, they not only spent money with us, they also reignited our passion for the industry.

While I was out buying more napkins and colas for our crop night, Clancy had stopped by. She reported the sales figures from our Faust booth to Margit. She also shared email addresses of folks who wanted to take classes.

I was sorry that I missed her.

Margit was actually "off" at seven, but since she was demonstrating her craft, she was happy to stick around.

I checked the schedule, hoping that Mert would be in. Although she had her own cleaning and dogsitting businesses, she worked a couple of hours each month, mostly to maintain her employee discount. Frequently, she chose to help at the crops. That way she and I could spend a little quality time together while getting paid for our presence.

223

But Mert's name had been scratched out on the schedule. I swallowed my disappointment.

"Laurel Wilkins" had been written in. Laurel could charm Rush Limbaugh into making a six-figure donation to the Democratic Party. She's also the most amazingly competent young woman I've ever met. And pretty? Shoot. We used to call her "Miss December" because she looks like a centerfold, but once we learned it hurt her feelings, we all apologized and stopped. As per usual, Laurel showed up looking stunning. She wore skinny jeans, a flowing gauzy top, and big earrings with the peace symbol on them. On her feet were ballerina flats. She helped put the colas on ice as our customers trickled in.

Bonnie Gossage bounced little Fernando on her hip as she spread out the supplies for his baby book. Her older son, Felix, was home with his father, Fred. Now that Felix was a toddler, Fernando was our resident "pass-around baby." Miriam Glickstein brought challah and a big pan of kugel. Rita Romano brought a cookbook she was making for her new daughter-in-law. She also made a big pot of Mexican rice. The scent of cumin made my mouth water. Kathy Berberich and Pat Davis were making memory albums to give to kids whose wishes had been fulfilled by the Make-A-Wish Foundation. I was delighted to learn that a wish is granted every 40 minutes. How cool is that?

Since Friday night crops ran well past midnight, almost everyone brought food. That was helpful on this Friday because I'd had so little to eat. As it turned out, Sheila hadn't baked another chicken. Or made more vegetables. I was mortified by my mother's piggish conduct and ashamed of Claudia's remarks.

Sheila had shrugged. "Robbie told me why you need to stay here. About the plan. Honestly, men! They love all this running around like secret agents. What they need to do is grab a gun and go put Bill out of his misery."

"I'm not excited about their scheme. In fact, I hate it."

"I don't see any other options. We need to get that monster out of our lives. I can keep Anya out of the way this weekend, but what can we do about your mother?"

"That's why I haven't told Claudia to leave. While she's around, Mom has a play buddy."

"If we're lucky, this will be over soon. Until then, your mother and Claudia are welcome to stay at my house."

I'd never heard her so conciliatory and I said so.

"Don't fool yourself. I don't care about your mother, and I'd love to plant my foot on Claudia's big behind and kick her to the curb. I just want this hassle behind us so we can all go back to some semblance of normal."

I agreed. "Is something bothering Anya? She seemed down in the dumps last night."

"She's been very quiet."

"She hasn't told you what's on her mind?"

"No. Mostly she spends her evenings in her room with Seymour. She's online a lot. I'm not sure that's a good idea."

"I hear you. At my house the computer is out in the open."

Sheila nodded. "I know it. But I don't think we can take her laptop away from her right now. She needs it for school. So many of her assignments are online these days."

"Is there something at school that's happening? Something I need to know about?"

"I don't think so. I was working on the invitations for the wedding yesterday. She picked up the list and wanted to know how many 'Lowensteins' are still around. Whether Harry had any brothers, and if they had any children or grandchildren."

Harry was Sheila's husband, Anya's paternal grandfather who died of cancer six weeks before she was born.

"And the answer is?"

"No. Both his brothers, Saul and Herschel, died at Auschwitz. As far as we know, so did all of his cousins."

"Is she still bothered about you changing your last name?"

Sheila shrugged again and picked the crease of her slacks. "Or you changing yours."

A sharp pain zipped through my temples. I put my fingertips to my head and rubbed. "I need to get back to work. I can't deal with this right now."

"I know you can't. Unfortunately, I can't either."

SIXTY-THREE

JENNIFER MOORE ARRIVED AT the shop late. I showed her the new May Day album. I only had a few pages to go. "Absolutely gorgeous. CALA definitely should sell these as kits. In fact, I'll tell the bookstore manager that I'll order a half dozen right off the bat."

"Thank you, Jennifer. That's really kind of you."

"My pleasure. I saw the memorial album you made for Edwina Fitzgerald. You did a great job."

"Have you heard whether Deanna and Peter liked it?" I motioned Jennifer into the backroom where we could speak privately.

"I don't want to gossip, but—" Jennifer chewed on a finger. She always nibbled herself to raw flesh whenever she became nervous.

Very gently I reached up and pulled her hand away from her mouth. "Then don't. I overheard people talking at the funeral. There seemed to be some concern about the company. Since you're on the board, I realize you can't talk."

She inhaled, long and slowly. "It's more than that. As a member of the board, I have a fiduciary responsibility. When that bumps up against my friendships, it's tough. I mean, I like Deanna and Peter, really, I do. I understand their desire to keep up with their neighbors. But pretending to be someone you aren't—that never ends well."

"How's Peyton doing? Anya's been awfully moody. You're lucky that Nicci opted out of participating."

Jennifer cocked her head and said, "Notice something weird about all the photos of Peyton? Anything unusual?"

I thought back. "They are all posed shots."

"That's right. Ask yourself why. You'll figure it out."

SIXTY-FOUR

As I TIDIED UP after the crop, Jennifer's challenge stuck with me. I could come up with various reasons for only including posed shots: (1) the subject resisted having her photos taken. (2) Peyton was difficult to capture on film and only a professional did a good job. (3) Peyton's usual grooming/attire wasn't up to the standards her family set. All right, there was (4) no one was interested in taking her picture.

None of these told me anything worth knowing about Peyton or the Fitzgerald family. Or did they? Jennifer was a smart cookie. She'd been trying to share important information. She trusted that I would get her drift.

If she was nibbling her fingers, the situation was tense. Ergo, I needed to sort this out right away.

How could I learn more?

I turned to the only resource I truly understood: pictures. I knew that Sheila's personal library contained copies of the school yearbook going back more than thirty years. Maybe a candid shot of Peyton would help me learn more about the Fitzgerald family dynamics. An unstaged shot might reveal a relevant piece of information.

But relevant to what?

Heartened by my plan, I turned off the store lights and flipped the sign on the front door to read CLOSED. After locking the back entrance, I gathered my dog's leash and strolled with her toward my car. Once I unlocked the passenger side door, I unclipped the Great Dane.

"Get in," I told my dog. "Up."

The night was still. A warm breeze tickled my skin. "Come on," I tugged at Gracie's collar. But instead of stepping into the BMW and plopping her backside down on the passenger seat, Gracie froze. She locked her legs, fighting me. She turned her head, stared over her shoulder, and growled.

"Come on," I encouraged her, pushing her toward the opening. She swung her blocky head left and right before sniffing the air. She sidestepped me.

"Come on, dog. I haven't got all night." I urged her forward with a tug on her collar.

But Gracie and I weigh the same. And she wasn't budging. I grabbed her collar and gave her a bit of a shove from behind.

She didn't move. Not at first.

Suddenly, she twisted free of my grip and jerked her collar out of my hands.

"Gracie! Come! Gracie, get back here!" I yelled at her retreating shadow. I tossed my purse into the car and took off running, following an instinct rather than an image, straining to keep track of the sound of my dog panting. I paused, listened closely, and heard the slap-slap-slap of shoes on asphalt.

Who was out there? Why had Gracie decided to chase that person down? Usually, she ignored passers-by. But not tonight.

Had Gracie sensed danger to us? What caused her to take off? Why hadn't she come back?

"Gra-cie!" I yelled into the black hole that was the night. I kept running in the direction she'd taken, but now I was totally immersed in the thick darkness of that spring evening, a night so humid it pressed down on me from all sides.

Gravel churned under my feet. I used my outstretched fingers like cat whiskers, trying to feel my way along. Where was I? Where was Gracie? I stopped and turned, making a complete U-ie, trying to get my bearings. The only direction I could discern was the south, because I could hear the rumble of engines and the singing of tires. By my calculations, Gracie had gone toward that busy road.

The thought chilled me. I had to get her back. Although her harlequin coat had splashes of white along with the black, she could be hard to see in the dark. I'd heard of drivers mistaking Great Danes for deer. She could easily get hit by a surprised driver. "Gracie? Wanna go for a ride?" I repeated over and over.

That was all I had to offer. I made a tight circle in the dark. Then I stopped. I heard crunching. I heard scuffling, followed by the hollow clanging of a trash can. A woman started cursing. The voice sounded familiar, but honestly, under duress don't we all?

"Crud," I shook my head. Could it be that Brenda Detweiler had stalked me? Was she the shadowy figure my dog had attacked? If so, would Gracie be okay? I didn't trust Brenda. Her drug usage and history was splattered with violent episodes. A panic rose in my chest. What if Gracie got hurt trying to protect me?

Or what if my attacker had been Bill? Or someone he hired? My underarms were wet with perspiration. My heart beat so hard I swear you could see my blouse shaking. My voice quavered as I called, "Gracie? Come! Here, girl! Come on!"

SIXTY-FIVE

Oh, RIGHT, LIKE MY feeble commands would make her race to my side.

Ha, ha, ha. The joke was on me.

My teeth started chattering. Was my dog okay? Why hadn't I kept a tighter grip on her? What if she ran out into traffic and got hit?

My only hope was to get in my car, roll down the windows, drive slowly around the block, and call out for her. She loved going for rides. Perhaps it would be enough of an inducement to lure her to me.

I started back toward the parking lot, feeling my way along with my feet. Squinting, I tried to find the edge where the alley intersected the pavement. I was concentrating so hard on my feet that the brush of fur against my leg startled me.

"Gracie! Where were you?"

From her new spot, she growled long, low, and loud. I gripped her collar and tried to haul her back toward the car. The ruff of hair around her neck met my knuckles; the fur stood up on end. She'd raised her hackles. She was seriously ticked.

A crunch from behind our building caused Gracie to surge forward, nearly yanking my arm out of the socket. "What the heck?" I muttered as I rubbed my wrist. "Come on, Gracie. That's enough of this nonsense. Get in the car."

I hoped that whoever was out there heard me. With luck my would-be assailant would slither off into the dark.

From across the lot I heard the slap-slap-slap of shoe soles hitting the pavement. A dark figure raced past me toward the alley. I could make out long arms flailing at the night. I heard the crackle and snap of small twigs breaking. I smelled a pungent perfume of broken greenery as the intruder burst through the hedge that separated the back of our building from the house that abutted our lot.

I tried again to get Gracie into my car. Now my job was harder because I was trembling.

In the distance, a dog howled. A beagle from the sound of it, making that eerie yodel that signals catching a scent.

Gracie twisted to look past me. Light from passing cars glinted off her eyes. She was tracking a moving target. I could feel her body relax, and I assumed her prey was getting away.

"Are we safe?" I asked her. My dog's big tail whopped me as she dug her moist nose into my hand. Translation: "It's okay. Whoever they were, I scared them off. I'm a good pup, huh?"

I slipped my arms around her neck and hugged her.

"You are a very, very good pup. What would I do without you?" I leaned into my car and rested one hand on the fabric convertible roof.

Sticky.

I pulled back and held my hand toward the streetlight. A glob of yellow egg yolk ran down my fingers.

Drat, drat, and double drat.

After I ran the BMW through a car wash, I drove to Ted Drewes. I bought myself a Terra Mizzou, a frozen custard mix-up so thick it was like setting concrete. Gracie lapped up frozen vanilla custard served in their signature yellow and green plaid paper cup.

As I chewed on a pistachio nut, I wondered. Who had been waiting for me in the lot? What would have happened without Gracie acting as my protector? Why had he or she egged my car?

Was this just a prank?

Or a warning, a threat I needed to take more seriously?

When would this be over?

Until then, I vowed to carry my gun close to my body. Especially when I was in and out of the parking lot. After all, why own a weapon if I wasn't going to use it?

SIXTY-SIX

I made a call to Detweiler to say good night as I was on my way back to Sheila's, but he couldn't talk. After I got Gracie situated, I went upstairs. Anya's bedroom light was on. I rapped at her door.

"Go away," she said.

I was not about to take that for an answer. I opened the door a crack. My darling daughter lay on her bed, curled up in a fetal position, playing with Seymour and a gray felt stuffed mouse that looked worse for the experience.

"Honey, what's wrong?"

"Mom? Oh, it's you. You're late."

"That I am. Who did you think it would be knocking at your door?"

"Grandmére. Or that creepy Claudia."

I bit my lip. As her mother, I was expected to encourage her to be nice. But at what expense? When we were growing up, my mother had insisted on having my sisters and me kiss—and kiss up to—people I didn't like. Systematically, I was taught to ignore my gut reaction. While I can understand our need to teach our kids civility, where's the line between civility and victimization? If Anya can't trust her gut, if I try to lie to her and get her to lie to herself, I've stripped her of a powerful protective instinct.

"Claudia creeps me out, too."

"How come you're letting her stick around?"

What could I say? Because we're setting a trap for Bill Ballard and I'm scared your grandmother will mess up our plans?

"I have a reason, and it's a good one. Actually I have two reasons, but I can't discuss them with you right now. Will you trust me to tell you later?"

Those denim blue eyes, so like her father's, blinked slowly as she debated. Finally, she said, "Okay. But I don't like her, Mom. I caught her in the kitchen opening drawers in Gran's china cabinet." Then she turned her back to me again.

"What did she say? I mean, when you walked in?"

"She giggled. She said she was looking for a pair of scissors. Ha. She planned to steal something. I know because she took a piece of Gran's silver out and stared at the mark on the back. I heard her talking to someone on the phone. She said, 'You should see all the loot in this place.' I mean, if that doesn't prove that she's a sneak and a thief, I don't know what would."

I snuggled next to my girl, spooning up to her. I reached over her and stroked Seymour, savoring his rumbling purr.

"Tell Robbie what you saw—and anything you see in the future. He can help keep an eye on her. In fact, I'll mention her behavior to him tomorrow. Claudia can't steal anything if she can't get it out of the house, right?"

Anya half-rolled over to stare at me. "How come Grandmére likes her so much? Claudia's not only a sneak, she's mean and nasty."

"She pays attention to Grandmére, and Grandmére likes that."

"But, duh, doesn't she realize that Claudia wants something? I mean, she's such a big brown-noser."

Out of the mouths of babes. "You see that. I see that. But Grandmére doesn't. I guess she needs more attention than we can give her."

We rested there, quietly. Anya's breathing became regular and slow. When I thought she'd fallen asleep, I started to disentangle myself.

"I still think about it," Anya said in a near whisper. "About all that screaming. How fast we had to run. I hear the shots in my head. We were lucky."

"Shh. Hush now, sweetheart. You're safe." I tightened my hold on her. All night we stayed like that, my arms wrapped around my daughter. I rested on top of the covers, but I didn't sleep much. Not at all. Were we really safe?

Not while Bill Ballard was in town. Not while he was alive.

Again, my thoughts returned to the little Kel-Tec that Detweiler had given me. What could it hurt if I started carrying it?

SIXTY-SEVEN

Saturday, May 8

A STRAND OF DROOL dangled from my mouth, as I slowly came around to consciousness. Anya grunted, rolled over, and stayed asleep as I got up and tippy-toed around her room. I hesitated in her doorway, enjoying a moment of watching my sleeping baby. I would do anything, anything at all to keep her safe.

Mert once told me, "When you feel like a victim, you act like one, too. That's how you decide to sign up for Round Two of abuse."

I decided to break the cycle.

I text-messaged Detweiler first thing and suggested we go to a local gun range. Target practice would go a long way to make me feel better about owning the Kel-Tec. I mean, lipstick I can manage, but a gun? Moving parts? Sheesh.

Using Sheila's computer, I pulled up info about gun safety and how to shoot. Admittedly, reading the directions wasn't the same as real practice, but at least it gave me a better grasp of the fundamentals. I thought back to the Lee Child books and how Jack

Reacher always slowed his breathing before taking a shot. I extended my arm and pretended that Sheila's Swingline Stapler was my gun.

"Take your time and aim," Detweiler said softly in my mind. "Most shooters splatter bullets. Even if someone has you in his sights, he's likely to miss because of adrenaline."

I thought back to the past winter and an Olympic sport called the Biathlon where contestants ran a course, then stopped and fired at a target, and then jumped up and ran again. The commentator remarked on how their accelerated heart rates made regulating their breathing—and controlling their muscles—difficult. Detweiler's suggestion made perfect sense.

He had continued with, "And if someone has a gun pointed at you, and you are aiming back at him, never, ever allow yourself to get distracted. That leaves you as a sitting duck. No matter what happens around you, keep your eye and your gun on your target."

Every inhalation and exhalation moved the "muzzle" of the stapler up and down.

Interesting stuff. Who knew?

While the printer spit out paper, I combed Sheila's shelves for her copies of the CALA yearbook, looking for a candid photo of Peyton. I'd just found one when Robbie stuck his head around the door frame.

"Got a minute?"

He motioned me outside to Sheila's back deck.

Robbie and I could talk in private here. Twice I'd caught Claudia listening in while I chatted on the phone with Detweiler. One time she'd actually been pressed against my bedroom door. When I opened it, she toppled over.

Robbie pulled an official-looking piece of stationery from his back pocket. "I took the liberty of running a background check on your mother's friend."

According to this report, "Claudia Turrow" did not exist. She certainly wasn't registered with any nursing agency or care-giving facility in the Tucson area. She didn't have an Arizona driver's license. Or a phone number registered in her name. Or a permanent address.

"A colleague of mine in the Tucson P.D. promised to poke around, but anything more you can supply about her would be helpful. We're drawing a blank here, and I have a bad feeling about this woman."

"Join the club," I said as we went back inside.

I text-messaged Amanda and asked her to see what she could learn. I decided that the next time Claudia left her purse unattended, I'd look at her driver's license and her checkbook. If she could snoop around, so could I.

There and then I decided to rummage through the trash. After all, Scotty didn't beam her down from the SS Enterprise. If she'd flown here from Arizona, there'd be an airline ticket stub. If she'd taken a cab or a bus, maybe there was a ticket or a receipt.

"Anything else?" I asked Robbie.

His weary eyes held mine, as he said, "Johnny met up with Bill last night. Bill offered him five grand to kidnap you."

My stomach cramped and I doubled over.

"You okay?"

I managed a weak, "Yeah. Just nerves. Haven't had breakfast either."

"You won't be in any danger, Kiki. Not ever. The decoy is ready to take your place. As long as everything happens on this side of the Mississippi, we're fine. Try not to worry. It'll all be over soon. How about if I make you scrambled eggs?"

I thought his offer very sweet and told him so before adding, "I'm meeting Detweiler for breakfast."

Robbie broke into a smile so sunny it brought to mind sunbeams parting clouds after a storm. "I'm glad. You two are good for each other. By the way, Dodie Goldfader filed a complaint about the mess Brenda caused at Faust Park. Your name isn't mentioned. That Mrs. Goldfader is a smart woman. Keeping you out of it."

Sometimes she is, I thought to myself. I debated whether to mention what happened the night before. I had no proof that Brenda had egged my car. Any evidence was washed away when I ran the Beemer through the car wash.

"You're my daughter now. Or you will be once Sheila and I say our vows. I won't let anything happen to you," said Robbie as he gave me a quick hug. "I promise."

I turned away so he couldn't see the tears in my eyes.

Finally, I was getting a dad who cared about me.

SIXTY-EIGHT

I TUCKED THE CALA yearbook under my arm and raced off to meet Detweiler. He got to his feet as I approached the booth in the diner. The look of him—long, lean, and exuberantly masculine—sent a thrill through me. When he pulled me close for a kiss, sparkles of electricity ran up and down my body. He smelled of Safeguard soap and the spray starch he favored for ironing his shirts. I sank into him, loving the muscularity of his chest, the sinews of his arms, and the loud lub-lub-lub of his heart. Wrapping his arms around my shoulders, he held me like I was the most precious thing on earth.

This was home. Wherever my physical address might be, this spot, the sheltering embrace of the man I loved, was the place where I found sanctuary and contentment.

All too quickly, a waitress walked up to take our order. We stepped apart and sank into the cushy seats of the booth. I ordered scrambled eggs well-done, whole wheat toast, and a cup of tea. He had the meat lovers' omelet, a side of bacon, and coffee. As we ate, he talked about the investigation into the sniper attack. So far they'd found nothing to link it with Bill.

"Doesn't make sense. He's talking with our informant. He's bragging up a storm, but he hasn't said a word about the shooting at CALA."

"Maybe you could find out whether he had a beef with the Fitzgerald family."

Detweiler shook his head. "We've pursued that angle. In fact, from every conversation we've had, we've heard that Bill actually liked Peter. They were golfing buddies. If that's the case, why shoot him? As for Mrs. Fitzgerald, why shoot at her in a crowd?"

"To make a statement?" I wondered out loud. "Like the terrorists were doing with the World Trade Center? It wasn't just an attack, it was an attack on two iconic buildings, and on the city that's the most ambitious in the world."

He nodded. "Which leads us to motive. If the goal was to get you, why risk missing you? With all those dancers milling around, you weren't an easy target."

"I still don't understand why a sniper would have delivered a kill shot and then missed so many other shots," I said. "I mean, you wouldn't try something like that unless you were very good and very confident, right? Let's say that Mrs. Fitzgerald was the initial target. How did the shooter then miss Peter? The crowd was still seated. No one had figured out what was happening. The sniper could have just as easily taken Peter out as he or she did Mrs. Fitzgerald."

Detweiler stirred his coffee and studied the clouds of cream. "There's a reason behind all this. Once we find the logic, we'll find the shooter."

I opened the CALA yearbook. "Jennifer Moore suggested that I study the photos of Peyton, the Fitzgerald daughter. You know, she started a rebellion against the May Day ceremony." I told Detweiler what I knew of that.

He studied her picture. We flipped to the index, found more photos, and I moved to his side of the booth so we could examine them together.

"Anything jump out at you?" Detweiler asked me.

I hated myself for what I was thinking. "Well, er, yes. Yes, I do. Peyton could easily be mistaken for a boy."

Detweiler sat back in the booth and whistled a low tone through his front teeth. "You've got that right. You say she didn't want to participate in the May Day ceremony? What would her part have been? I know there's dancing."

I thought a second. "Senior girls wear long white gowns. Bridal gowns."

"I thought women dreamed of their wedding day. My sisters always made a big hairy deal out of their dresses and their attendants. Why wouldn't a girl want to pretend to be a bride? What else is expected of them? A little dancing around. Wearing a long formal dress."

"They are presented to Elliott McMahan. Sort of like a cross between a wedding and a vestal virgin ceremony. He nods to acknowledge them," I said as I studied the candid shots of the girl. She seemed to have lots of friends. According to the information under her formal photo, Peyton was involved in honor society, the science club, choir, and debate.

"So, it's like Mr. McMahan is a stand-in for the groom at a wedding," mused Detweiler.

I jerked my head up as a thought came to me. I glanced back through the photos. In every photo where Peyton appeared, another girl appeared as well … Neenah Sterling. Neenah always stood very, very close to Peyton. I looked up Neenah's activities. She was in honor society, the science club, choir, and debate. Except for photos where she appeared with Peyton, Neenah wasn't pictured in the album.

I phoned Jennifer. It was early, but I knew her habits. She was up with the birds. "Quick question. Does Peyton Fitzgerald have a boyfriend?"

Jennifer cleared her throat. "No."

"Is she gay?"

There was a silence on the other end. Jennifer's son, Stevie, was gay and she was a very protective mother.

"I'm not trying to out her," I said. "I'm only wondering because, well, if I were a young woman who was gay, the idea of trotting around in a wedding gown and curtseying to an older man would be, um, repellent. I mean, I'm not gay and I have to admit the whole presentation thingie is a little bit … creepy."

Jennifer laughed. "Creepy? Sort of like offering yourself up as a sacrifice, right?"

"Yeah, exactly," I said before I told her goodbye. It wasn't until after I hung up that I realized Jennifer never answered my question about Peyton.

SIXTY-NINE

W E   D R O V E   T O   T H E   shooting range in two separate cars. I hadn't told Detweiler about my run-ins with Brenda, but we both understood that being in a car together was risky business. I ached from holding back. Of all the rough spots in our relationship, this push-me, pull-you, seesawing back and forth, where we were intimate one minute and strangers the next, was the toughest to take.

Detweiler helped me load my gun. "Pretend that's Bill," he suggested as he pointed at the target. "Aim for center mass. Remember, a gun doesn't do you any good if you won't use it."

I took a black marker and wrote "BB" over the red bullseye on the paper target. Before I squeezed the trigger, I measured my breathing. In, pause, out, pause. Easing the trigger back, I fired my first shot with my new weapon. The gun pulled up, but I'd expected as much.

"Son of a gun, you hit that perfectly," Detweiler said with a tone of wonder in his voice. "Let's see if you can do it again."

I did. When the magazine was empty, we reeled the target back in and unclipped it.

"That's fine shooting. I have to say I'm impressed and surprised."

"Why?"

"This is your first time with that gun, and you're doing great. You sighted the gun correctly, you slowed your breathing, and you squeezed the trigger. How'd it feel to you?"

I admitted the process seemed more natural than I would have expected. The sound was louder than I would have guessed. The smell—thick and peppery—coated my nose. "Is that cordite?" I wondered.

"Nope. Only very old ammunition uses cordite. You're getting a whiff of nitroglycerin and sawdust."

"But people always talk about the smell of cordite."

He grinned at me. I loved how his top incisor was slightly crooked. "One of those phrases that we adopt and use without thinking. I think you should take this target home to Anya. She'll be impressed. That reminds me. Mom and Dad want to have you both over for dinner. The middle of next month, I'll have been separated from Brenda for six months. That's long enough for them to feel it's official. They know it's over. Although she doesn't seem to be getting the hint that I've moved on."

"What do you mean?" I chewed my bottom lip to keep from blurting out all my grievances.

"She keeps showing up at my apartment. Calls me. Sends me text messages. A few days ago she even texted me twenty-two times in ten minutes."

I double-checked my gun for bullets. When I was sure it was empty, I slipped it into my purse. "So, she's stalking you."

"Basically."

"She threw you out, now she wants you back."

"Sweetheart, Brenda doesn't know what she wants. She's an addict. She's unstable and violent, and she refuses to go to regular meetings to help her stay on the straight and narrow. If she doesn't clean up her act—fast—she'll be out of a job. Not to mention, she's on the verge of being cut loose from the nursing management program she's been taking."

"Wow." I'd been counting on her moving away. If she didn't complete her degree, that wasn't likely to happen. The specter of a life where Brenda could show up anytime, anywhere, did not thrill me one bit.

I didn't tell him about the eggs on my car. It just didn't seem like that big of a deal. I felt discouraged. It wasn't that I expected life to be easy. It never is. But I hadn't realized we could be dealing with Brenda for a very long time. Hadn't Princess Di complained about there being three people in her marriage? Brenda was our own personal tiresome third wheel. If she didn't finish her degree and move to Colorado as planned, there was no reason to think she'd ride off into the sunset.

After we kissed goodbye, he held me at arm's length and studied me. With a gentle touch, he stroked my forehead. "Don't frown, sweetheart. Everything will be all right. We've got each other. That's enough. We'll get through all this mess with Bill and Brenda, and someday when we're old and sitting in rocking chairs outside of a Cracker Barrel, we'll have a good laugh about all this."

I nodded. The lump in my throat caused a pain that kept me from talking.

He drove off first. I took a deep breath and backed out slowly. Before I pulled out of the parking lot, I reached into my purse and touched the Kel-Tec. The cold plastic reassured me.

At a stoplight, I paused and rested my forehead on the steering wheel. Lately, the urge to nap overwhelmed me. I was tired all the time. I badly needed to recharge my psychic and physical batteries.

I missed my friendship with Mert. I missed Clancy's usual good humor and support. I missed Dodie's steady nature and calm reassurance. I missed living in my own house, having my own space, and not worrying if Claudia was listening in. As much as I loved Detweiler, a mild irritation crept under my skin. He wasn't worried about Brenda, but did he have any concept of the havoc she was causing in my life?

A tap on the horn startled me into action. I waved at the car behind me and started through the intersection. As I did, my phone rang.

SEVENTY

"KIKI, IS THIS A bad time?" my sister's voice came across as urgent.

"No, no. It's fine," I said. I was thrilled to hear from her. I pulled off into an empty parking lot and put on my blinkers.

"How's it going with Mom?"

"I'm worried about her. She has to tinkle a lot. I know that's common in older women, but she's also so- —so—"

"Weird?" asked Amanda. "Wasn't she always?"

"Yes, but she's an animal lover and—"

"She got mixed up. She put your daughter's kitten into the microwave thinking it was the cat carrier, I bet."

Put that way, it sounded like a simple mistake. But I didn't think it was that easily explained away.

"Amanda, when did Mom have her last checkup? She's not just confused. It's like her personality has changed. Maybe you haven't noticed it because you live with her, but I'm shocked. She used to be such a stickler about manners. Now I can't stand to watch her eat. And personal hygiene? That's gone completely by the way-side."

Amanda blew out a sigh. "You're right. Look. I'll find her medical records and fax them to you. Email me a fax number, okay? Meanwhile, Claudia showed up on your doorstep? How did that happen?"

I'd been thinking about that. "My cell phone disappeared a couple of times. I guess Mom phoned her. What did you find out from the McMurrays?"

"Nothing. Mrs. McMurray is in a coma. Doesn't seem like the time to pepper them with questions about Claudia. I know her daughter is here working with hospice, caring for her mother."

"That reminds me. I can never thank you enough for keeping a roof over Mom's head. I guess I've been pretty wrapped up in my own life. Now that she's here, well, I have a better appreciation of what that might be like for you. What I'm trying to say is, thanks. Thanks a lot."

She was quiet for a moment. "Yeah, well, I owe you an apology, too. I guess I wanted to believe you had it made. I thought you were Mrs. Got Rocks and you just didn't want to help Mom out. Is it true you live in a garage?"

"It's been converted. But yes, that's what it was. Things are tough, but I'll get by."

"What do you think we should do about Claudia?"

I drummed my fingers on the steering wheel. "I don't know. If she stays here until Mrs. McMurray dies, she won't have a reason to return to Tucson, right?"

"Theoretically. I guess she could try to come back and move in with Mom. Sponge off of her until she finds another elderly person to pillage. Of course, Claudia might want to stay in St. Louis—and keep away from here. I've got a feeling that when Nancy McMurray realizes that Claudia took some of her mother's things, she'll press charges."

I stared out at the cracked asphalt and the spindly weeds poking up through broken bits of pavement. "Claudia is a survivor. She'll find a way to explain away the situation."

"How can she live with herself?" asked Amanda. "She's preying on old folks! And how come Mom can't see that?"

"She's giving Mom what she wants: attention. That's all that matters to Mom. Maybe she did the same for Mrs. McMurray. Maybe when you are old and all alone, you'd gladly trade a few possessions for companionship and attention."

Amanda's tone turned husky. "Then all of us share the blame, right? Claudia's guilty of taking advantage of the situation, but it's our fault that our aging parents are so lonely."

SEVENTY-ONE

GUILT. WHAT A CONCEPT. I should have no trouble finding a new job as an activities director at a guilt-trip cruise line. Now I felt awful about Mom's plight. Had Amanda and I pushed her into Claudia's greedy grasp?

I could think of only one sure-fire way to get Claudia out of our lives. We had to catch her at something illegal.

I pulled into Sheila's driveway and turned off the car, steeling myself for what was ahead. This wouldn't be the first time I'd gone Dumpster-diving. Or the last.

I had a plan. All I needed was a change of clothes. When Anya heard what I was doing, my kid offered her assistance, even calling her friend Nicci to say she'd be a bit late coming over. Nicci volunteered to swing by and pick Anya up, as her older brother, Stevie, could do the driving.

I changed into old pants, a stained tee, and latex gloves. I found one of Linnea's aprons and stuffed a flashlight into the big front pocket. A couple of clear zippered plastic bags were in my pants pocket. Working together, Anya and I spread a plastic drop cloth on the ground to keep the mess to a minimum.

I lowered the large plastic trash bin onto its side. Since Sheila lined all her small trash containers with plastic bags, I quickly sorted the bags by room of origin. Anya helped me paw through the contents of Mom's trash.

The assemblage of oddities told us a story. We found three receipts from Walgreens for snacks, colas, and a couple of bottles of cheap wine. Claudia was signing Mom's name to these credit card slips. There was also a receipt for pizza, and this, too, had an unfamiliar script.

"That's not right," grumbled Anya. "That's forgery."

I agreed. "But I bet Mom would say it was okay with her. What we have so far is not enough to bring any pressure to bear on Claudia."

SEVENTY-TWO

WE WERE PAWING THROUGH the contents of a second bag when Nicci and her brother, Stevie, hopped out of Stevie's Volvo, a boxy blue late-model vehicle that I knew Jennifer had chosen for its safety features. Anya explained to the Moore kids what we were doing. They volunteered to dig through the garbage, too. I recognized another trash bag from the upstairs bathroom. We opened it, but all we found were used tissues and more receipts for food.

Stevie rocked back on his heels and stared at the slips of paper. He was blonde and thin like his mother, and nearly as particular about his clothes. I was impressed that he was willing to help us with such a gross task. Although he'd been very fastidious about wearing latex gloves and handling the paper gingerly, he'd still dripped a bit of coffee on one of his perfectly pressed Dockers. I also noticed a smudge on the crisp placket of his pink Oxford cloth shirt.

"Is this woman smart? I mean, really smart?"

"Sort of. Why?" Anya looked toward him thoughtfully.

"Does she know you suspect her?" he raised an eyebrow.

Anya shrugged at me. I pondered this. "Maybe. I've caught her listening in on my conversations. When she saw me pulling out the latex gloves, she followed me to the back door. She asked what we were doing in the trash. I told her I lost a receipt I need for a refund."

"And she didn't seem alarmed? Worried?" Stevie asked.

"Nope."

"If I wanted to hide receipts or other stuff, I would be careful about putting anything into the garbage, wouldn't you?" asked Stevie.

Nicci rolled her palms over in a gesture of defeat. "I'm not sure we'll find anything here."

I started to set the garbage bin back on its feet.

"But she hasn't been out of the house. At least I remember Anya saying she doesn't have a car. So if she's bought anything or gotten anything or written anything down, where has she stashed those papers?" Stevie held open a big black trash bag.

"I'm planning to look in her purse," I admitted. I hated telling my daughter and her friends that I was going to perform an act I didn't approve of. "It's wrong, but I need to protect my mother. There's something going on here, and I intend to get to the bottom of it."

Stevie grinned. "Looks like you already did. Sort of."

We all laughed as he pointed to the trash can.

"She keeps her bag with her. I mean, she's very careful about it," said Anya. "See, Mom, I had the same idea. I've been watching, waiting for a chance to get a look at her driver's license, but she's really keeping an eye on that purse."

"What did you hope to find?" Nicci picked up receipts by their corners and dropped them into the small bag they belonged in.

"Something signed with her real name."

"That would be on paper, right?" Nicci asked.

"Recycling!" we all shouted at once. I ran into the garage and grabbed the blue plastic bin with the white logo on the front. Once again we tipped the contents out onto the plastic tarp.

Since Sheila didn't separate her recycling, we sorted through a motley mess of cans, paper scraps, plastics, and newspapers. Most of it was intact, but Stevie found several pieces of paper that had been shredded by hand. Those we slipped into my plastic bag.

"She might have figured by shredding her stuff, you wouldn't put the pieces together. I mean, that's what I would have done," said Stevie.

I thanked him, his sister, and my daughter. The kids were going back to the Moores' house to watch marathon sessions of *Community*, their current favorite television show. I didn't worry about Anya while she was at the Moores' home. Jennifer knew all about Bill, and the Moores' personal wealth caused her to be naturally cautious.

"Stevie, do you share any classes with Peyton? How's she doing?" I handed him a moist towelette so he could wipe his hands.

"Actually, she's doing pretty well. See, her grandmother didn't approve of—of her friendships. She threatened to cut Peyton out of her will if she didn't go to prom with a suitable guy," said Stevie with a heavy emphasis on the word "guy."

"That must have been tough. Trying to be her own person and feeling that disapproval." I held open a trash bag so he could toss in the dirty wipe.

"It's tough on anyone who's the least bit different," he said. His eyes echoed his sadness, but a small smile played around his mouth.

It's not easy to be young, I thought as I waved goodbye to the departing Volvo.

SEVENTY-THREE

HOW MUCH DID PEYTON resent her grandmother? Had the pressure that Edwina Fitzgerald put on her granddaughter finally caused the child to crack?

I phoned Detweiler and told him my theory. "Deanna came from a family that's familiar with firearms. What if she passed that interest on to Peyton?"

He was quiet for a second. I could tell he was gathering his thoughts. "Okay, but I'm confused. If Peyton Fitzgerald didn't participate in the May Day ceremony, why did her parents and grandmother go? I mean, parents attended to see their daughters dance. But she wasn't dancing. I don't get it."

"I do. You see, even if Peyton didn't perform, the Fitzgeralds went because this is a tradition. Most importantly, Mrs. Fitzgerald—Edwina—really loved the ceremony. And her word was law in that family. Remember? I told you she threatened to cut off funding if CALA discontinued it."

I could tell he was thinking this over.

"So if Peyton wasn't performing, she could have been the shooter."

"It's a possibility," I said. "Look, I have to return the family photos to the Fitzgeralds. I'll see what I can find out—"

"No!" said Detweiler. "Leave it alone, Kiki. I mean it. We can't afford to have you compromise our investigation, much less the situation with Bill."

Taking that cue, I changed the subject, telling him about the shredded papers I had. I promised to text message him any information I found about Claudia.

The morning went by quickly at the store. The nice spring weather encouraged folks to drop in and buy colorful, floral paper for projects. A steady stream of customers kept me hopping.

Taping together the torn receipts we'd found in the trash would have to wait until Clancy came in at 3 p.m. to help. She'd worked the early shift with Margit and Dodie over at Faust Park. As usual, Clancy wore a classic style that complemented her trim figure. Her taupe linen pants were topped with a tangerine-orange silk blouse and a matching jacket. A tortoiseshell barrette held her hair to one side. She could have doubled for a young Jackie Kennedy Onassis.

"How are things out at Faust?"

"Okay, I guess. We've sold a lot of page kits. Dodie asked me to have you make more up, please." From her pocket she pulled a list of styles and themes.

"Gee, I better get cracking. But first, how's your mother?"

Clancy avoided my gaze. "Don't ask."

"I am asking. Hey, Clancy, it's me. What's up?" I motioned her over to the paper racks where I could start pulling what I needed to make more page kits.

Her lower lip trembled, but she stiffened her spine and said, "She's insisting that I move into her house."

"What are you planning to do?"

SEVENTY-FOUR

She raised her shoulders and let them drop. This admission of defeat changed her posture, causing her to slump over and hang her head. "They gave me the name of a geriatric psychiatrist. Dr. Bernard Terra. I've got a call in to him."

"But you don't think it will do any good?"

"No, I don't. My mother isn't interested in talking to him. She keeps demanding to go home. Then she turns on me and tells me what a selfish child I am. How she gave up everything to put me through school, and how I'm too self-centered to help my dear old broken-down mother. She's even said that I want her dead. That I am selfish and cruel and I'm breaking her heart."

"Ouch." I paused while collecting embellishments. Clancy isn't much of a toucher, usually, but I patted her shoulder anyway. I figure that even if she doesn't shower me with affection, I'll offer her mine. As long as it doesn't make her uncomfortable, I plan to keep on being me.

The store was empty, so I didn't worry about anyone seeing her in distress or overhearing our conversation. Otherwise I might not have pursued the subject.

Clancy sniffed and dabbed at her eyes. "They brought in a social worker to talk with Mom. She had been by the house to see the setup. The social worker told Mom it would need to be overhauled to be safe. We'd need to remove all the area rugs and add handrails. That's in addition to putting a bathroom downstairs. Mom, of course, is refusing to consider those changes. I suggested she could move in with me, as my house would be easier to modify. I have a bath on the first level. The hallways are wider. There's already a safety rail in the shower."

"What does she say?"

"She refuses to consider it. She says that I'm after her house."

"Wow. It doesn't get much worse than that."

"Why would I want her house? I've never taken anything from Mom. Ever. I have my own house, and I'm willing to share it so she can remain independent. But she refuses to listen. Nothing I say is right. My mom's on the warpath." Clancy paused to wipe tears from her face with a trembling hand. "She's lying there in a hospital bed looking fragile and tiny, but she's never been so powerful. I've never seen her so angry. I understand she's scared and dependent, but I've always been there for her."

"Right, but now she can't do for herself. I bet she's choosing to feel angry instead of feeling helpless."

Clancy nodded. "That's what Dr. Terra said. Rage is common in the elderly, especially when their world gets smaller and their options less appealing. They get angry with the people they know won't desert them. So the caregiver gets the brunt of the emotion."

"So what exactly are her options?"

"She could move into an assisted living facility, she could move back to her old house, or in with me. Frankly, I don't want her with me, but I'll do that rather than have her in a care facility. All this is dependent on her taking physical therapy to regain her mobility."

"Is fixing up her house a realistic option?"

"No. There are six concrete stairs out front, the bathroom is on the second floor, the wood flooring is slick, the lighting is dim. Honestly, it's the worst possible choice for someone who is elderly." Clancy gave a bitter laugh. "You can't imagine all the money I've spent to fix Mom's air-conditioning, to re-roof that old monstrosity, and to cover her checks when she's bounced them. Plus, the amount I pay to have her car serviced regularly and to put on new tires, even though the Buick sits in her garage because she's too blind to drive it. Yet Mom keeps saying that I want her money. That I'm trying to take the house and sell it so I can pocket the dough."

"You didn't get receipts for all that work? Don't you keep a ledger?"

"She's my mother. Do you run a spreadsheet on your family? No, I didn't think so. None of us do. But maybe we should."

Time to change the subject. I knew Clancy was good at puzzles and word games. I showed her the torn slips of paper. "See if you can make heads or tails of this."

When she finished, she called me over.

"Boy, you are good," I said with a low whistle. "Really good."

SEVENTY-FIVE

Sunday, May 9

SUNDAYS WERE ALWAYS A special day for Anya and me. Because Robbie had done such a great job with breakfasts all week, I made German pancakes for everyone. Claudia polished hers off and had both seconds and thirds. I also poured coffee for her and for mom.

"That hot chocolate you made for us last night was really good. Is it a secret recipe?" asked Claudia.

"I put mocha flavoring in it," I explained. Mocha flavoring in the form of Ex-Lax maximum strength. By my calculations, any minute and we'd have blast off. I know I should have felt guilty, but I didn't. Not one bit. Ever since she'd arrived, old Claudia had stuck to my mother like a pilot fish latches onto a shark. She had no respect for the concept of family time or privacy or boundaries. Several times I'd asked Claudia to excuse us so Mom and I could talk, but Claudia just laughed and said, "Why? Luci and I don't keep secrets from each other."

The Ex-Lax trick was harsh, I'll admit, but finally I'd had enough. That's when I decided to teach old Claudia a thing or two. I hoped Sheila had a good supply of toilet paper.

"Mom, how about coming with Anya and me to Laumeier Park? It's a cool outdoor sculpture park that I think you'd really enjoy. You always love art." No sooner than I'd gotten the words out of my mouth when Claudia interrupted.

"Of course, Lucia and I would like to go. We've been cooped up in this house for days. Honestly, I am so bored."

"I figured we'd leave in an hour or so. I have laundry to do first." I needed to give my "hot chocolate secret recipe" a little more time to work.

As I washed and ironed clothes, I heard the toilet flushing repeatedly in Mom's room.

After ten minutes went by—and the flushing didn't stop, Mom toddled down the stairs. "I'm ready, but Claudia won't be joining us. She has an upset tummy. Do you have any Imodium?"

I shook my head. "Sorry, no, I don't. Maybe we could pick up tablets while we're out."

"I hate to leave her here when she's not feeling well."

"We won't be gone long. I have to work this afternoon. We're having a Mother's Day card crop at the store."

Anya stared out the window. She was a bit too old for outings like this, but she was taking a photography class and needed outdoor shots. I reminded her of all the cool stuff at Laumeier, including the huge eye, the walking roots, the Leelinau, and the poets. On any given Sunday in the spring, Laumeier's winding walkways would be filled with visitors. I'd even come here on frigid winter days and found I was one of many who admired the austere beauty, the dramatic juxtaposition of bare branches against sculptured steel, concrete, sod, and other materials I couldn't identify. Today proved no exception; we were joined by many who wandered happily among the sculptures.

Mom found the grounds enchanting. "I love the fact you can walk around all these pieces."

Anya ran on ahead while my mother and I walked. We hadn't gone far when Mom complained that she needed to tinkle.

"Mom, you seem to be having to go a lot," I said. "Maybe we need to have you checked out by a doctor."

She admitted that might be a good idea. "Claudia says I'm fine, but it is getting annoying." I promised to make her an appointment or at least start making calls on Monday. We found a restroom, she tried to relieve herself, and we started back along the pathway.

Pulling papers from my pocket, I asked, "Do you know anyone by the name of Beverly Glenn?"

SEVENTY-SIX

"No. Why?"

I didn't tell her that one of the receipts we'd pieced together had this name as a signature. The handwriting matched Claudia's.

"Hmm. How did you meet Claudia? She seems to care a lot about you." I nearly choked on the words, but I managed to spit them out.

"I thought you knew. She worked for Rena McMurray. Rena is in my bridge club. She about drove Claudia nuts," said my mother with a chuckle. "Rena is nothing but an old hillbilly with shoes on. She doesn't know much. Hasn't been anywhere exciting. But I've always been kind to Rena, so I continued to stop by even after Rena got sick again."

"Got sick again" was my mother's euphemism for getting cancer. My mother had been a smoker most of her life, and she refused to believe that cigarettes could cause tumors. She would still be a smoker if she hadn't had pneumonia ten years ago. The combination of fluid in her lungs and wheezing made smoking impossible, so Mom quit.

"Gosh, Claudia must have a background in nursing. I mean, she cared for Rena, didn't she?"

"Claudia doesn't have a medical background. She doesn't need one. She was there to help Rena because Rena couldn't do for herself. But that's not why Claudia hurried here to be with me. I called her from your phone, you know. You see, she puts my needs first," said Mom with a sly grin. I caught the zinger but ignored it. "She's not here because I need her. She's here because she loves me."

"Loves you," I repeated. I couldn't believe we were having this conversation. My mother had gone bats-in-the-belfry, totally whack-o, cuckoo for coconuts. I wished I'd brought along a tape-recorder because no one would ever believe this bizarre turn of events. "Claudia loves you." I said it again to make it more real.

"Yes, she thinks I'm fascinating. I'm the first celebrity she's ever met. Why she could listen for hours to my stories about being on stage!"

I cleared my throat and spoke carefully, "Um, so if you couldn't pay Claudia, she would still want to spend time with you."

"Of course. However, she and I have discussed my finances. I've come to realize you're not capable of helping me. So, I'm perfectly happy to sign my part of the house I share with Amanda over to Claudia. That way dear Claudia will always have a place to live."

SEVENTY-SEVEN

I MANAGED TO CATCH Amanda on the first ring. When I told her what Mom and Claudia planned, she whispered, "You HAVE to be kidding? Where would that leave me? I've kept a roof over Mom's head for ten years! The promise was that when she died, I'd recoup my expenses by inheriting her share of the house!"

To my amazement, Amanda burst into tears. "That's all the thanks I get? For making sure Mom has a place to live? Kiki, I've paid all the utilities and taxes on this house for years. And now our mother is more worried about where Claudia Turrow, or whoever she is, will live than she is about the quality of my life? It's … it's … unbelievable." For the next five minutes, Amanda fumed and sputtered. I didn't know my baby sister could curse like that.

"Amanda, she's a sick old woman. It's not about you. It's about Mom and this person kissing up to her."

"I know," said Amanda. "But she's not so sick that I can use my power of attorney. Mom's in her right mind. Even if what she's doing is wrong. I'll go over and talk with Rena McMurray's daughter

271

today. I hate barging in on them at a time like this, but we can't wait."

"What if they ask Claudia for her social security number? Maybe they could say they have to send her a tax form? That might help us track down her real identity."

"She's been paid in cash, Kiki. I know it because Rena told me so, and Claudia did, too."

"There's always the I.R.S. Maybe we turn Claudia in to them. I thought of another angle. Claudia seems to be very religious. Maybe if you find out what church she attends, they might have a directory."

"Tried that. She's listed as Claudia Turrow. That's it, that's all."

A few minutes later, I walked through the back door of the store. We weren't officially open for another half hour. I took the CALA yearbooks out of my satchel and flipped to the pages where Peyton Fitzgerald was pictured.

Peyton wore her hair in a boyish crop, tucked behind her ears with multiple piercings. She hid in baggy shirts that hung off her slender frame. Every photo showed the girl in cargo pants. On her wrist was a Swatch watch.

I tried to put myself in her shoes. She obviously felt uncomfortable with girly togs and the affectations associated with femininity.

I decided to call Jennifer. She answered cheerfully and told me she was actually en route to the store.

"I give. What were you trying to tell me about Peyton?"

"As you can see, Peyton isn't the typical CALA student. She absolutely refused to attend the May Day ceremony. Said it was barbaric, which it is, in a way."

"Right, so I heard."

"Edwina threatened to cut her off. Told her she'd have to pay her own way through college. Said she wouldn't inherit so much as the dust bunnies rolling under the beds."

"There seems to be a lot of that going around. Fortunately I don't have any money, so I guess Anya won't ever have to worry about me threatening her like that."

"I think you're both lucky. I hope that Sheila never tries what Edwina did. What a huge riff! Deanna and Peter found themselves stuck in the middle. They tried to get Peyton to change her mind, but she wouldn't. After one particularly nasty battle, Edwina marched into the alumni office and said she would cut off funding to CALA if they didn't force all the girls to participate."

"But they couldn't do that, could they? Remember, Bonnie Gossage said there was an attorney who took the case and supported the students' civil liberties."

"That's right. Guess who it was who found that lawyer?"

"Peyton?"

"You've got it."

"That's quite a story, and then Edwina gets shot at the very ceremony she insisted the school have. How's that for irony?"

Jennifer laughed. "Edwina and her granddaughter were evenly matched, huh? Two tough cookies. The apple didn't fall far from the tree, and all those other clichés. That reminds me. I'm hungry."

I groaned. "Me, too."

"I can run by Bread Co. and pick you up a sandwich."

"I'll pay you back."

"My treat," said Jennifer.

"One more question. Since Peyton didn't participate in the May Day ceremony is it remotely possible she could have been the shooter?"

"Whoa," said Jennifer. "No way. You're barking up the wrong tree, Kiki. The kid's a vegan. She doesn't believe in killing anything, not even to eat. Besides, she has the perfect alibi."

"What?"

"She was at my house with Stevie and a group of CALA students. They're hoping to start a Gay/Straight Alliance Group at the school. They asked me if I would start a PFLAG chapter for parents and friends of lesbians and gays. You know how I feel about families forcing kids into molds that just don't fit."

I did, indeed. She'd lost a brother because her father forced him to be someone he wasn't.

"Hey, I'm almost at Bread Co. Let's talk more when I get to the store. Since I'm spilling the beans, I might as well tell you about Peter's job. Or lack thereof."

SEVENTY-EIGHT

As EAGER AS I was to see Jennifer, I admit I had another reason for wanting to chat with her before the crop this evening. I suffered from nerves. My anxiety was at an all-time high.

As the clock wound down, and my fake kidnapping grew closer, I became increasingly edgy. Worse yet, I couldn't talk to anyone about it. Mert and I weren't on speaking terms. Johnny and I were keeping our distance. Detweiler was busy with case work and dodging Brenda.

The more I thought about it, the more comfortable I felt with the idea of carrying my Kel-Tec. In the backroom, we had an old gun holster, the kind that slid on your belt. Dodie's husband, Horace, had brought it in for me to use with my glue gun. Sounds corny, I know, but the tip of the glue gun gets really, really hot. Slipping it into the holster kept me from burning myself several times over.

I found the holster and threaded my belt through it. Lately I've been wearing loose blouses because I've gained weight, and this proved to be advantageous because the extra fabric totally concealed my holster.

Robbie said I would never be in any real danger. Even so, someone had been sneaking around in our parking lot. Who had it been? Why hadn't the police kept a better watch on me then, huh?

How I missed calling Mert! She would have consoled me or set me straight. The loss of her friendship made a huge hole in my heart.

A litany of "what ifs" crowded my mind. What if Bill hurt Johnny? What if Bill got wind that Johnny was a spy? What if a scrapbooker or another worker was here at the store and that person got hurt? What if my decoy didn't look enough like me?

I locked myself in the bathroom and took my gun out of my purse. I turned it over and over in my hands. I never thought of myself as a person who owned a gun. I never joined the NRA. I never shot anything in my life. Heck, I once released a field mouse who had gotten his tail caught in a mousetrap at our house in Ladue.

What was I doing with a gun?

What sort of man gives his girlfriend a gun?

Would I ever use it? I mean, if push came to shove, could I fire this thing?

SEVENTY-NINE

I splashed cold water on my face, put the gun in my holster, and gave my reflection a stern lecture: "Stop it. Grow up. You're perfectly able to defend yourself. Carry the stupid gun. When this is over, you can stash it away. But for now, do like a Girl Scout and be prepared!"

Thus fortified, I started sorting die cuts for tomorrow night's crop. We planned to make Mother's Day cards, so I'd cut flowers of all shapes, sizes, and colors.

Edwina Fitzgerald wouldn't be getting a bouquet this year. I remembered the blood blooming on her chest and shivered. Had I really been the target? I doubted it.

The door minder interrupted my depressive musings. Jennifer breezed in, bringing the fresh scent of a floral perfume, the rich aroma of a turkey sandwich, and an air of happiness that filled the store with light.

She started exactly where we'd left off. "Succession is a common problem with family-held businesses. Often the entrepreneur won't turn over control, but the kids expect to maintain their positions or to be promoted to run the company. When there's a board involved, those people can be expected to rubber stamp succession."

I swallowed my iced tea impatiently. "What does this have to do with Poor Peter Fitzgerald?"

"He's been singularly ineffective and he certainly doesn't have the skills necessary to run the family business."

"So, he'll inherit money and keep his old job, right?"

"No, he'll inherit stock, he'll become the majority stockholder, and he's probably convinced he's in line for a promotion. If he takes the helm, I think the company will go under. It's a tough economic environment, and an inexperienced CEO is a recipe for failure."

"But he never wanted to be a businessman. From what I've heard, he always wanted to be an artist! Why doesn't someone go talk with him? Offer to buy him out?"

Jennifer smiled, "That's good thinking. I mean, it's pretty obvious, but I guess I've been listening to board members gripe for so long that the straightforward approach eluded me."

"Hey, if he's not good at business or bookkeeping or whatever it takes, he won't want the job. If you are honest with him, you can point out that he's been neglecting his real talents all these years. If he doesn't fight you, if you can put an experienced CEO at the helm, Peter will have plenty of money without all that stress."

Jennifer flipped open her phone. "Peter? How you doing? Back from church? How's the leg? Hey, could I stop by? I thought maybe we could talk about, well, stuff. Would it be possible for us to speak in private? Great. I don't want to hurt Deanna's feelings, but I need to know I can talk candidly with you. Right. I'll be over in five minutes."

Jennifer picked up her purse. "You don't owe me anything for this lunch. If I play my cards right, I might owe you lunches for the rest of your life."

KIKI'S FLORAL FANTASY

Flowers are hot, hot, hot in the craft world. They add so much color and texture to your paper projects. Fortunately, they are also simple to make. They look great placed solo on a card or bunched together in bouquets. It's easiest to make a lot of them at one sitting and keep them in reserve for other projects.

Here are a few of my favorite ways to create flowers:

Simple Punch Flowers

1. Punch multiple flowers the *same size* out of different shades of paper. Stack. Pin together with a brad. Curl the petals.
2. Punch multiple flowers of *varying sizes and shapes*. Stack. Pin together with a brad. Curl the petals. (Tip: Use a sharpened pencil and curl the petals around the lead tip.)

Circle Flowers

1. Punch circles of paper in descending sizes. (Tip: This looks particularly nice with patterned paper and even newsprint!)
2. Stack the circles in descending sizes.

3. Adhere in the middle with a brad.
4. Ruffle the edges by running the open blade of scissors along the outside of the circles.

Sweet Peas

1. Punch two sizes of hearts out of contrasting paper.
2. Fold the hearts in half vertically.
3. Roll the right lobe of the heart in toward the center. Repeat with the left. (Tip: Wrap the lobes around the point of a pencil.)
4. Glue a small heart inside a larger one and add to a stem of wrapped floral wire.

EIGHTY

Monday, May 10

"I'M NOT GOING TO school until I find Seymour." Anya planted herself in the foyer and crossed her arms over her chest. With a sniveling sigh, she added, "I know something's wrong, Mom. He loves his breakfast. He nudges me if I don't get up and make it for him."

"Okay, sweetie, let's think of the house like a grid. That's what they do in the mystery novels. We'll start in this corner."

"But I already looked there!" her voice cracked. A tear leaked down her cheek.

"The grid is 3-dimensional. We'll look up and under stuff. Maybe he's blocked in," I said, as I removed several cushions from Sheila's sofa.

"He could cry, couldn't he? I mean, he's got a loud mew."

"Right." I didn't want to share what I was thinking. After my mother put Seymour into the microwave, I'd had unhappy visions of finding him in a toilet or in the trash can.

Face it, Kiki. She's nuts. You need to get her to a doctor. At least you'll know what you are dealing with. If you take her in for the bladder issues, maybe the doc can also check her reasoning.

I moved through the living room like a whirling dervish. I tossed pillows, I pulled out furniture. I called, "Here kitty-kitty-kitty," until my throat was hoarse. Finally, I dropped to my knees and looked under the sofa.

There he was, lying on his side, barely moving. I slipped both hands under his tiny body and pulled Seymour out. I quickly realized how cold he was to my touch. He blinked at me. I pulled back his lips. His gums were white, which I knew to be a very, very bad sign.

"Anya? I've got him."

She bounded down the stairs. "Seymour, where—"

A strangled cry escaped Anya. "Mom, is he—? Is he dead?"

"No. But we need to hurry."

Fortunately, Gracie was already waiting in the car. I moved the seat so Anya could climb in the back. She held Seymour carefully, gently. I noticed a trickle of blood streaking her blouse, but I didn't say anything. I couldn't tell where the blood was coming from, and there didn't seem to be any point in mentioning it to my sobbing child.

I flew out of the driveway, revving the car as fast as it would go in reverse.

"Buckle your seat belt," I yelled to Anya.

I knew exactly where the animal emergency clinic was, a mile and a half up the road. I also knew the back way there, because that was an alternate route to CALA. I paused at stop signs. I ran the tail end of a yellow light. I managed to dial 411 and get the operator to connect me with the clinic.

"Emergency. Our five-month-old kitten was found lethargic. He is cool to the touch. There's bleeding. Gums are white. We're on our way."

"Bleeding?" Anya wailed.

"Shh. Don't upset Seymour. It will only make it worse for him. You have to be strong, Anya."

At the clinic, I double-parked, tossed my seat back, grabbed Seymour, and flat out ran. A woman in scrubs met me as I raced in. She took Seymour out of my hands.

After I got Anya and Gracie settled, I gave the receptionist my information, what we knew about Seymour, and my credit card. Wordlessly, the receptionist handed me a sheet with costs on it. When I saw how much they were charging, my legs turned to instant pudding.

But I wasn't about to let that kitten die. I'd find a way to pay the charges, no matter what it took.

I called CALA and told them Anya would be late. I left a message on the phone at Time in a Bottle, explaining I would be late. My daughter and I read old magazines for more than an hour. When we weren't reading, we were pacing. We must have walked a mile and a half, going from one end of the clinic waiting room to the other and back.

Finally the stainless steel doors swung open. A man in white scrubs pulled a white filter mask from his face.

"That was close," he said, craning his neck and making that awful popping sound. "Your little guy is going to make it but we'll have to keep him overnight at least. Who's the numbskull who left Advil out where the cat could get them?"

"I'll kill her," hissed Anya. "I've seen her drop pills on the floor twice. Gran and I both asked her to be more careful."

I put a staying hand on her shoulder. "We'll talk about it tonight. Let's get you to school."

The doctor shook his head. "Some people shouldn't be pet owners."

EIGHTY-ONE

I FELT THE BLOOD drain from my face. "Excuse me? How dare you! My daughter is a terrific pet owner. Unfortunately for all of us, my aging mother is living with us temporarily. And she's the numb-skull who dropped the pills on the floor. It's certainly not my daughter's fault! If you had any compassion, any decency, you wouldn't, you couldn't, you—"

A nurse came scooting out from behind the desk. "Dr. Lazarus, um, why don't you go grab a cup of coffee?"

After she pushed him behind the swinging doors, she turned to us. "I am so, so sorry. He's a phenomenal doctor. Really he is. But he's awful with people. Just horrid. I can't apologize enough."

Anya's mouth trembled. "I hate my Grandmére. Hate her. She's mean and nasty and now she almost killed my cat!"

The nurse shook her head. "Believe it or not, Dr. Lazarus saved your kitty's life. He's an absolute genius with animals. He says things like that because he gets so emotionally involved with his patients. That doesn't make it any easier, I know."

"What makes him so sure the kitten ate an Advil?" I asked.

"A portion of the bright blue gel cap was stuck to the inside of his teeth."

I gritted my teeth. I knew my mother had an enormous bottle of the liquid painkiller capsules. And yes, they were all bright blue.

I put my arm around Anya and pointed her to the door. I stopped halfway there. I turned and spoke to the nurse. "You tell him that if he ever, EVER, ever speaks to my child again, he'll be talking an octave above soprano. I will personally reshape his future and his profile with my own two bare hands. There's no excuse for his rudeness. None. As for our cat? He better be just fine or I'll hunt Dr. Lazarus down. I'll make him pay. He'll have nowhere to run and nowhere to hide from me. You tell him that."

"Ye-ye-yes, ma'am. I'll be sure to tell him." The nurse nodded vigorously.

After hustling Anya into the car, I turned over the engine. My daughter stared at me with big blue eyes. Anya said, "Mom? You okay?"

"I am perfectly fine." I backed out of the lot carefully. "Sort of." Then I bumped us down the curb and onto the road, scraping the bottom of my bumper as I went.

"Um, how about if we stop and get you a latte from Kaldi's? Or whatever. I mean, I know caffeine ramps people up, but, uh, I'm thinking you need something. A Diet Dr Pepper? What would help? Are you feeling okay? Do you need an aspirin?"

"Anything but an Advil," I said.

EIGHTY-TWO

"You are two hours late! This is unacceptable!" Margit shook a finger in my face.

"Family emergency," I said. Before I dropped Anya off at school, I'd given her an extra long hug. Despite Robbie Holmes' protests that I was totally safe, that the sting operation would go without a hitch, I felt terribly vulnerable.

"Kiki, honestly. Why didn't you call?" Dodie turned a mournful head toward me. "We've been running around like crazy. That Mother's Day class started a run on flower-making materials. You can't imagine how tough it's been to cover the floor and do paperwork!"

I had called. I'd left a message on the machine in the back because I called early. I could only assume that neither woman had arrived at her appointed time either.

"I could not wait on them all. You were supposed to be here!" Margit's voice climbed a notch. "That is your job, to wait on customers. If you cannot do your job, you can be replaced."

Her strident manner was totally at odds with the cheerful yellow polyester pants suit she wore. Underneath her jacket was a white knit shirt covered with jaunty black-eyed Susans.

I waited for Dodie to tell Margit that replacing me would be impossible. I was the only person on the staff who created projects, packaged them, and pioneered new techniques. I was also the only person who taught on a regular basis. Besides all that, I'd stood by Dodie when she had cancer. I'd always been fair and honest. For the most part, I was dependable.

I expected Dodie to ask me what had happened. She knew I wouldn't blow off my shift.

When she didn't say anything, I repeated myself. "I. Had. A. Family. Emergency."

"It's always something, isn't it? Your life is a circus without a ringmaster," snapped Dodie. "My daughter needs a job. Maybe you don't."

The words slapped my face. I thought about all the times I'd covered for her, about how many hours of extra time I'd put in while she was getting treatment. She seemed to forget all that. Or maybe it never registered on her.

I thought about the evening ahead, and how dangerous it sounded.

I thought about my mother and all the extra stress she added to my life.

I remembered Sheila saying that Linnea made more money than I did.

To my credit, I said nothing more. I walked past both women, put Gracie in her crate, and pulled up a chair at the sorting table in the back. After I made a few calculations, I knocked on the door of Dodie's office.

"This isn't working, is it?" I stood in front of her desk. "I obviously don't have any rights—or say—as a minority owner. I didn't realize that when I bought stock in the store. Now that I understand I am powerless, I want to sell out. Please give me back my money. I would like to go back to being an hourly employee. I did the math. I would make more money if I had a second part-time job than I did with the bonus you gave me last year. When I came to work here, it was on the condition that family came first. This morning, you didn't even ask what my emergency was, and you actually made fun of my life.

"That's intolerable. I will work the crop tonight, and I understand you need notice to replace me, but I'm giving you two weeks starting now."

I delivered this whole speech while looking at a spot on the wall right above Dodie's head. I didn't wait to hear a response. I walked out. I grabbed a cold Diet Dr Pepper from the refrigerator and started pulling together materials for the special technique I planned for the evening's crop. Trying not to cry, I threw myself into my work.

I heard Dodie close the door. I heard her talking on the phone. I was still hunched over the work table when Horace came flying through the back door. He entered Dodie's office and slammed the door behind him.

I hated the idea that they were mad at me. This had been a great job for me. I had learned so much, and I'd made so many friends.

Once upon a time, I would have put up with being ridiculed and scolded.

Not anymore.

KIKI'S TAPE TRANSFER TECHNIQUE

This is a cool way to transfer an image so you can use it on a scrapbook layout or on a card. It's so simple kids will enjoy trying it.

You'll need: packing tape, a color image, a bowl of water.

1. Find an image you like in a magazine or advertising insert or on a package.
2. Cover the image with packing tape. If the image is wider than the tape, overlap two pieces or more to cover the image. (Tip: Tear the tape pieces off in advance and have them ready. Try not to get any wrinkles in the tape as you stick it down.)
3. Burnish the tape. Rub it flat repeatedly with the back of a spoon or a bone folder to get all the air bubbles out.
4. Soak the tape and the image in warm water. After about five minutes of soaking, you can rub off the paper with your thumb or a dish scrubber. The image will stay adhered to the tape. The only part you are detaching is the excess paper pulp.
5. Lay the tape flat on a piece of paper towel and let it dry.
6. Trim and use as desired.

EIGHTY-THREE

THIS I BELIEVE: THERE really is a fickle finger of fate. It spins around and lands on us, bringing trouble, trouble, trouble. When that finger points your way, absolutely everything will go wrong.

The fickle finger pointed my way.

Dodie and Horace left together. Slipping out the back door. The fact that they said nothing to me confirmed my worst fears: They were actually glad I had thrown in the towel.

Margit came out from her new "office" area. Dodie had gotten Margit a desk, a bulletin board, and a comfy chair so she could sit in the back and call in orders.

Wasn't that special? Whereas I didn't even have a locker for my purse or a shelf in the refrigerator. No, there was no special area that I could call my own. None.

"Time for me to go. I am taking two orders I must mail. To-day's postmark guarantees us free shipping." The ring of her cell phone interrupted. "*Ja?* She is? All right. I am coming."

"My mother expects me," said Margit in a stiff, formal voice.

I thought about walking out, then and there, but I still cared about the store and our customers. However, the unfairness of the situation rankled. I couldn't be late because of an emergency, but Margit could waltz in and out as she pleased!

Clancy called two minutes after Margit drove away. "I can't make it in. Mom got up last night to use the bathroom and fell again. She's in surgery now."

Amanda called. "Rena McMurray died this morning. Obviously I can't ask her daughter for the scoop on Claudia. I guess we'll have to wait to find out who Beverly Glenn is and what the McMurrays know about her."

The vet's office called. "Your cat is on the mend, but we'll need to keep him two more days, instead of one. We need to make sure he's hydrated." The woman named a cost for this extra day of care that would max out my credit cards.

Sheila called. "Your mother and her sidekick ran up $125 in pay-for-view movies. I got the bill today!"

Lane called. "When will you be done with the memorial albums? I thought you'd be done by now. I really need to get the Fitzgeralds their copy. Can you have them done today? Tomorrow at the latest?"

Right when I thought life could not possibly get any worse, Mert dropped in.

"Here," she said as she pushed a key ring at me. She wore her usual work uniform of black slacks and a white blouse. "I don't feel right about keeping your house key."

"So that's it? After all these years of friendship?" I couldn't swallow, the lump in my throat was that tight.

"You hurt my brother. Hurt him something fierce. And it don't seem like you. I ain't never seen you act like that. Not to no one, no how. Since what happened in the park, he's been going out and drinking to all hours. I know that ain't your responsibility, but you had a hand in it. I need time to think. To sort this through."

She turned and walked away without a backward glance.

EIGHTY-FOUR

THERE WAS NO WAY that I could finish both the Fitzgerald albums and get the store ready for the evening crop. I was feeling totally overwhelmed and it wasn't even ten o'clock yet.

To my vast relief, the fickle finger must have been moving on to ruin someone else's life. I called Laurel. She picked up quickly and promised she could come in less than a half an hour. Of course, she arrived looking like a page out of a Victoria's Secret catalog with her shiny black boots, tight-fitting pants, wide black belt, and ruffled cream-colored, low-cut blouse. She wore a light fragrance that formed an aura around her person like a fresh spring zephyr.

"What can I do to help?" she asked. I set her to work cutting paper for the crop. That gave me the time I needed to finish the Fitzgerald album. As I worked, I tried to compartmentalize, to avoid thinking about my rendezvous later this evening.

Stop it. Robbie Holmes has this all planned out. You'll never be in danger.

But would Johnny be? And if he got hurt, what would Mert do? I couldn't stand to think about it. Luckily, we had a run of customers. For the next two hours, I located flower punches, coffee filters (they make great flowers when dyed), templates, and fake stamens. Being busy helped keep my mind off the fact I was leaving the store.

"We're completely out of the punch that spits out flowers in three parts," said Laurel. "I took a customer's money and told her the order would arrive on Tuesday."

That was worth double-checking. If a customer made a special trip, only to find we didn't stock the desired item, she might justifiably get miffed. I told Laurel what I planned to do and went into the backroom to track down the order sheet.

I'll give Margit this, she was well-organized. I found the order form in no time, partially because it was sitting out on the top of her desk. With the other order form. Both of them needing to be postmarked with today's date.

Drat. If they didn't go in today, we'd miss out on the free shipping.

I couldn't send it in. That would step on Margit's toes.

But I also couldn't walk away. I still cared about Time in a Bottle. Sure, I was leaving, but I wanted to leave with my head held high. With any luck, Dodie and Margit would realize they'd lost a valuable partner.

How could I both ensure the order was processed and be respectful of Margit's role?

I could run the form by Oak Haven. I could drop it off at the front desk or even sit there and wait for Margit, if need be. Laurel had the store under control. The croppers wouldn't arrive until

5:30. I decided that it was the right thing to do, an action that would prove me to be a bigger person than Dodie and Margit.

Ten minutes later, I entered the spacious lobby of Oak Haven. It had, as do all such places, the strong smell of pine-scented cleanser with a pungent undertone of urine. But the brightly appointed foyer and cheerfully attentive receptionist also told me the place was tiptop. I paused at the front desk and explained my mission.

"Mrs. Eichen and her mother Gretel are here in the garden," said the receptionist. "Sign in, take this visitor's pass, then follow the signs."

EIGHTY-FIVE

I SET OFF THROUGH the huge power-assisted door that led outside. Once there, I could smell the perfume of petunias. Tall purple spikes of salvia, roses in tight buds, and pink flowers I couldn't name added to the visual profusion of color. White wrought iron tables and chairs sat in clusters along the brick walk. Several families moseyed around, enjoying the lovely sunshine and mild weather.

Margit's back was to me. She sat across from an older, more wrinkled version of herself. Between the two women was another chair. On it sat a large, gold and black stuffed tiger. The toy leaned to one side and threatened to fall to the ground so I grabbed it as I approached the twosome.

"Kiki!" Margit's voice was breathless with surprise. "There must be a problem at the store!"

"Sort of." I handed over the documents. "You needed to get these orders in by five, and you walked off without them—"

Before I could finish, Margit's mother half rose out of her seat and grabbed the stuffed animal out of my hands. In a thick German accent, Gretel Westheimer said, "It is *verboten* to touch Adolphus! He's mine! He does not like strangers."

"Um. Sorry." I looked around. "Gee, this is a great place for you two to spend time together."

"Tell her to go away! Adolphus does not like her!" With that Gretel made a shooing motion toward me. "I want *Mutti*!"

My co-worker turned her face to me, her eyes begging for understanding. "Kiki … I … she …"

"*Mein Mutter und mein Vater*! Where are they?" Gretel's voice grew louder and louder.

At first, I was confused. Never once had Margit mentioned her mother's mental health. That was the key, wasn't it? Your body wasn't much good to you if your mind wasn't functioning right—and Gretel definitely wasn't "all there."

But Margit had pretended, visiting her mother regularly, acting as if nothing was wrong. Was that just for her mother's benefit or for her own?

Hard to tell, and not really any of my business.

"I'm sure your mother and father will be coming along soon, *Fraulein*. In the meantime, isn't it nice that Margit is here?" I put on my ultra-cheery voice, and my most sincere face.

Gretel carefully placed Adolph back on his chair, as she grumbled a bit. "She can not have my *kuchen*."

"I won't eat a bite of it. I promise." Margit sighed. "I baked it for you. Just for you. It was my own mother's recipe. My own darling *Mutti* used to make it for me."

EIGHTY-SIX

MISSION ACCOMPLISHED.

Sort of.

Margit walked with me to my car. "I keep this routine because it is good for her. That's what they tell me. It is marked on a calendar with a big red letter 'M,' and the nurse crosses off the other days and reminds *Mutti* that I am coming."

"Is she ever, you know, more lucid?"

"More and more she forgets who I am. But I know who she is and I know what she did for me. She worked two jobs so I could go to school. She helped me raise my children. She taught me to cook and to knit."

Margit wiped her eyes. "This is the time of our lives when children become parents and parents become children. This is how we honor them, by forgiving and giving and putting the past behind us. I ask myself, how could I live with myself if I ignored her now? What would I feel when I bury her? That ache is one I could not bear. So I visit three times a week."

"Why did you pretend? You could have told us. We would have understood."

Margit adjusted her cats-eye glasses. "I do not pretend for your sake, but for mine. Each of us must find a way to live through these things. Dodie pretends she is not sick. She tries to be strong, maybe too strong. You pretend that you are not afraid, but when you think we don't notice, your face shows your terror. You are also pretending not to be pregnant. *Ja?* Why is that?"

"I don't know that I'm pregnant."

She stared at me.

"Okay, all right." I dug at a piece of loose gravel with my toe. "I haven't decided how to handle it. I mean, of course, I'll have the baby. It was an accident. Equipment failure, I guess is what you'd call it. But I know Detweiler. He will insist we get married."

I squinted up at a tree, the young green leaves fluttered like a dancing mist against the blue, blue sky. A faded daffodil drooped at the foot of the trunk, its pale blossom brushing against hopeful grass blades. "I don't want to repeat my mistakes. I don't want to wonder if he's marrying me because of the baby. I want him to marry me for me. And if I wait, the baby will be a Lowenstein, in name at least. That will comfort Anya."

"We all do the best we can. Sometimes it isn't enough. Most of the time, thank God, it is."

EIGHTY-SEVEN

I GAVE MARGIT A hug that she returned heartily and then I climbed into my car.

Before I started driving, I called Laurel and she told me, "All the technique kits are done, the tables are ready for the crops, and I ordered pizza for the crowd tonight. I also took Gracie for a walk. She's such a sweetie. I left Rita Romano in charge of the store for the five minutes while we were gone."

"Laurel, you are a wonder."

"Happy to do it for you, Kiki. Look, I know I shouldn't bring this up over the phone, but is there a problem between you and Mert?"

I sighed. "Yeah. I hope to get it straightened out tomorrow. She's my best friend. I know she's upset and disappointed in me, but there's nothing I can do until then. I miss her terribly."

"It'll be okay," Laurel said. "She knows you care about her. I'm sure you two will work everything out. Take your time coming back to the store. I'm sure you could use the break."

As I hung up, I wondered how Laurel knew that Mert and I were on the outs. We hired Laurel at Mert's recommendation, so their relationship must pre-date Mert's and mine. But that was odd because I'd known Mert for nearly ten years. She'd never spoken of Laurel until that day when I mentioned we were looking for part-time help.

Oh, well.

I dialed Clancy. "Mom's still in surgery. Kiki, can you do me a favor? She had an appointment with Dr. Terra this afternoon at three. Could you call them and cancel it for me? I don't have his number with me."

I had a better idea. I drove by Sheila's and ran inside. I could hear the shower running upstairs.

"Mom?"

She sat in front of the television, half-asleep. Her skirt sagged a little, but she was dressed in a nice outfit and her hair was neatly brushed. My day was definitely getting better. "I'm tired," she whined.

"Mom, I managed to get a doctor's appointment for you with the best doctor in town. It's a last-minute opening, so we have to hurry."

"What about Claudia?"

"We'll write her a note. Since she loves you so much, I'm sure she'll be thrilled that you'll be seen by a specialist. Besides, we don't want to hurry her through her shower, do we?"

"What should I wear? Claudia always helps me choose."

I pushed hangers around in the guest closet. "How about this? Or that?"

Mom shook her head. "I can't decide. I need Claudia."

"I have a better idea. How about if we take two or three outfits? You can decide on one after we have lunch." I picked up a canvas bag and slipped the clothes inside.

Mom looked at me dubiously. "I am hungry."

"Great! So am I. We can bring food home for Claudia. Won't she be pleased? It will be so nice for her. I bet she loves surprises."

"She does."

Good, because we've got a doozy planned for her. I smiled to myself as I thought about the text-message I'd received from Robbie Holmes right as I swung into Sheila's drive.

"Beverly Glenn" had a warrant outstanding for her arrest. She'd skipped bail in Mesa, where she'd been arrested for theft. Robbie was processing the paperwork. Using a dirty water glass from the house, he'd managed to match "Claudia's" fingerprints with those on file for "Beverly Glenn." With any luck, "Claudia Turrow" would soon be out of our lives forever.

EIGHTY-EIGHT

"Your mother is absolutely amazing!" Dr. Terra's gap-tooth grin reminded me of a jack-o-lantern. With his carrot-top mop of hair, he looked a bit freaky-deaky, but there was a sincerity about him that immediately put a person at ease. "I've never met anyone like her. In fact, I hope you'll give me permission to use her as a case study. I'll obscure her identity, of course."

Crud. She pulled the wool over his eyes, I thought to myself. I bit back a sigh. So I'd been wrong about her. She was normal and I was the one with a problem.

"She maxed out the test. That's … that's just astonishing."

"What test?"

"Actually there are several, but that doesn't matter. What matters is the diagnosis, and I didn't even need the testing to see that your mother is a craving narcissistic personality to the nth degree. Hey, how much therapy have you had?"

"Not enough."

"My hat's off to you. Growing up with a narcissistic mother, well, it must have been horrible. No empathy. No concern for your feelings or emotions. Always living in her shadow. People telling you how terrific she is, but she's so different at home. The backhanded compliments that were really slaps. I bet she pitted you against your siblings, right?"

My mouth was so dry all I could do was nod.

"Was she always like this? Narcissism tends to get worse with age, so I'm thinking it wasn't always this bad." He grinned at me.

"It's always been this bad. Always." I stopped and reflected. "Maybe it's worse."

"Boy, that must have been rough. And with the infection, she's been even more moody and confused, right?"

"What infection?"

He seemed surprised. "I thought you knew. She has a raging urinary tract infection, a UTI. Any sort of UTI in an elderly person can affect their cognitive abilities."

"You're kidding. You found that out already?"

He gave a self-deprecating shrug. "She came in with a mild temp. I examined her, and she squealed when I pressed on her belly. We took a urine sample. It was foul smelling and cloudy with a little blood in it, so we sent it out for a test, but I'm positive she should be on antibiotics."

"Oh." She must have been hurting and I didn't know.

"We should have the results in an hour or so. I'll write you a script now because that'll give you time to get it over to a pharmacy. You'll want to get her on the antibiotics right away."

All of this came at me so fast that I had trouble processing what he was saying. But after he handed over the prescription, I found my voice. "You are telling me that my mother is mentally ill? And she always has been?"

"Yes, ma'am. Growing up in a house with her must have been an absolute nightmare. Let me guess: You were dead last, you never got any credit for anything you did, your mother one-upped you at every turn, and anything that you needed or wanted was labeled selfish."

My head was reeling. He'd recapped my entire childhood in less than fifteen seconds. "So, it really was hard, wasn't it? I wasn't just imagining it or being a whiner."

"Let's put it this way, I wouldn't wish your childhood on my worst enemy. Do you have siblings? Your mother never mentioned any of her children, and she talked non-stop for more than an hour."

"Yes, two sisters."

"Are they functioning? I mean, do they have successful lives?"

I thought about that. Amanda never married. She shied away from relationships, avoided getting close. Catherine? She ran away years ago. I hadn't heard from her in years.

I told Dr. Terra this.

He nodded. "Not surprising. The child of a narcissist never learns to stand up for himself. Or herself. Never learns to ask for what they need so they have problems getting their needs met. Your mother taught you that you were not important. Unfortunately, you might even perpetuate the cycle by teaching your own child—if you have one—that she's too important. It's a difficult foundation on which to build a successful, fulfilling life."

"What can we do about it? Now?"

He gave a bitter chuckle. "Not one thing. She's too old to change. She doesn't want to change. She has no reason to change, and even if she did, we have very little success with problems like this. The best advice I can give you is take care of yourself. More and more you'll be called upon to be her caregiver. Think about what they tell you on the plane before you take off."

"Buckle your seat belt?"

"Put your own oxygen mask on first."

EIGHTY-NINE

ON OUR WAY TO the pharmacy, we ran through the driveup at Wendy's. Thinking ruefully about "Claudia," I bought an extra salad and put it in the cooler I keep in my trunk. If I'd had the courage to let it sit in the heat, maybe our problem with Beverly Glenn would get solved … fast.

Dr. Terra's nurse phoned to confirm that my mother did, indeed, have a UTI. The prescriptions would be ready for pick up when we arrived at Walgreens. One was for pain and the other was an antibiotic.

"Poor thing. Don't be surprised if your mother sleeps a lot after she takes her medicine. I bet she's been up and down all night with the urge to go. Not to mention the discomfort," said the nurse. "And her fever."

I felt like the world's biggest jerk. Here I'd been so angry with her, so put out—as had we all—and Mom had been feeling punk the entire time. Punk and tired.

But had I thought to get her a thorough checkup?

No, I hadn't. I made a mental note to remind Amanda once again to send me all Mom's medical papers. The nurse suggested, "Go buy a plastic folder for each member of your family. Keep all their medical papers inside. List prescriptions, procedures, doctors' names, and insurance policy information. It's much easier than trying to reconstruct stuff when there's a problem."

Here I called myself a scrapbooker, and I had never thought of that. What a simple and smart way to have all that information at the ready. Gosh, if Anya was taken to the hospital, I'd have to scrounge around for all her paperwork, like what she was allergic to, when her last doctor visit was, and so on.

I vowed to make amends and to rectify the situation.

I picked up Mom's medicine and a bottle of water for her to wash down the pills. Racing up and down the aisles, I also bought her a couple of magazines, a pint of Häagen-Dazs Chocolate Chip Cookie Dough ice cream, and a bag of those chocolate-covered pretzels she loved so much. On my way up to the checkout counter, I grabbed two paperbacks for her as well. All in all, I collected quite a haul.

Good thing I'd be getting back my investment in the store. At this rate, I would need it to cover my bills.

"I'm sleepy," Mom said, clutching the plastic bags with the Walgreens name on them. I helped her crank back the passenger seat so she could snooze. As I leaned over, the gun poked me in the ribs. Even so, the pang of pain comforted me. Reaching down, I patted the six-round magazine I'd slipped into my back pocket.

Still there. Six little bullets ready to do battle.

We were only six blocks away from Deanna and Peter Fitzgeralds' house when Mom started snoring. Because we were so close, I decided to return their old albums, the ones I had borrowed to make the enlarged portraits of Edwina and to complete the memorial album CALA had commissioned. Returning this stuff would be one more item to cross off my "to do" list. After losing the May Day album, I was a bit paranoid—holding onto the Fitzgeralds' original materials made me nervous.

Now was the perfect time to drop these off. I had everything I needed to complete their album and hand it in to Lane Carlée this afternoon. Then I could tell Margit to submit the bill for my services and the materials.

There was a broad patch of shade at the far end of the Fitzgeralds' long circular driveway. I pulled in and parked my car under a generous maple tree. Since Mom snored loudly and looked so comfortable, I decided not to wake her. Instead, I rolled down all the windows on the BMW. I ran up to the imposing double front doors and pressed the doorbell.

Derrick, his face set in a weather-beaten scowl, answered the door. "Yes?"

You'd have thought we'd never been introduced. He stared at me like I was a door-to-door salesperson trying to peddle my wares.

"Look, Sissy wants to be left alone," he said as he moved to block the doorway. "You and all your pals at that fancy school should respect that."

"I understand, but I needed to return these albums. Remember? You loaned them to me. I wanted to thank Deanna."

"She can't come to the door right now. She needs her rest. Folks have been pestering her." Noticing the package in my hands, he reached out and took the albums from me, but fumbling and dropping them on the porch.

"Oh, no," I said as I bent down to retrieve them. Wincing from the way the Kel-Tec jabbed me in the side, I picked up the stack. On top was the photo of Derrick and Deanna with the dead buck.

I passed them to Derrick, and his eyes caught mine. The hairs stood up on the back of my neck and my heart pounded so hard I thought that surely he'd notice.

I knew.

I understood everything. The pieces fell into place. I managed to say, "Thanks so much. I'm sorry for your loss. I bet your sister is really torn up about losing her mother-in-law. Anybody would be."

"Right." Derrick glowered at me.

"Have a nice day," I said in the cheeriest voice I could muster. Using all my willpower, I turned toward my car, and walked to it slowly, trying not to break into a run.

I hadn't seen Derrick at the May Day ceremony. If he'd attended, he would have been sitting next to Deanna and Peter, because that's what families did. But Derrick hadn't been there—although he had been here in town. He said he'd arrived a few days before the ceremony.

I remembered Deanna screaming for help. If her brother had been standing beside her, she wouldn't have called out to strangers, would she?

NINETY

So her brother hadn't been with them.

I phoned Lane Carlée.

"Hi, Lane," I chirped. "I thought maybe we could go to lunch tomorrow, and I'll bring both the Fitzgerald albums. My treat."

"You don't have to do that. Let me treat you. Or more to the point, let CALA buy us both lunch. Tomorrow will be fine."

Exactly what I hoped she would say. "All right, if you insist. I hope Deanna likes what I've done. I returned her old albums to her."

"She didn't say anything to you? I feel awful that I missed the funeral." Lane sounded concerned.

"She wasn't available so I gave the materials to her brother, Derrick. Have you met him?"

"Yes, he's a very nice-looking man, isn't he?"

"He sure is. I wonder why he didn't come to the May Day ceremony. I would think Deanna would want to show him off."

"I sure would!" Lane laughed. "Unfortunately he had other plans. Deanna told me he was meeting with an old friend who was going through a rough patch. Under the circumstances, it's probably for the best. That's one less person in the family who was traumatized by the tragedy."

I bid her goodbye after she promised to email the particulars for our lunch date. I pushed the "end call" button, then phoned Detweiler.

"Hey, sweetheart," he said, "How are you? Ready to have this hassle with Bill behind us?"

"Um, yes, but that's not why I called. Do you have a minute to talk?"

"Only a minute. Guess what? Good news! Brenda is coming over to sign the divorce papers."

At last we were catching a break. I felt my shoulders relax although I hadn't realized how much tension I held there. "That's… that's wonderful. What a relief."

For a second, I thought about telling him that I was pregnant. Or at least that I thought I was. But I decided against it. I hadn't taken a pregnancy test. Considering what we planned for this evening, maybe it was best to keep my personal news to myself. I didn't want Detweiler to call off our plan. Not when Johnny had put himself in such a precarious position for me.

So instead of saying, "I'm pregnant," I said, "I want to share a theory with you. I think Derrick Roper killed Edwina Fitzgerald."

"Okay, I give. Who is Derrick Roper?"

"Deanna Fitzgerald's brother. See, Peter Fitzgerald was totally ineffective in his job, but he hung in there because he was making so much money."

"And you know this how?"

"I have my sources," I said.

He chuckled. "I'm well aware that you do. So why would Mrs. Fitzgerald's brother shoot her husband in the leg? Was he cheating on her? And why take out the older Mrs. Fitzgerald? Or was she collateral damage?"

"Edwina Fitzgerald ruined her son's life in order to keep him as part of the family business. But lately, the board of directors has been getting nervous. The board knew that the business couldn't survive with Peter at the helm. At least it couldn't survive now, given the economic climate. But if they got rid of him, Peter could never get another job at this level. He and Deanna wouldn't be able to keep up their standard of living. I bet if you check, there was a board meeting coming up, a meeting when they would be discussing the issue of succession."

Detweiler made a "hmm" sound, a noise that showed he was following. He asked, "So Mrs. Deanna Fitzgerald's brother climbs a tree, shoots Mrs. Edwina Fitzgerald, kills her, and shoots Peter Fitzgerald in the leg... why?"

"It drew suspicion away from the family. See? Derrick Roper is an excellent marksman. He grew up hunting and shooting to feed the family. That's why he hit Edwina first with a killing shot. He didn't miss and hit Peter by accident. That shot to the upper thigh was done on purpose. Get this for irony—the killing occurred during the celebration Edwina adored. In fact, I'd venture to say she loved it more than she loved her family."

"I see," said Detweiler in a thoughtful voice. "Let me check into this, Kiki. But I think you're onto something. Got to go."

Really, as crimes went, it was very nearly perfect.

NINETY-ONE

MY MOTHER SNORED LOUDLY as I pulled into Sheila's driveway. I decided I'd carry in the food for "Claudia" and Mom's extra clothes before waking her up. That would give her a little more time to sleep. I'd given her the first pill immediately after I left the drugstore. She wouldn't need another for six hours.

I felt an unexpected surge of love for my mother. Curled up, she looked childlike and vulnerable. She hadn't wanted me, had gotten pregnant with me before her marriage. My presence was a constant reminder of her shame. Once in a fit of anger, she told me how humiliated she'd been by the whole ordeal.

Something similar had happened to me. But I had wanted Anya. I'd fallen in love with my child even before they settled her in my arms. Everything about her thrilled me, from the tiny curled toes, to the translucent fingernails, to the pulsating top of her head, to the pucker of her sweet pink lips. Anya was perfection.

Whereas, I had been a painful scarlet letter on my mother's forehead.

Still, my mother had done her best. She wasn't a bad person. She was confused, and she was unhappy, but that said much more about her than it could ever say about me.

I vowed to redouble my efforts to be a good daughter. I knew I couldn't please her, but I also knew I didn't want to look back and regret my behavior. I wanted to be able to live with myself after she was gone.

That reminded me of what was ahead.

Robbie Holmes told me that I would be safe during their planned escapade. Detweiler seemed to think so, too. But it was my life, and I would be stupid to cede all responsibility to them. Odd as it seemed, feeling the Kel-Tec at my waist gave me a sense of confidence. I couldn't imagine using a gun on anyone. Waving it around would have to suffice.

However, I could wield a mean pair of scissors. That was more my style. I pulled a small pair of orange-handled Fiskar scissors out of my purse. At five inches long and two inches wide, I could palm them and no one would ever know. They weren't long enough to be lethal, but they were sharp and strong enough to be dangerous. I stuck them in my back pocket.

Mom snorted in her sleep. A vein pulsed on her hand as the blood moved through her thin skin. I noticed how scarce her hair had gotten and how her shoulders protruded through the fabric of her blouse.

Her fragility moved me. All I'd ever wanted was her love, and now she was slipping away from me, moving on without me. If she didn't notice me soon, see the hunger for love in my eyes, it would be too late.

But Dr. Terra's warning came back to me. "For whatever reason, she's limited in her ability to care about others. Especially if you don't make her the center of your universe. Love her for herself. Realize she's limited in what she can give. Try to be content with it."

Mom didn't have the capacity to put other people first. It wasn't part of her nature. Because she hadn't shown that concern for me, I grew up unsure how to care for myself. But that was then and this was now. Since George's death, I'd been forced to become self-reliant.

I knew better than to count on other people. I would look after myself.

NINETY-TWO

ALTHOUGH SHE WAS DROWSY, Mom woke up enough to stumble into Sheila's house and curl up on the sofa in the great room. I preferred not to have any interaction with "Claudia," so I didn't call up the stairs to say that we were home. That left me with the task of retrieving Mom's belongings by myself, but I didn't mind. Sheila would be back from her nail appointment any second, and she would keep an eye on my mother.

I popped open the trunk, stuck my head inside, and fished out the bag of clothes. I lifted the lid off the cooler and retrieved "Claudia's" lunch. My plan was to take these items inside and then try to move Mom upstairs to her bedroom.

But I didn't get that far.

A car pulled into the driveway. I figured it was Sheila, but I was wrong.

"Put your hands in the air," said a woman's voice from behind me. "Or I'll shoot you where you stand."

"Okay, Brenda," I said as I lifted my hands slowly.

"Keep your hands up and get in the driver's side of my car," she said. "We're going for a little ride."

I shook my head. "Shoot me here where I stand, but I'm not getting into a car with you." I knew the statistics. Victims who are abducted are less likely to survive. I doubted Brenda's ability to murder me in cold blood, but I wasn't about to ride around in a car with her.

"I figured you'd be stubborn. Take a look at this," she shoved her iPhone into my face.

I gasped at the image.

Sheila sat on a metal folding chair. Silver duct tape sealed her mouth. Yards of the stuff strapped her hands and feet to the seat. Most people would have read the look in her eyes as defiant, but I knew her well enough to tell that she was both terrified and ticked.

My stomach knotted and my knees went weak. I couldn't imagine any harm coming to her, especially if I were the cause.

"Either you come along like a good girl, or Sheila gets it."

"Gets what? What are you trying to do, Brenda? Have you lost all your marbles? Sheila hasn't done anything to you." I really didn't need this drama. Not now. Sheila would be hopping mad about this, and Brenda was goofing around with the wrong woman. When Robbie Holmes got wind of what happened to his fiancée, he'd throw Brenda's skinny white bottom into jail faster than she could say, "My bad!"

By way of response, Brenda shoved a gun into my ribs.

"Oomph." I groaned. I looked down to see it was a Kel-Tec.

Seriously, Detweiler had to start giving better presents. Shoes? Maybe. Flowers? Definitely. Guns? No way.

"Come on, Brenda. Where is she? You've got me now. Let's drive there and you can let her go. This is between the two of us." I sounded reasonable, but inside I was going nuts. Where was Sheila? How could I find her? Should I pull my gun on Brenda? Would I have time to retrieve the clip and load it? Would that put a scare into Brenda or goad her into shooting me on the spot? Could I force her to tell me where Sheila was?

"You can't count, blondie," snarled Brenda. "There are more than two of us. Tell her hi, Bill."

On the phone screen, Bill Ballard stepped behind Sheila. "Hey, Kiki," he waved to me with a big grin. "Watch this." He dropped his hands onto Sheila's throat and squeezed. I could see her face turning red from the pressure and her eyes bulging with the effort of breathing.

"Stop it! I'm coming. You don't want her! You want me!" I raced to the driver's seat of Brenda's white Camry. The decision had been made for me. Pulling my gun on Brenda might cost Sheila her life.

Brenda opened the passenger side door and threw herself in. Holding the gun to my ribs, she said, "Give me your cell phone."

I reached into my purse, fished around, and found it.

Brenda threw it out her window. "Take 40 and go across the river."

I groaned inwardly. That would take us into Illinois. Robbie Holmes would have no jurisdiction. Brenda's father would have friends there. Detweiler could come after us, but he'd have no backup available. Johnny was nowhere to be found.

I was sunk.

NINETY-THREE

I'D BEEN CAR-NAPPED BEFORE by Bill, but back then he forced me to drive to Babler Woods where the hilly road gave me a chance to escape. There was no way I could free myself on Highway 40, which is really Highway 64, but not according to the locals. With its multitude of lanes, the zooming pace of traffic, and its newly revamped entrance and exit ramps that fed more cars onto the pavement faster, the best I could hope for was a gigantic multi-car crash to divert us.

I was desperate, but I'm no fool. I had no right to endanger the lives of innocent people as I fought for my own.

There would have to be some other way.

But how? What? When? Where? I went over my options and came up dry.

Brenda yakked on and on, happily, telling me that she and Chad Detweiler belonged together. "Sure, I threw him out," she said, "but he knew I didn't mean it. He loves me. Always has. Always will. He was just fooling with you."

She was so high, she was out of her mind. I didn't bother to argue with her. As my Nana once said, "Never try to teach a pig to sing. You'll annoy the pig and lose your voice." Fussing with Brenda wouldn't help my situation.

"Um, how did you wind up working with Bill?" I asked when I couldn't take much more of the "Chad loves me and only me" baloney.

"He contacted me. He'd heard about you and Chad. He knows you are trying to ruin our marriage. He's decided you need to pay for how you messed up his life, too. You really are a slut, Kiki. Everyone agrees. Even Chad's sisters. They have no use for you. None."

Ouch. That hurt. I hadn't met Detweiler's sisters, and now I doubted that I ever would. His parents had been very nice, but maybe that had been a pretense of civility.

"You have the morals of an alley cat, Kiki," said Brenda. "You're really disgusting. Bill thinks so, too."

Wasn't that just ducky? The man who cheated my husband, snuck around on his pregnant wife, and killed his lover had problems with my morals? The woman who had a drug addiction, threw her husband out, and then abused me was calling me names?

All I could do was take it. I thanked my lucky stars that Mom was safe in Sheila's house. I sent up prayers of gratitude that Anya had elected to stay after school and work on a science project. As for Sheila? Once Bill had me, he could let her go. She'd be honked off, and Robbie Holmes would make Bill pay, but she'd be okay.

Or would she?

With a jolt, I realized: Bill couldn't let her go. He had too much at stake.

"Brenda, you don't want to be involved in this. When Bill kidnapped Sheila, he crossed a line. You do realize she's engaged to marry Police Chief Robbie Holmes, don't you? He will hunt you both down. But if you make sure she's freed, he'll put in a good word for you."

Brenda laughed as she twisted a piece of oily hair around her finger. "I didn't kidnap Sheila. Johnny Chambers did that."

I struggled not to show my surprise. Fortunately, she kept talking.

"There's no way anyone can prove I was involved. You got into this car by yourself. No one can put me with Sheila. All I have to do is drop you off."

"Um, where is Johnny right now?"

"He's with Bill. Johnny's got a real hate-on going for you. Even his sister is angry at you. He says she wants to wring your neck."

I fought tears, struggling against the burning lump in my throat. Whatever happened next, I hoped that Mert would learn I hadn't meant to hurt Johnny. That my actions had been part of a plan, and that he'd agreed to it. I couldn't stand the idea of Mert thinking I'd betrayed her. She'd been my best friend for years. If something happened to me, I wanted Mert to continue to be a part of Anya's life. How could that happen under the current circumstances?

I sniffled.

Brenda saw the effort I was making not to cry. "Yeah, that's right. You've done it now. I got in trouble with my supervisor for what happened in the hospital. Did you know that? You love creating problems for people, don't you? Well, you're finally getting your comeuppance. Guess what Bill plans to do with you?"

"I have no idea," I said, and I didn't.

A peace settled over me. This was the end. I was tired, so tired. I hadn't been sleeping well. Dodie's quick acceptance of my resignation hurt. I'd had morning sickness and the inevitable exhaustion that followed. I dreaded telling Detweiler that I might be pregnant. I felt bad for my daughter. If I was gone, she wouldn't have to put up with my mother. As long as Sheila went free, Anya would be taken care of. Sheila could parent Anya. I'd named her my daughter's legal guardian months ago. Sheila had the funds to take good care of Anya, and with her upcoming marriage to Robbie Holmes, Anya would have a surrogate father. However, if both of us died, my sister Amanda could claim custody—and Amanda didn't have any experience raising a child. Anya would have to move to Arizona, and that would surely break her heart.

I had to rescue Sheila. No matter what the cost to me.

Once my mind was made up, a peaceful feeling descended upon me.

I couldn't keep fighting on all fronts. Whatever Bill planned to do with me, I hoped the end would come quickly. And I hoped my body would be found so that Anya could go on with her life.

"Bill plans to drown you. That dead husband of yours told him how scared you are of water. He wants to make you suffer. Because we've all suffered. Thanks to you. Yup, payback is a pain. You're going to get yours."

NINETY-FOUR

WHY HADN'T JOHNNY TOLD me about the change in plans? Why had he gone along with Sheila's kidnapping? Why hadn't he called Robbie Holmes to warn him? Or let Sheila know so she could be prepared?

There could be only one reason: He'd switched sides.

Perhaps Bill offered Johnny enough money to make him change his loyalties. Or maybe Johnny really was angry with me. I thought that our spat was for show, but quite possibly I hit a nerve. Bill had the resources to help Johnny disappear—and Johnny often joked about moving to Cuba where he could drink rum and smoke cigars. I knew that everything Johnny made went to pay off his legal bills. Maybe that had gotten old.

I could fight one man, maybe. I could kick Bill hard or wrestle myself free and run away. But I couldn't escape from two men. And what was Brenda's part in this? Was she just the courier and I was the package? She had no beef with Sheila.

I needed to free Sheila. But how? With all that stupid duct tape, she couldn't make a run for it. If Johnny was on my side, he might help me get her free. But if he had switched sides, that would be two men against me and a hog-tied Sheila. Providing that Brenda dropped me off and left.

How could I tell where Johnny stood?

I gritted my teeth. My palms slipped on the steering wheel because they were wet with sweat. I had to believe in Johnny. Or else all was lost.

Sooner or later Detweiler would figure out I was missing. Even if we crossed the river, he'd come for me. If Robbie called Sheila and didn't get an answer, he'd know something was wrong. Surely he had friends on this side of the river. All I needed to do was stall.

"You listening to me?" Brenda poked me with the gun barrel.

"Um, could you repeat what you said?" I sounded conciliatory.

"Turn onto 270 North. Take that over the Mississippi. We're going to Piasa Island."

———

One thousand two hundred years ago, Native Americans painted a mural of a monster bird on the limestone bluff overlooking the Mississippi River. The original limestone was quarried and taken away, so now the image is repainted regularly to preserve it.

I love the piasa bird. I think it beautiful and passionate and wildly entrancing. Although legend said that the name meant "monster that eats men," I didn't believe it. I believed the bird was a guardian over the lands occupied by the Miami-Illinois Indians.

"Piasa Island," I said, squinting up at the bird on the rock face. "What's so special about it?"

Brenda gave me a smug smile. "It's the only place with free boat access between Alton and Grafton. It'll be really easy to launch, and no one has to know we were here."

"I never figured you for a murderer, Brenda. Honestly. You trained as a nurse. A lifesaver. Now this. How can you be so sure Chad won't find out about your part in this? That he won't come looking for you or me? Or both of us?"

She laughed. "Because he's sound asleep and will be for quite some time. I met him at his apartment and brought him a latte laced with Ambien."

My stomach twisted into a tight knot, and suddenly it was hard to breathe. There would be no last-minute rescue by Detweiler. The whole promise of signing the divorce papers had been a ruse. Not that it mattered.

What was I going to do?

NINETY-FIVE

AT HER DIRECTION, I pulled into a deserted parking lot. Johnny's truck was nowhere to be seen. I wondered if this had all been one big bluff. I wouldn't put anything past Brenda. Maybe I should have looked at the photo on her phone more carefully. Maybe it hadn't been Sheila, just someone dressed as a decoy.

"Get out, and leave the door open. Turn around with your hands up and your back to me."

I had to hand it to her, Brenda was smart. With my back to her, I didn't know if she had me in her sights or not. I heard her crunch her way around the gravel. I felt the round, hard barrel of the gun pressed against my back. I wondered if she'd search me. I expected her to, but she didn't. It must not have occurred to her that I might be armed. Score one for looking blonde and dumb.

"Walk toward that stand of trees," she said.

I moved slowly, hoping to buy time, although I wasn't sure what good it might do me. As we neared the clump of sycamores, I spotted a man and a woman. The light glinted off the woman's body and face. That was the duct tape, reflecting the sunshine. I noticed a third figure behind the woman. From his stature and posture, I knew I was looking at Johnny. He stood up and I noticed the roll of duct tape in his hand.

Bill held a revolver on both of them. Or so it looked. Johnny handed the duct tape to Bill, and Bill lowered the gun. At least he didn't have Sheila in his sights anymore.

This was bad. Much worse than I expected. I couldn't tell who was on my side.

My stomach took an express elevator ride down to the ground floor. A late-breaking wave of morning sickness hit me so hard that I stumbled, doubled over, and heaved my guts out. When I was through, Brenda grabbed me under my armpit and hauled me to my feet.

"Get up. Stop it." Her voice was harsh with disapproval.

"Hi, ya," Bill called out, "Glad you could join us, Kiki. Welcome to our little goodbye party. Bring her over here, Brenda."

Beyond him waited a small rowboat, sporting patches of faded blue paint. Partially submerged trees formed a fence around the boat. Weeds nearly covered it.

I shivered as Brenda shoved her gun into my ribs. "Start walking."

Sheila sat in a lawn chair, one of those folding aluminum jobbies with the woven mesh seat and back. Her shoulders were slumped, and her posture was beaten. She seemed despondent, and when she raised her eyes to mine, they seemed devoid of any life at all. As I'd seen on Brenda's phone, Sheila's arms were trussed behind her back. Her white silk blouse wore a vibrant smear of red across the bust. I could see that her legs were taped together loosely. She might be able to make hobbling steps, but she couldn't run. A trickle of blood ran down her left temple. From the looks of it, she'd been hit on the side of her head hard enough to split the skin. A dark maroon crust formed an angry crescent along her face. She stared at me a minute and then hung her head, a gesture oddly submissive and apologetic.

Poor Sheila. She had been the bait to get me here.

NINETY-SIX

"JOHNNY? PAT HER DOWN, won't you?" Bill tipped his head toward me.

"With pleasure." Johnny gave Brenda a small nod. "Step aside, I need room. And for goodness sake, don't point your gun at me."

Mert's brother ran his hands up and down my legs, in a lascivious manner, snickering at my quick intake of breath. When he reached under my loose blouse, I could tell he found my holster, but his hands never stopped, never gave any sign that I was armed.

So he hadn't gone over to Bill.

I had a chance!

"She's clean," Johnny told Bill, giving me a small push forward. "What you want me to do with her?"

"Yeah, what are you going to do with her?" snickered Brenda.

"Come on over here by me, Brenda," said Bill. She loped over, her long legs covering the distance quickly. "You did a great job."

Her face beamed with the warming glow of approval.

"Let me see your cell phone." Bill held out his hand.

"Wh–why?" Brenda reached for the phone clipped to her waistband, but she didn't pass it over to Bill.

"So I can erase the phone log. Don't want anything linking us. That would put you in danger." His hand entered her personal space, his eyes locked on hers.

She shrugged and handed it over. "All right. That makes sense. Thanks for looking out for me."

With a quick pivot on one foot, Bill turned and tossed Brenda's phone into the lake. *Plunk!* The water splashed up, making a picturesque spray in the glinting sun.

"How could you do that?" Brenda stomped her foot.

"I'm only protecting you. What if your husband put a GPS on your phone?"

"Chad won't wake up until tomorrow. He's totally out of it. I drugged him good."

"What if someone at the station calls him, huh? What if when he doesn't answer, they send someone over to his place? If they see he's drugged, who will they suspect? You. You aren't very smart, Brenda. Leave the thinking to me."

That was Bill, always the diplomat. *Not.* His patronizing attitude toward women hadn't changed one bit since he and I tangled more than two years ago.

"Time for you to hit the road, Brenda. We can't afford to get caught, and someone might be looking for your car."

"Aw, come on," said Brenda. "I did what you wanted, and now you're making me leave."

"Get out of here while you've got the chance," he said. "Or else. I don't want that car of yours to cause trouble."

NINETY-SEVEN

KICKING GRAVEL AS SHE walked, she stomped over to her Camry. She hit the gas so hard that her tires spun. Dust and dirt flew everywhere. As she zoomed out of the lot, Bill laughed. "Good riddance to bad rubbish," he said, "What a total pain in the butt. Druggie."

His voice sounded hoarse and he looked awful. His hair was badly cut, dirt crusted his nails, and his clothes were shabby and dirty. Life on the lam didn't suit him. I wondered how his attorney got him out of jail so fast because Bill—once a dapper man with champagne tastes and a *GQ* wardrobe—now looked like thirty days of hard time. In his right hand, he waved a gun.

"Johnny, tape Kiki's hands. Let's get her in the boat." Bill walked over to the tied-up vessel and checked its outboard motor.

I heard the tape ripping from the roll, and I felt Johnny pressing the tape against my back and lifting it several times. I knew what he was doing. It was an old scrapbooking trick. By pressing the tape against fabric, it lost much of its adhesive grip—but it could still stick. He wrapped the tape around my hands individually and joined the two pieces behind my back. I could still pull my hands apart if need be.

"Got her," yelled Johnny. He took my elbow and I took my sweet time, fighting him every step of the way. Twenty feet. Fifteen. Ten. Five. I now stood right next to Sheila.

She tilted her head slightly to look into my eyes, and what I saw there was sadness … and love. Really, it wasn't surprising. We'd come to appreciate each other, to see the qualities that made George love us both. I blinked three times, and she gave me a sad smile, the tape moving slightly upwards and her eyes crinkling. She knew I was mimicking the three squeezes Anya and I often shared. So she blinked three times back at me.

In all these years, we'd never said, "I love you" to each other. Now here we were, at the brink of death, declaring an affection that both of us craved so much. We'd found a place in each other's hearts.

I had to save her.

Bill walked over to Sheila. "Fun and games time. I've been looking forward to this!" He grabbed her by the hair so hard that he pulled her right out of the lawn chair. With a muffled shriek, she staggered to her feet.

I lurched toward her, but Johnny held me back. "Let him fiddle with her. Then you can draw on him."

Bill didn't hear this because Sheila was shaking her head at him and trying to yell, kicking at him as best she could with the tape binding her feet.

"Go get in the boat!" He pulled his gun out of his waistband and pointed it. He gestured toward the short pier, a walkway of loose boards, maybe a yard in total length. Johnny and I were only fifteen feet away from it. Bill and Sheila were six feet closer. But Sheila didn't move. Her feet were tethered to each other.

"I said get in!" he yelled.

When she refused to move, he jerked her by one arm and dragged her to the walkway.

I couldn't stand it. I tugged free of Johnny's grip. "Leave her alone, Bill" I said. "Your quarrel is with me." The duct tape still linked my hands together behind my back. I hadn't pulled it hard enough to separate the two pieces.

Bill turned to answer me—and Sheila reared back and head butted him. Her skull smashed into his face with a satisfying splat.

"Ow!" yelled Bill. His hand flew to his busted lip but he didn't drop his gun. With a vicious shove, he pushed Sheila forward, propelling her down the short walkway. Her loosely bound feet made walking difficult. Because her arms were tied behind her back, she couldn't use them for balance. With blood streaming down his face, Bill stepped behind her and gave her a second shove toward the boat.

The force of his blow whiplashed her head back and forth. Sheila tumbled forward to the side of the pier and the pylon where the boat was tethered.

Johnny kept his grip on me, wrapping one arm around my waist. He tapped my gun holster with one finger as a reminder. But I couldn't do that. I couldn't shoot anyone. There had to be another way. And waving the Kel-Tec around empty didn't seem like a good idea.

"You've got to do it," he hissed.

"It's not loaded," I whispered.

He cussed.

Bill gave Sheila one more push—and this one sent her sprawling. She fell face first into the boat with a sickening *CRACK!* The little vessel rocked back and forth violently, before yawing out in a half-circle of protest.

Sheila slumped over a seat, face down, with her forehead resting against the wooden floorboards.

"That'll teach you," snarled Bill. He tucked his gun in his belt and smiled.

NINETY-EIGHT

SOMEWHERE IN THE DISTANCE came the sound of a car, traveling this way fast.

We all turned to look. Well, all of us but Sheila.

I prayed it was help. Had someone come at last? My heart leaped in my chest. Would it be Robbie Holmes? Or even a groggy Detweiler? Maybe an Illinois law enforcement official? I stood on tiptoes and watched, listening as the tires crunched along the small lane that connected this spot with the highway.

The car rounded the curve, and my heart sank.

It was Brenda Detweiler. Back again. Her Camry pulled into the gravel parking area, spewing rocks as the tires spun.

I nearly cried with disappointment.

Why has she come back? As soon as I thought it, I knew the answer: *She's nuts! And she's high. And she hates me!*

She hopped out of her car and screamed, "Hey! I've got a right to be here!"

"Brenda, get! Go on! Scram! I told you to leave—now do it or else!" Bill lifted his upper lip in a sneer.

"No!" she stood there defiantly, her arms crossed over her chest and her expression petulant. Her lower lip stuck out like a ledge.

"Johnny, use that tape on her. Since she's so proud of that car, tape her into the passenger seat."

Johnny nodded. "Okay, boss." But first he walked me over to the lawn chair where Sheila had been sitting—and shoved me into a seated position.

"Hey, old woman. You're taking up the entire boat!" Bill grabbed Sheila by her hair and hoisted her into a seated position. "We've got other passengers on this pleasure cruise," he chuckled.

She moaned with pain.

I couldn't stand it.

His mistake was turning his back on me. First I jerked my hands apart. Then I jumped up from the lawn chair. As I ran, I pulled the small pair of Fiskars out of my pocket. I threw myself at Bill, slamming my hand down with all the force I could muster. Those small Fiskars scissors snuggled tight between my fingers like a brass knuckle. I had a killer grip on them.

The fabric of Bill's shirt gave with a loud rip. His cry of pain was nearly simultaneous. I felt the scissor blades meet resistance as they slammed against his right shoulder, his scapula. The blades vibrated against my palm with the force of my blow. I didn't let go. Instead, I twisted the handle, hard. Hot blood spilled over my hands, turning them slick and useless. But I didn't turn loose of the scissors. I wrapped my fingers through the grip and held onto them.

Bill sagged away from me as he squealed in pain. He swung at me but the movement activated his shoulder muscles and intensified his agony. In response, he staggered but he didn't drop his gun. He did try to raise it, but when his arm reached his waist, he turned white and groaned, losing his grip on the gun.

"You … you …" he sputtered at me, his face a washed-out color as he fought to control his body. I'd struck a good blow, and unless he could shoot with his left hand, I doubted he could fire at me even if he found his weapon. It would hurt him too much to raise his right arm. The boat he and Sheila were in rocked crazily.

"Let me go!" Brenda's fists rained down on Johnny.

I turned to the sound of her voice. "Then leave!" he yelled at her.

"I won't," she screamed back. They wrestled with each other, hand to hand, but I had no doubt he could hold his own. I thought about telling him to take the car—he could hop in and drive off.

But what would happen to Sheila? How bad off was Bill?

The exchange between Johnny and Brenda couldn't have been five seconds, but in that time, Bill regained his senses. Still standing in the boat, he raised his left fist and smacked me up the side of the head.

I saw stars and my ears rang. The world tip-tilted, and dizziness overcame me. I grabbed one of the supports of the pier and held on tight. That was all that kept me from falling into the water.

NINETY-NINE

"Eeeooowww!" A cry came from somewhere deep inside of Bill. His angry blow to me cost him dearly. He nearly sobbed from the effort. His knees buckled and he cried out. But he didn't fall over.

I stepped over to the spot where he'd lost his gun. Scanning the ground, I found it and kicked at it. But my aim wasn't very good. It didn't go far. Just tumbled toward the gravel lot. But at least it was farther away from him. Now he'd have to get out of the boat, run down the short pier, and search for it in the weeds. Immediately, I realized how stupid I'd been. I should have grabbed the gun and tossed it in the water.

With a roar of anger, Bill hopped off the boat and ran toward me, his head down, in the manner of a raging bull. I ducked out of his way and he ran past me.

I whirled and was on him, stabbing the scissor tips into his right bicep. Twisting those trusty orange handles, I dug them deep in his flesh, ignoring the hot blood squirting all over my hand. Bill screamed out in pain.

He swung at me with a clumsy sweep of his left arm and he hit me high in the chest. Knocked me off balance.

I stumbled backward. My arms windmilled in the air. I slipped on the gravel and went down. Landing hard, the wind wooshed out of my lungs. I gasped and coughed. I couldn't take in any air.

Bang! A gunshot split the air.

Johnny staggered away from Brenda's car. His hands were splayed against his gut. Crimson blood leaked through his fingers as he clutched his belly.

"Oh, no, no," I cried. I sprang up and ran to his side.

Brenda screamed, a frustrated cry like a thwarted child. "I didn't mean to! It went off in my hand!"

"Get help!" I yelled to her. This was the worst possible scenario—seeing my best friend's brother dragged into this ugly vendetta. I imagined how Mert would take the news he'd been shot. Johnny's feet refused to cooperate and he wobbled. Taking his weight on me, I helped him to the ground. "No," I sobbed. "No, please, no."

"It was an accident," Brenda stood over me, crying.

"Then go get help. Hurry!"

She hopped back in her car and roared out of the parking lot.

A steady stream of blood flowed from the hole. How could I stop the flow? I knelt and pressed my hands on top of Johnny's, covering his wound and praying for help.

Mert would never forgive me for this.

I would never forgive myself.

Johnny's eyes locked onto mine, and I felt the desperation in them. "Johnny! Johnny! Hang on, buddy. Hang on!"

"Shoot him," Johnny gasped. "Shoot him ... or he'll kill all of us. Get his phone."

Detweiler's voice echoed in my head: "Don't pull your gun unless you plan to use it."

"Where's your car? Or his?" I asked. Maybe I could load him up, grab Sheila, and drive away.

"Came by boat," said Johnny, his voice fading and his eyes dimming.

I know nothing about boats. Nothing. And I do hate the water, except to look at it.

I yanked the Kel-Tec out of the holster and reached in my pocket. I could hear Bill stumbling through the undergrowth, hear his feet crunching twigs as he searched for his gun. I pulled the clip out of my hip pocket. My hand shook, but I succeeded in loading the clip.

If we were going to survive, I had to save us.

ONE HUNDRED

BILL WAS ON HIS hands and knees, searching the area by the pier. By my calculations, he was about two feet from where I'd kicked his gun. I could see the blood drenching his hand. The hole I'd torn in his bicep sent a steady stream of blood-red geysers down his arm. His back sported a slower leak, a widening circle of red. He had to be weakening. If I stayed hunched over, I wouldn't draw attention to myself. Bill would think I was tending Johnny.

I wiped my sweaty palms on my pants.

"Take your time, babe," said Johnny. I could barely hear him. "Aim. You might get just one shot." I stayed hunched over my fallen friend, hoping Bill would think I was tending him. To staunch the flow of Johnny's blood, I took off my blouse and stuffed it under his hands.

"Love that black bra. Now I can die a happy man," said Johnny.

"Don't you dare!" I turned and looked over my shoulder. Bill's hands parted the purple-headed irises. Any minute now, he'd have his gun.

Sheila suddenly yelled, "Help! Somebody help us!" She must have chewed through the duct tape over her mouth—or maybe Johnny hadn't attached it securely, using the same trick he had to bind my hands.

"Got it!" Bill said, standing up slowly. I saw the gun in his hand.

"Help! Help!" Sheila screamed.

"Shut up, old lady," Bill said and he crossed the distance to her in a hurry. "Hey? What's that? A ring!"

In her struggles, she'd exposed her diamond ring. Johnny had taped over her hands to hide it, trying to protect Sheila. Oh, how proud she was of that Mary Pillsbury engagement ring! Now it became a liability. I turned and saw it sparkle in the sun, a beacon casting a brilliant rainbow of colors.

"Help," she whimpered.

Bill staggered back to the pier. Holding on to a post, he dropped into the boat.

"I told you to shut up! Give me that ring. Take it off." He bent over her and grunted. I could hear Sheila's elbows bumping against the boat as she fought him. He wrestled her, his arms moving as he tried to snatch the ring.

Slowly I stepped closer to the boat, getting myself in position. Detweiler had taught me to shoot for center mass. But as I calculated the trajectory of my bullet, I knew that a center mass shot could go right through Bill and hit Sheila.

Instead of shooting, I waited. Patiently. My target moved up and down. I stood my ground, computing the angle of my gun. Figuring the path of the bullet. Taking my time for the kill shot.

I heard gravel crunching. I remembered what Detweiler said about distractions. Even so, I glanced over my shoulder. Brenda

Detweiler's car raced into the parking lot. Back again. Her Camry spit out gravel as she braked to a stop. I ignored her. Maybe her conscience had gotten to her. She was a trained nurse. How could she drive off and leave Johnny bleeding? Especially when it was her fault?

I put all my attention on Bill. He would kill Sheila unless I intervened. No doubt he'd toss her overboard as soon as he took her ring. I sighted my gun. I slowed my breathing. I heard the Camry door open. This time I didn't turn.

Inhale—pause—exhale—pause. The rhythm steadied me. The barrel of the gun quit moving between breaths. A Zen-like calm flowed over me.

I can do this!

Bill pinned Sheila to the seat of the boat with a loud *thunk!*

"Give it to me," Bill's voice was tight with anger. Totally focused on getting the ring, he'd forgotten all about me. Besides, where would I go? I wouldn't leave Johnny. I didn't have a car. Or a phone. Or a gun.

He underestimated me. People often do. Kiki Lowenstein, alone, with a gun.

"Noooo!" Sheila's muffled cry was hard to decipher.

I heard the crack of bone. Probably her finger. She howled in pain. Bill stood up triumphantly. Now he was clear of Sheila, or at least his head was. He held the ring on his thumb. His hand wasn't raised high, but it was still a gesture of defiance. In his other hand I saw his gun.

This was my best chance. I took a breath, paused, sighted the back of Bill's head, squeezed the trigger, and *BANG!*

A red mist sprayed from his head, creating a demonic halo. His knees crumbled, he listed to one side, and fell out of the boat with a decisive splash.

From behind me came an answering *BANG!* Almost an echo of my shot. A searing pain laid a trail along my right temple. I smelled flesh burning. My hand touched the spot that hurt, and a hot trickle ran over my fingers. I turned to see Brenda Detweiler, her gun held high, still aiming at me. She grinned.

Everything went black.

One Dead, Three Injured in Shoot-out

ALTON, IL—One man was found dead and three people were injured in what police are describing as a bizarre revenge-love triangle shooting at a secluded boat access on the Mississippi River, one mile north of Alton, Illinois. William Thomas Ballard, a former resident of Ladue, was pronounced dead at the scene. Ballard suffered a gunshot wound to the head. Three other people were taken to St. Anthony's Hospital in Alton. Johnny Ray Chambers was admitted with a gunshot wound to the abdomen. He is in guarded condition. Sheila Lowenstein suffered a broken collarbone and other injuries. Kiki Lowenstein was found with a gunshot wound to the temple. Both women are in stable condition. A fourth person, Brenda Detweiler, was taken into custody and charged with attempted murder and kidnapping.

Off-duty East St. Louis policeman, Sergeant Bradley Wiberg, was birdwatching with another off-duty policeman, Corporal Greg Leljedal, when the two men heard gunshots. "My doctor recommended I find a peaceful hobby. Greg was stressed out, too, so we decided to take up birdwatching. When we heard the shots, I turned my binoculars toward the sound. Greg rowed us closer and we quickly realized we'd stumbled upon a crime scene."

After notifying the Alton authorities and requesting help, Wiberg and Leljedal climbed out of their boat and approached Brenda Detweiler. "We were unable to prevent her from shooting Mrs. Kiki Lowenstein. However, our appearance caused her to run for it. Mr. Chambers was already on the ground and bleeding. Mr. Ballard's head was blown off. Mrs. Sheila Lowenstein was injured, unconscious in the bottom of a boat. We applied first aid to Mr. Chambers and both women," said Leljedal.

Illinois police apprehended Mrs. Detweiler as she was driving Highway 64–40 back to St. Louis.

Wiberg and Leljedal plan to take up another hobby.

ACKNOWLEDGMENTS

Special thanks to Larry Elliott of Executive Defense Technology, LLC, for explaining how the justice system handles parolees. Visit him at www.execdeftech.com. My pal Alan Orloff helped me with a sticky plot point. Sally Lippert and my sister, Jane Campbell, explained to me UTI symptoms in the elderly. Al Hallonquist talked me through what police procedures were likely to be in the event of a sniper attack. My tai chi friend Margit Hanna was kind enough to share her recipe for plum kuchen.

A big shout out to The Mystery Book Club that meets at the Barnes & Noble in Fenton, as well as Deborah Horn and Lynn Oris, booksellers extraordinaire. A bouquet of virtual flowers to Lane Carlée, who won both character naming privileges and my armadillo vase in an auction to benefit the Boynton Beach City Library. Kathy Berberich and Pat Davis deserve kudos for all the work they do for Make-A-Wish Foundation. Mega-thanks to Wendy Jo and Angela, two of my great Fiskateer friends.

Jane Campbell, Paula Dear, Shirley Helmly, Judge Bill Hopkins, and Sharon Hopkins were kind enough to help proofread this book. Big thanks to Connie Hill, my wonderful editor. Any mistakes here are mine.

For caregivers or adult children of the elderly, I suggest the book *Coping with Your Difficult Older Parent: A Guide for Stressed-Out Children* by Grace Lebow and Barbara Kane with Irwin Lebow. If you have a family member with a terminal illness, contact your local hospice. Hospice workers are angels who walk among us.

© Glamour Shots

ABOUT THE AUTHOR

Joanna Campbell Slan is a scrapbooker who has written seven technique books on the hobby. In fact, she loves crafts of all kinds. She is the author of twelve nonfiction books, including a college textbook, and her essays appear in five of the Chicken Soup for the Soul books. Joanna lives on Jupiter Island, Florida. Visit Joanna at: www.JoannaSlan.com.

WWW.MIDNIGHTINKBOOKS.COM

From the gritty streets of New York City to sacred tombs in the Middle East, it's always midnight somewhere. Join us online at any hour for fresh new voices in mystery fiction.

At midnightinkbooks.com you'll also find our author blog, new and upcoming books, events, book club questions, excerpts, mystery resources, and more.

MIDNIGHT INK ORDERING INFORMATION

Order Online:
• Visit our website www.midnightinkbooks.com, select your books, and order them on our secure server.

Order by Phone:
• Call toll-free within the U.S. and Canada at
  1-888-NITE-INK (1-888-648-3465)
• We accept VISA, MasterCard, and American Express

Order by Mail:
Send the full price of your order (MN residents add 6.875% sales tax) in U.S. funds, plus postage & handling to:

> Midnight Ink
> 2143 Wooddale Drive
> Woodbury, MN 55125-2989

Postage & Handling:
Standard (U.S. & Canada). If your order is:
> $25.00 and under, add $4.00
> $25.01 and over, FREE STANDARD SHIPPING

AK, HI, PR: $16.00 for one book plus $2.00 for each additional book.

International Orders (airmail only):
> $16.00 for one book plus $3.00 for each additional book

Orders are processed within 12 business days. Please allow for normal shipping time.
Postage and handling rates subject to change.